"We are not entirely alike, you and I." Patrick's voice was low.

How could Suzanne ever have thought they were? She was too aware of how his hand felt against her, a touch promising warmth, sweetness, glowing pleasures.

The hand at her neck curved around her face, urging her to him, and he bent his head to meet her.

His kiss was warm, just as she knew it would be. But it was cautious, giving her time, letting her decide if she should pull away, letting it be, if she should so choose, nothing more than a kiss of affection.

But how could Suzanne move away? How could she draw back from him? He who was her other half, everything she was, except he was male; strong where she was soft, thrusting where she was welcoming, man where she was woman....

ABOUT THE AUTHOR

Kathleen Gilles Seidel was born in Lawrence, Kansas, and attended the University of Chicago and later Johns Hopkins University for her Master's Degree and a Ph.D in English Language and Literature. Before turning to writing full-time, Kathy taught English at a small community college near her home in Virginia.

Books by Kathleen Gilles Seidel

HARLEQUIN AMERICAN ROMANCES
2—THE SAME LAST NAME
17—A RISK WORTH TAKING
57—MIRRORS AND MISTAKES

These books may be available at your local bookseller.

For a list of all titles currently available,
send your name and address to:

Harlequin Reader Service
P.O. Box 52040, Phoenix, AZ 85072-2040
Canadian address: P.O. Box 2800, Postal Station A,
5170 Yonge St., Willowdale, Ont. M2N 5T5

Mirrors
and Mistakes

KATHLEEN GILLES SEIDEL

Harlequin Books

TORONTO • NEW YORK • LONDON
AMSTERDAM • PARIS • SYDNEY • HAMBURG
STOCKHOLM • ATHENS • TOKYO • MILAN

for Mickey Mantle

Published June 1984

First printing April 1984

ISBN 0-373-16057-7

Chapter One

David Stern, his hands poised in front of him, was waiting to take the basketball in bounds.

"Watch out for that guy in green," Patrick Britten cautioned as he tossed him the ball.

"I noticed." David grimaced as he began dribbling down the brightly varnished floor of the court.

With the understandable arrogance of men who were as fit in their late twenties as they had been a decade before, David and Patrick were impatient with men who were out of shape but tried to play like they weren't, siding at every stop, losing their balance with every lunge. Patrick and David didn't care if such a man injured himself, but they worried that one day they would find themselves in the path of one of those clumsy, crashing falls.

But most of the players were in adequate condition, and the vaulted gym echoed with the squeak of basketball shoes and the rhythmic thud of the ball as these young lawyers, accountants, consultants, and investment bankers sought relief from the stress and pressure of their Boston jobs with a quick, hard game.

At the mid-court line, the man in green tried to guard Patrick, but Patrick easily shook him. Now unguarded, he knew that David would get the ball to him.

They had been playing together for years, and out on the basketball court, they thought alike.

Patrick pivoted and gathered in David's crisp bounce pass. Dribbling hard, he charged at the basket. His green-shirted guard was far behind, and so he slowed for a pointedly nonchalant lay-up. Leaping easily, Patrick laid the ball softly off the glass backboard, watching it fall precisely through the hoop.

But from the corner of his eye, he caught a glimpse of green and then felt an impact, a rocking, jarring momentum, cutting his legs out from under him, thrusting him crashing down against the floor...and then a sharp crack burst into fiery pain.

"How's the cripple?" David brushed the snow off his shoulders and looked down at Patrick's left leg, now a smooth corduroy-covered column, swollen by the plaster cast that swaddled it from instep to thigh.

"Lousy," Patick complained. "This is supposed to be a walking cast, but I don't exactly call this walking." He demonstrated by lurching into his living room. "And I had to plead to even get this."

Patrick had the first floor and a half of a townhouse on Beacon Hill and on this dark, snowy December Sunday, the living room seemed like a warm and comfortable place, brass lamps throwing circles of yellow light against the brown leather wing chairs and the mahogany butler's tables. At least it might have seemed inviting if its resident had not been in such a dour mood.

"This had better be good, Stern," he continued, lowering himself back into one of the wing chairs, lifting his cast up to a footstool. "It's a major undertaking for me to get to the door." To open the front door involved going down three steps, and Patrick and steps were not, at the moment, the best of friends.

David had been carrying a cardboard box when he had arrived and he gestured at it now. "That Cabernet we liked so much last month was on sale so I decided that we should split a case of it." The two of them regularly shared cases of wine, each taking six bottles.

David pulled out a bottle and passed it to Patrick, who examined the label. "I do remember this," he said and then his expression brightened. "But not well enough; I think we should open one now."

David laughed and went back to the little kitchen to get the glasses and corkscrew. "Every so often, I forget why I like you, Britten, but you do have a certain charm—as well as the most ridiculously well-organized kitchen on the face of the earth," he finished from inside that room.

This was a common refrain. David's habits tended to be cheerful and careless while everything Patrick touched—his desk, his drawers, his attaché case, his kitchen cabinets—were maintained in rigorous order. The two were very good friends, but they never could have lived together.

As David handed Patrick a glass, he glanced down at the three-ring binder open on the end table next to Patrick's chair. "What's that? The India proposal?"

Patrick nodded.

"Did he screw up as badly as everyone is saying?"

Patrick and David were both management consultants, working for Southard-Colt, a firm that designed computer systems and did policy and program analyses for other businesses and government agencies. Many of the contracts that they worked on were awarded only after a bidding process during which a number of consulting firms competed with one another. Thus, writing proposals and submitting bids was an important part of what David and Patrick did.

Recently the government of India announced that it wanted to hire a consulting firm to computerize the inventory and supply system for its navy. It would be a multimillion dollar, two-year contract, and Stan Daren, one of the firm's newest vice-presidents, had been in charge of the proposal. Daren's marriage was falling apart, a fact no one at the firm knew until one of the junior people saw his draft and had the courage to go over his head. On Friday of this week, the company's senior vice-president read the draft and immediately ordered Daren off on vacation. The proposal was turned over to Patrick Britten with the instructions: "See what you can do." At twenty-nine, Patrick was not a vice-president, but he was known around the firm as one of the fastest and best writers with abilities that Patrick had been quick to assure people were unimpaired by his newly broken leg.

"The system concept is okay," Patrick now told David. "The big picture is fine, but the detail isn't there, and the writing is nearly incomprehensible. And there's just an amazing amount of work left to be done."

"But you could come out of this smelling like roses."

Patrick lifted his glass. "That thought has crossed my mind," he said dryly.

"Would you go to India if they wanted you to manage it?" David asked.

"Wouldn't you?"

Ambition burned bright and clean in Patrick. He wanted to be a vice-president and he didn't want to wait one minute longer than he had to. Spending a year or so in India did not seem like a high price if it purchased him a vice-presidency.

"We've got to win the project first," he added, "but

even if we don't, having all this writing to do will give me a good excuse to work at home. Getting to the office on Friday was a bit of a struggle, and I did have to promise the doctors that I wouldn't walk very much for the next few weeks. But most of this proposal I can do here just as well—probably better."

"Can you get Katie to ferry things back and forth for you?" Katie Bowers was the secretary Patrick shared with one other consultant.

"Are you kidding?" Patrick laughed. "Katie has enough trouble ferrying herself back and forth." Katie was an excellent typist, one of the best in the firm. Beyond that, she was a trifle scatterbrained and often drove Patrick crazy.

"Actually," he continued, "she isn't going to work on this. Harrison Colt is on vacation until after Christmas, and so, for whatever reason, his secretary is doing it—at least until he gets back."

"Lawrence?" David was clearly surprised. "She's doing it? She probably hasn't typed a proposal in three years. Why's she doing it?"

"Beats me." Patrick shrugged. "But that's what Laughlin said, that *Miss* Lawrence will be typing it... and, by the way, I do think that you and I are supposed to call her 'Miss Lawrence.'"

"You can't keep calling her 'Miss Lawrence,' not if she's showing up here for three weeks."

"Maybe *you* can't, but we all know what kind of manners you New Yorkers have. We New Englanders can behave properly. Anyway"—Patrick dropped his lofty tone—"it's not like I have a lot of choice. I'm not entirely sure what her first name is."

"I think she's Suzanne, but don't quote me on it."

"I don't intend to," Patrick returned. "Especially as I devoutly hope she doesn't come showing up here. I'd rather risk my other leg stumbling to work than have someone over here a lot.''

Patrick was a very private man; although he had a number of friends, he liked being alone and he treasured his privacy.

"What's wrong, Patrick?" David knew his friend well. "Wouldn't you like Katie to come hang out here for a couple of weeks? She could bring her radio and her cat posters and you could become such good friends.''

Patrick groaned. "At least this Miss Lawrence is older and should have a little more sense.''

David looked at him curiously. "Are you sure? Not about her sense, but her age. I don't think she's much more than a year or so older than Katie.''

"She's not?" Patrick was surprised. Katie was twenty-five—at least that's what her personnel records said. By every standard other than chronology, she wasn't a minute over seventeen. Patrick would have guessed that the poised Miss Lawrence was older than he was.

"No." David shook his head. "We're clearly talking under thirty here. Haven't you ever looked at her skin or her hands?''

"Why on earth would I have done that?"

"Because she's female, Britten, and sometimes females are just a great deal of fun to look at.''

"Are they?" Patrick raised his eyebrows ironically. "I didn't know that."

David matched his tone. "I thought even you knew that. I mean, baby preppies do have to come from somewhere. Where do you get little progeny to leave your wealth to if you don't like looking at females?''

"From the bank, David, we get them from the bank," Patrick replied immediately. "When your trust fund matures, they let you choose between a set of antique hunting prints or an infant you can start another trust fund for.''

"And you chose the hunting prints?"

"You better believe it."

This too was another familiar joke between the friends. Not only were their habits different, but they were from different backgrounds. David's family was Jewish, and his father was a first-generation American, while the Brittens had been in Massachusetts since before the Revolution. There was some money in Patrick's family, but neither of his parents had much interest in financial matters, and his father, a history teacher in Concord, collected eighteenth-century engravings with an enthusiasm unchecked by the least bit of financial realism. Except for the trust fund that his grandfather had set up for his education, Patrick did not imagine that any family money would ever come to him, a situation which he did not object to in the least. He felt entirely able to make his own way.

The difference in the two men's backgrounds was immediately apparent to anyone looking at them. They were nearly the same height, but David was thin and dark with curly hair and deep-set eyes. Patrick on the other hand had a strong jaw, clean features, and blended eye color—his were a gray-green—that came after generations of stewing in the great American melting pot. Although his thick, straight hair was auburn rather than the regulation sun-streaked brown, he still managed to look, in the words of his friend, like an ad for crew-neck Shetland sweaters.

Warmed and encouraged by the wine, the two men might have continued to prod and tease each other if the doorbell hadn't rung.

"Do you want me to get that?" David asked, gesturing at Patrick's broken leg.

"Please."

David returned almost immediately escorting a small, red-haired woman bundled in a shapeless down parka that made her almost square. "Do you know this young person, Britten?" David asked. "She's making the most remarkable claim about who she is."

Patrick struggled to stand up. "It's anyone's guess what she's pretending to be, but in general, she's my mother."

"Don't get up, Patrick," his mother ordered. "I don't know where you learned such manners."

"Not from you, that's for sure," her son laughed good-naturedly as he sank back into his chair.

David helped Sally Britten take off her parka, an act that revealed a faded "Save The Whales" T-shirt covering a slight body that might have belonged to a fifteen-year-old.

Sally Britten was an attractive person—almost in spite of herself. She was utterly without personal vanity; she wore no makeup, gave little thought to her hair, and frequently wore shirts that had belonged to one of her four sons. But she had an energy, an enthusiasm, a sparkle that engaged nearly everyone who met her.

Including David Stern. "Didn't I read about you in the Guinness Book of Records?" he joked. "You were seven when Patrick was born, weren't you?"

"Close," Sally returned. "I was eighteen. That's why Patrick's so screwed up; he spent his formative years with a pair of undergraduates."

David shook his head. "Patrick's the sanest person I know."

"That's just it," Sally agreed cheerfully. "Nobody can be as rational and calm and sane as he seems to be and not be totally messed up." She kissed her oldest son and perched on the arm of his chair.

"Mother, be careful," Patrick immediately cautioned, having little faith in his mother's sense of balance. She was entirely capable of getting so involved in her conversation that she would forget how precariously she was perched and come crashing down on him, doing untold damage to his leg.

"You can come sit on my lap, Mrs. Britten," David offered encouragingly as if there weren't plenty of places to sit in Patrick's living room.

"For heaven's sake, call me Sally," she announced. "It's Patrick who's got proper manners, not me. It was that blasted prep school his grandfather made us send him to. Thank God none of the other boys went."

Patrick had been born six months after his parents had been married, and at eight pounds, six ounces, no one could pretend that he was premature. Sally and Nathaniel Britten had loved him, but as they now freely admitted they hadn't been particularly good parents. They had both continued with college and it wasn't until they had graduated and worked for a while that they started what Patrick understandably sometimes thought of as their "real" family, his three younger brothers.

Patrick no longer resented his brothers—although it was with a certain regret that he saw how much more spontaneous and lively they were than he was. He was more reserved than they, more distant, more detached. None of his brothers had his ambition or his drive; they were not likely to achieve as much as he, but ordinary human happiness was a goal they would probably reach more easily than he ever would.

Patrick did like his parents, at least as people, if not as parents. Certainly one thing that Patrick had discovered very early was that his life tended to be a lot more complicated when his charming, disorganized mother took it upon herself to act like a mother.

As she was doing at the moment. "Now, Pat," she was saying, "here are your jeans. I fixed the leg seam for you." Few of Patrick's trousers would fit over his cast. "Don't you want me to do your good slacks?"

"Thank you, Mother, but David took them into the Harvard Coop for me. They have a tailor." Patrick examined the seam of one pair of jeans. It was a good thing, he thought, that she didn't have to make her living as a seamstress.

"What's wrong?" she asked. "Don't you trust me?"

Patrick grinned at her. "Don't push it, Mom."

"What an ingrate you are." She wrinkled her nose at him. "Nonetheless I've got an illegally parked station wagon full of food for you so you don't have to move around in your little kitchen with that leg." Sally Britten tended to cook a couple of times a year, spending several marathon days in the kitchen, then feeding her family out of the freezer while she occupied herself with projects she found more interesting and important.

By the time Patrick's freezer was full of Tupperware, boilable plastic bags, and squares of aluminum foil, all of which were utterly unblemished by anything so mundane as an identifying label, it was after five and rapidly growing dark. Sally helped David and Patrick finish the bottle of wine, but with a drive back to Concord ahead of her, she had to leave. She stood up, offering to drop David off on her way. Reluctantly David confessed to having a car of his own, which he said he would happily torch if Sally would consent to running off with him.

Ignoring David's threats of becoming his step-father,

Patrick bid farewell to this now chummy pair and clumped awkwardly across the room, settling down to the desk which his brothers had carried out of the study. They had arrived en masse the day before and moved things around for him, making up the bed in the first floor study, bringing his clothes down there, generally making it possible for him to avoid going up to the second floor where his bedroom was.

It was not until after midnight that he quit working and as he slowly and awkwardly got ready for bed, he thought about the secretary who would start working with him tomorrow.

Although he had hid it from David, he had been surprised when they told him she would be working on the project, but he had decided there was no reason to question what was undoubtedly a piece of good fortune. She had to be good; she couldn't be doing the job that she was doing if she weren't—especially if she were as young as David had said she was.

She—Miss Lawrence, Suzanne, whatever she was to be called—was secretary to the firm's senior vice-president although Patrick guessed that her duties were hardly secretarial. She probably never did a moment of filing and would type only the most confidential memos. He wasn't sure exactly what it was that she did, but one of the office jokes was that she and the three other executive secretaries—the only people in the firm that everyone called "Miss" or "Mrs."—ran the place; the four members of the Management Committee, the men who had founded the firm, just did as these women told them. It was very odd, Patrick now reflected, that one of them should volunteer to do the grunt work on a proposal, and she must have volunteered; this was not the sort of work anyone would order her to do.

As he slowly unbuttoned his shirt, Patrick tried to remember the few times he had seen Miss Lawrence. His encounters with her had not been frequent; the business unit he was in did not report to her boss, and he rarely had reason to go up to the tenth floor where she worked. But one time he had gone into the fourth floor supply room for a box of pens—Katie was not entirely reliable about fetching supplies—and a group of secretaries had been clustered around the big Xerox machine trying to unjam it. Suzanne Lawrence's blond head was in the center and it was clearly she who knew what she was doing. Patrick found himself remembering a pair of brown eyes, the quick competent movements of a small hand, and a very fine gold chain around a slender wrist.

How different she had looked than the other secretaries around that machine, he thought now. All four of the executive secretaries dressed better than any other woman at the firm, including the female professionals. Since clients rarely visited the firm's offices, the dress code among the secretaries on the lower floors was casual, stopping just short of jeans. But the women on the top floor were on display and they dressed like it, wearing suits or dresses with blazers. In fact, you hardly even noticed whether or not they were attractive women, Patrick reflected, they seemed so fiercely well-groomed that any natural beauty seemed entirely beside the point. Certainly when she was with the other secretaries her own age, Suzanne Lawrence was dressed so much more formally that it did almost seem as though she were of a different generation.

Yet, even when the four executive secretaries entered a room together—Patrick remembered some party for a departing employee when for the very brief time they were there, the four of them all stood together, looking a bit like four grown-ups in a room of children—Suzanne Lawrence did not entirely blend in with them either.

For there was no mistaking that she was twenty years younger than the other three. Even without paying close attention to the texture of her skin, that was obvious.

With very uncharacteristic curiosity, Patrick wondered if she were conscious of the impression she gave—although never standing out, she never quite fit in either; it was as if she were always observing people from a distance, never completely involved.

He shook his head and finished undressing. That was pure projection on his part; because of her age and the way she dressed, she looked the way he always felt, like a bit of an outsider, a little bit distant, a little bit removed from everyone else. There was no reason to assume that she shared any of these actual feelings.

But—one more thought distracted him as he tried to find a comfortable position for sleep—why was she a secretary? She had to be terribly competent to be working for Harrison Colt. Young women that capable usually did better for themselves these days.

Oh, well—he shrugged—it was certainly none of his business.

Suzanne Lawrence would have agreed. It was none of his business why she was working as a secretary. None at all.

When she had accepted a job with that title, she had sworn to herself that she would never apologize for it, never explaining, as so many other secretaries felt they had to, that this was a stepping-stone, only something she was doing for a while. When people would assume from the way she dressed that she was one of the professional staff, she would look at them directly and in a calm voice tell them no, she was Mr. Colt's secretary. Or when she'd run into old college friends, she would never hide behind the title of assistant, administrative aide, or office manager, any of which she could reasonably claim, and would just endure their disbelief unflinchingly. "You?" they'd exclaim. "A secretary?"

"Yes, me," she'd answer. After all, she was working hard at an honest job—and getting very well paid for it. What was there to apologize for in that?

Suzanne Lawrence had made two major mistakes in her life so far. One was borrowing money to go to college. The daughter of elderly parents—her mother had been forty-two when she was born and her father fifty—she had gone to her mother's alma mater, Mt. Holyoke, an excellent and expensive women's school in Massachusetts. When her parents developed costly medical problems, Suzanne's academic advisor had suggested that she take out student loans to pay for the rest of her education, advice which she had taken almost unthinkingly. By the time she finished Mt. Holyoke, neither of her parents were living, and on graduation day she found herself with a splendid education, an impoverished writer for a boyfriend, and many thousands of dollars in government-guaranteed loans.

Suzanne hadn't fully realized when she had signed her name to those loan notes, that these were real dollars and cents that she was borrowing and would be expected to pay back. Mt. Holyoke gave young women a solid background in liberal arts, training them to think critically, exposing them to the finest achievements of Western civilization, introducing them to the delights of cognitive activity. Common sense, however, was not one of the college's strong suits.

To her credit, Suzanne was, after graduation, horrified by her indebtedness. It weighed heavily on her, and cursing her naiveté, she resolved to pay it off as quickly as she could. Only after she had paid her debts, would she allow herself to make any other plans.

Suzanne had been an English major. She knew all the kings of England and the difference between the first generation of Romantic poets and the second. She had read all of Jane Austen's novels and most of Dickens's. She knew exactly what effect World War I had had on the history of English letters.

She loved knowing these things, but she soon realized that no one was going to pay her a salary just because she did.

With a shrewdness that they didn't teach at Mt. Holyoke, Suzanne took stock of her other abilities. She didn't have the kind of dynamic personality that a person needed for teaching these days, but she was the most organized person that she knew and she could take anything and turn it into clear, readable prose. However, the interesting little jobs in publishing that her friends with similar skills were taking didn't have interesting enough salaries.

So she swallowed hard, borrowed a little more money and took a crash summer program at Katharine Gibbs, polishing her already good typing skills and learning about office procedure. She then set out to sell herself and her abilities to the highest bidder. She found exactly what she wanted at Southard-Colt, a firm that rewarded their support staff not with flattering pseudoprofessional titles but with cash.

Suzanne was even better than she had expected to be. It had, of course, taken her awhile to understand exactly what the job was; some of her most important functions were never discussed or described. It soon became clear to her, for example, that the reason the

tenth floor executives managed to get anything done
was that their secretaries maintained such a formal,
forbidding manner. It was, she reflected, remembering Humanities 234: "Approaches to the Myth," the
White Goddess style of office management.

This aloofness meant, of course, that Suzanne had
made no real friends at Southard-Colt. The other three
executive secretaries cared for her very much, but the
age difference was too great for genuine friendship.
That was all right, though; Suzanne had more than
enough friends—and some of her friendships were absolutely exhausting her; she was at the firm for the
money.

And money was why Suzanne was standing on Patrick
Britten's doorstep on Monday morning. One reason
that Suzanne jealously guarded her title of "secretary"
was that it meant that she was a nonexempt employee;
certain Labor Department regulations about regularly
scheduled hours and the like applied to her. As a result,
she, unlike the professionals, got paid overtime. She
normally worked fifty hours a week, always getting in
at least ten hours at time-and-a-half pay, and Colt's office was busy enough that she could frequently put in
sixty hours or more without wondering if she were taking advantage of the company.

But during Colt's vacation the last three weeks of
December, there wasn't any overtime. Most secretaries
relished their bosses' vacations as a chance to take it
easy. Not Suzanne; she just resented the lost chance to
swell her paycheck. So when she heard what a mess the
big India proposal was in, she decided to work on it.
Another thing Mt. Holyoke had not taught her but she
now knew was the smell of a project with lots of overtime. This was clearly one.

Part of Suzanne's success at Southard-Colt was that

she was never unprepared. She took each task as seriously as she had her Senior Honors Examination at Mt. Holyoke. So as she patiently shifted the stack of folders, listening to the heavy thud that was almost surely Patrick Britten's leg cast coming to the door, she already knew a great deal about him.

She had pulled his resumé. He was twenty-nine, had gone to prep school and then on to Harvard, both for college and an M.B.A. from the Business School. He was unmarried, childless, and had listed his health as "excellent"—an evaluation that, at the moment, did not seem to apply.

She had also put in a rare tap on the office grapevine. He was on the fast track. Made a principal last year, he clearly had his eye on being a vice-president long before he was thirty-five. He was good with clients although not wonderful. His best asset was that he wrote well and fast. The grapevine further labeled him one of the easiest people to work with; he wasn't terribly friendly, but he was never impatient, abrupt, or temperamental.

And finally Suzanne had flipped through Katie Bowers's files and found one of his manuscripts. His handwriting was neat, she noted with relief; he could spell, and although his punctuation was a little old-fashioned, tending toward a few too many commas, he was at least consistent. Despite his reputation, his writing was not perfect. He did write well, but his verbs were a little weak and his topic sentences were occasionally off—although it was nothing, she thought calmly, that she couldn't easily fix.

When she was through with her research, Suzanne probably knew more about Patrick Britten's place in the firm than he did himself. Certainly he did not know the extent to which his tall athletic form had been discussed when the women's softball team had all gotten very drunk after their final game last summer. Nor did he know that two of the female consultants found his reserve, his steady refusal to ever talk about himself, absolutely fascinating, and they longed to spend some time outside the office with him.

Of course, Suzanne had complete confidence in her ability to handle nearly anything one of the consultants might try, but she was still pleased that the grapevine marked Patrick Britten as an utterly unflirtatious man. It would make stopping by his home easier. In fact, she thought with a shiver, the only possible disadvantage of working with him would be if she froze to death waiting for him to hobble to his front door.

Chapter Two

"Miss Lawrence?"

"Mr. Britten."

"I do appreciate your bringing these." A stack of folders changed hands.

"It was no trouble, I'm sure, and I will be glad to pick up your revisions tomorrow."

". . . and we found this outline on Mr. Daren's desk. I was sure you'd want to see it."

"Yes, yes, of course. But, Miss Lawrence, I'm sorry you keep having to run over here. This is the third day in a row."

"It's all right. I take the Red Line so I can get on at the Park Street station; it's really no problem."

"I'm sure that isn't true, but you are saving me an enormous amount of time, and I appreciate it."

"My God, Suzanne, come in. You're absolutely white. Is it really that cold out?"

"It's a little brisk." She was trying not to shiver.

"I feel just—"

"Will you stop apologizing?"

". . . and I thought you'd want to see these resumès."

He shook his head. "What a marvel you are. I was

just cursing myself for not asking you to bring them. How did you know I wanted them?"

"It was only logical."

"We should play basketball together."

"I beg your pardon?" Suzanne's eyebrows arched.

"Basketball. We should play together. We think alike; that's important in team sports."

"Fine. So long as thinking alike is all we have to do. Just don't expect me to touch the ball."

He leaned back against the wall of the foyer. "I take it you aren't much of a jock."

"Not in the least. I'm terrible at sports."

"Really? It seems like you would be good at everything you do."

"No. I just don't do the things I'm bad at."

"... now if you can finish this by noon, I can get it on my lunch hour and—"

"Suzanne, this is ridiculous. Isn't there something you can work on here?"

"Not without a typewriter."

"Then get a typewriter and starting tomorrow, set up shop here."

"Work here?" She was surprised.

He shrugged. "Why not?"

"I would never want anyone working in my home, not ever."

"Normally, I wouldn't either, but you're hardly anyone."

"That's a typewriter? Four boxes and two deliverymen for a typewriter?" Patrick's living room was being rearranged.

"Of course it isn't a typewriter, Patrick. No one in their right mind uses a typewriter anymore. It's a word processor."

"You make that many mistakes?" He was teasing.

"No, but I'm expecting that *you* will."

And so entirely at his own instigation, Patrick had what he had sworn he didn't want, a secretary coming to work at his home each day.

It went extremely well. As they had guessed from their phone conversations and quick meetings at Patrick's front door, their work habits were entirely compatible. They worked quietly, steadily, with few breaks and no chatter.

Suzanne soon realized that he was not used to working with secretaries as competent as she. Several times she had to take a folder from him and say firmly, "I can take it from here."

Or another time Patrick stared in surprise at some neatly formatted charts and graphs. "I thought I had only made the notes for these."

"That's right," Suzanne answered. It seemed unnecessary to say that she had finished them, and from then on, he automatically handed her the notes, knowing she could finish the graphs herself.

They were both much more productive without the continual distractions of office life—phone calls, lunches, people sticking their heads in one's door and then staying for twenty minutes.

Of course, working in his home, there was inevitably some overlap between the personal and the professional.

After a few laborious trips to the front door, he had given her a key. Sometimes if he had worked very late, she arrived before he was up, and as she began to type what he had written the night before, she could hear him moving about in the back bedroom, getting dressed.

Clearly, there were things he needed help with, and

quietly, unobtrusively, Suzanne did them. She made coffee, fixed lunch, and washed whatever dishes were in the kitchen, overriding his protests by saying that she'd rather do them herself than listen to him clump around in that tiny space. If she had her own errands to run at lunch, she did things for him. "I have to go to the drugstore," she would say. "Are you out of anything?" And although she knew that his first impulse was to say no, he would hesitate and say, "I've been taking a lot more aspirin than usual. Would you mind getting me some more?"

His leg did hurt, she could tell that. He never complained, but some afternoons she would notice his lips tighten and he would unconsciously press a hand against his cast as if that would help. She offered no sympathy, knowing that he wouldn't want it, but she felt sorry for him.

She tried hard to keep the atmosphere as professional as possible. She respected his privacy absolutely, never commenting on anything she noticed in his home. She knew that few other women would have been so circumspect. "Oh, Patrick, this is the cutest picture, who is it?" "Why do you have three kinds of mustard and no mayonnaise, Patrick?" "What this room really needs is..."

It would have driven him mad.

She screened his calls just as she always did for Mr. Colt. Suzanne had long since discovered that if Harrison Colt felt like wasting his own time, she couldn't stop him, but she could certainly keep other people from doing it for him. She saw no reason to alter her policy because the man she was working for didn't have a corner office and a high-ranking title.

Patrick had looked surprised when she had first told someone he would return a call.

"How did you manage that?" he asked. "I'm sitting right there and he has to know that. I mean, where else would I be?"

Suzanne guessed that Katie Bowers had trouble convincing people that he was in a meeting when he genuinely was. "You've got to be tough to work on the tenth floor," she replied.

He laughed. "I can imagine."

Suzanne soon learned to let all of David Stern's calls through. She noticed that Patrick always returned his calls first and that the brief, rather cryptic conversations were often accompanied by deep, soft laughter.

One day she answered the phone. "Mr. Britten's residence."

"Miss Lawrence, are you in love with me?"

She knew the voice. "I'm not entirely sure I would recognize you on the street, Mr. Stern," she answered truthfully.

"Well, why am I the only person that you let talk to Britten?"

"I also let any of the vice-presidents speak to him."

"Person, Miss Lawrence, I said person. That doesn't include the vice-presidents."

Suzanne laughed. "Would you like to speak to him now?"

"Is he still calling you Miss Lawrence?"

"Ask him," she returned and handed the phone to Patrick who had been listening interestedly.

"Ask me what?" he growled into the receiver.

She also let all personal calls through; this was, after all, his home, and so when a caller seemed startled and confused by her crisp "Mr. Britten's residence," she turned the phone over to him without asking any questions.

But as she handed the phone to him Friday morning,

she was curious; the voice had seemed familiar, naggingly familiar. And as she worked, getting one of the first complete sections ready to print, she listened to Patrick's side of the conversation.

"I know it's a Christmas party, but it's hard for me to get around; it really is. I can't drive.... I know that...but I've already told them I'm not coming.... Yes..."

Suzanne smiled; this had the sound of a man allowing himself to be talked into something. It was no wonder. He must be getting very restless, staying at home every day. A party probably sounded very appealing at the moment, although she guessed in general he went to parties only because he felt he had to.

"... it's hard for me even to do that...well, yes, but...all right, eight thirty."

He hung up and grimaced a little sheepishly. "This is probably a big mistake."

"You need to get out," Suzanne replied.

"Yes, but going to a big party with a bunch of people who will get too drunk to drive home is probably the worst way to do it."

"Just be sure you have cab fare home," she said as she turned back to the word processor and then glanced back up as he laughed. She shook her head. "I'm sorry! I must have sounded like your mother."

"Not *my* mother; she's not half that sensible," he said cheerfully. "No, it's just that to know how good that advice is, you'd have to know Bunny and Carter Landau."

Suzanne stopped dead, the disc halfway into the word processor. Bunny and Carter Landau. She slipped the disc into place and closed the little door. She pushed "P" for print and obediently answered all the machine's questions about spacing and page numbering.

She did know them. Bunny had lived down the hall from her for three years at Holyoke. She hadn't known that Bunny was in town, but if she was, it was very unlikely that she would be going to any other party Saturday night than the one that Suzanne herself was going to.

So what? What difference did it make that she and Patrick were going to be at the same party? The only way it would be at all worth remarking was if she didn't tell him she was going.

"Oh, are you going to Nan and Ted Montgomery's?" she asked, her voice carefully casual over the printer's clatter.

He didn't answer and she looked up. He obviously hadn't heard her. He was reading one of the pages that was spitting out of the printer, his expression carefully blank.

"Is something wrong?"

"This isn't what I wrote."

His voice was quiet, too quiet. Suzanne knew he was angry only because this was exactly how she acted when she was angry.

She tensed. She hated confrontations. And above all she didn't want one with him. This week had been calm and productive without emotion or stress. That was the way she liked things; that was the atmosphere she functioned best in, with everyone detached, rational, and uninvolved. She thought he was like that too. But now he was angry.

"You should not have changed my work without discussing it."

He was right, of course he was; she knew that, but she just hadn't thought. "You're right," she said immediately. "I shouldn't have. I'm sorry."

No one listening to either one of them, to their even,

quiet voices, to their polite words, would have ever guessed that they were fighting. But they were.

"I am sorry," she repeated, "but this is what I always do; I forgot that you would be surprised by it."

She was refusing to admit that she shouldn't have done it, just that she should have told him.

And he knew it. "I'm sure you've saved my draft."

He was making it very clear. She was to remove all her changes, and for a moment, she was tempted to do just that. With the word processor, she could put his heavy nominalizations and awkward abstractions back in before the afternoon was over. That's what word processors were for—to fix mistakes.

Except her revisions weren't a mistake. To take them out would just be the impulse of hurt pride, and Suzanne Lawrence, like a good many New Englanders, prided herself on not acting on silly impulses.

"Would you look at it first?" She knew she had to speak carefully. He had probably been told at every salary review that he was one of the best writers in his business unit. He wasn't going to like hearing a secretary tell him he could be better.

Of course he couldn't refuse to read her changes, not without admitting that he was being stubborn and irrational, and so he started reading but in a moment, he stopped shaking his head. "I need to see the original; I can't tell what the changes are, just that it isn't my writing any more."

Suzanne had already gotten out his original manuscript. She laid it next to the printed version and resting one hand on the desk beside him, leaned over and explained the differences. "I really did only two things. You use forms of the verb *to be* too often in your predicate," she explained, entirely unaware of how much like an English teacher she sounded. "Let your verbs carry the sentence. That used to be 'Developing system skills will be easy for most users.' 'Most people can learn to use the system easily' is less tiring for your reader. And the other problem is that you qualify your point before you make it so I've just switched a few of your paragraphs around and changed your topic sentences a little."

Suzanne straightened and let him examine her changes. His right foot was tapping quickly, but gradually slowed and stopped. Unconsciously he scratched the back of his neck, ruffling the thick auburn hair.

It was so stupid of her not to have anticipated this. Now they were in an awkward position. Men had such trouble admitting that they were wrong. Sometimes it didn't seem fair to make them do it; they were so bad at it. Some couldn't do it at all. If Patrick Britten was one of those, they were in trouble.

He was slow, but he got there. "Yours is better," he said finally.

"It's just a few stylistic changes, that's all." She tried to minimize what she had done. She certainly didn't need him to grovel. "And I should have warned you that I was going to do it." She smiled politely and turned to go back to her desk.

"Wait a minute, Suzanne. Did you say you always do this?"

She shrugged and started to change discs so that the next section could be printed.

But Patrick was too alert for this brush-off. "Are you saying that Colt's...You know how everyone new wants to work with Colt because he helps you so much with your writing...That famed memo with all that useful specific advice about your style—that's you, isn't it?"

Suzanne didn't answer; those memos were treated as gospel, just as they should be, she thought confidently, but some people would pay a lot less attention to the sometimes harsh advice if they knew that Colt only approved them.

"Do you write those memos?" he repeated.

"Oh, Patrick," she sighed, knowing that he would tell no one. "You know what his time is worth, and those take forever to do."

He shook his head slowly, his gray-green eyes flooding with a surprised respect. "But why are you pretending to be a secretary?"

"Because I am. That's just one of the things I do. I also answer the phone and make coffee and type things."

"Doesn't it bother you that nobody gives you credit for doing this?"

Suzanne smiled; his ambition was showing. "I do get credit for it. I am very well paid. And with overtime, I certainly make a lot more than I would in a regular editing job."

"But how—"

He had stopped, but she knew what he was asking. "I am not entirely uneducated."

"Where did you go to college?"

She answered that question as she always did. "In Massachusetts."

He looked at her directly. "I hate asking people favors, and you've already done so much this week..."

"What is it?"

"I know it's Friday, but could you possibly stay a little longer and go over this with me? I'll be writing all week-end and I'm sure I can do this myself if you'll show me."

Suzanne was not one to refuse such a request. She loved working with people on their writing. "I'll be glad to...if I may use your phone?"

She dialed and Nick answered with his usual abrupt, "Moretti here."

And halfway through the conversation she realized how her half must sound to Patrick. "...and don't forget you have that reading at Radcliffe tonight. There are clean shirts in your closet and if you want something to eat, there's chicken from last night..."

She hung up and turned to him, pulling her chair over to his desk, getting ready to talk about sentence structure.

"I thought you weren't married."

"I'm not."

"Oh." He sounded puzzled.

A rare flicker of impatience, a distaste for having the domestic details of her life overheard, goaded her into reply. "Don't be naive, Mr. Britten. That was the man I live with."

If taking out loans for school was one of Suzanne's two mistakes, Nick Moretti was the other.

She had met him in college—he had been a student at Holy Cross—and from the first, it had been the attraction of opposites. He was lively and quick, with a spontaneous enthusiasm that her reserve and caution made her incapable of. His mind was imaginative while hers was analytic. He wanted to be a writer and she was awed by the dark energy of his work. In turn, he had admired her systematic nature, her organized competence—to say nothing of the fact that to Nick, Suzanne was the sort of fragile, patrician blonde that working class immigrants' sons only dream about

This working class immigrants' son was Suzanne's one act of rebellion. But she was clearly entitled to at least one. Her parents should never have had a child; they certainly didn't plan on her. A full generation older than her friends' parents, they had no sense at all of the needs of a child and an adolescent. So they fulfilled their obligations as parents by laying down many strict rules for her and continuing their lifelong absorption in the art museums they worked in. Nick and his unmannered energy would have horrified them.

But Suzanne's involvement with him was only part rebellion. She did truly love him, and when she finally slept with him, it was with the certain knowledge that someday they would marry.

But after graduation, it was Suzanne who refused to marry Nick. She distrusted his traditional background. He was entirely capable of insisting that his wife stay home; his brothers had done exactly that. And Suzanne felt the weight of her debts too keenly to transfer them to someone else, especially to someone with the potential earning power of a beginning writer. But she still loved him, and when he decided he didn't want to go back to his native New York City, they took an apartment together on Garden Street in Cambridge.

Their relationship deteriorated. Suzanne found it difficult to live with Nick. He was a messy, disorganized person while she was fastidious. But she adjusted to his clutter better than she did to his complete disrespect for her privacy, something that she had not noticed before they started living together. He read her mail, flipped through her briefcase, and insisted that she repeat word for word seemingly every conversation she had.

He wasn't jealous or suspicious. He was just curious. As a writer, the little details of people's lives fascinated him, and no one fascinated him as much as this quiet, lovely blonde. He wanted to know everything about her, and she hated it.

A "well-meaning friend" told her that Nick was not faithful to her. She confronted him, and he admitted it, but insisted that these occasional encounters didn't matter to him, they were meaningless and casual.

At heart, she believed him, but this seemed as good an excuse as any, and Suzanne packed to leave. Nick begged her to stay. He was in the process of selling his first book. He was terrified of his agent; the thought of having to read and sign a contract was almost as awful as the thought of not getting a contract at all. So she agreed to stay, with the understanding that she was to have her own room and that he was never to enter it unless she was there.

But soon he stopped coming to her room even when she was in it, and eventually, without their ever discussing it or deciding, their relationship became asexual.

Actually, they were both relieved. The sexual side of their relationship had always been difficult, a source of more tension than pleasure.

When she had first started sleeping with him, Suzanne had, like thousands of other college girls, started taking birth control pills. But the pills reacted with something in her system so that gradually she lost whatever interest in sex her repressed Bostonian upbringing had left her with. As much as she loved Nick, she simply felt nothing when he touched her.

Neither she nor Nick knew that her lack of response had anything to do with the Pill. The gynecologists had not warned her. So the two of them would lie, side by side, in silent darkness, tormenting themselves with unspoken thoughts of failure. It was hardly surprising that he was desperate for a more willing embrace, wanting not the physical pleasure so much as some reassurance that Suzanne's lack of interest was not entirely his fault.

Once she moved out of his room, Suzanne quit the Pill and within a few months, found in herself the stirring interest a normal woman has for men. A chance magazine article had suggested what might have happened, and a sympathetic doctor confirmed that yes, a few women did experience this as a side effect. "Or rather they used to," he added. "You were on the old high-dosage pills which aren't prescribed anymore. Would you like to try the new ones? They don't cause this problem."

Suzanne shook her head. By then it was too late for her and Nick. Much too late.

Nick's first book was a surprising hit, not a bestseller by any means, but the dark, bitter laughter in it was very well reviewed and he became something of a cult figure among a certain type of college student. He was prolific and his income was much steadier than anyone would have ever expected for him.

He wanted Suzanne to stay. Basically, he wanted someone to take care of him. He wanted someone to go to the grocery store and read his proofs, someone to do the laundry and talk to his agent, to make appointments with the lawyers and keep track of which expenses were deductible. If she would do all that, he offered to pay all their household expenses. He knew how she felt about paying her loans quickly.

As a lover, Suzanne could never have been bought. But, she decided, as a housekeeper she could be. And she knew she would earn every cent Nick spent on her.

So Nick, the man she once loved, was now another responsibility, something to keep track of, just like she kept track of the progress of some of Southard-Colt's big projects. But every month that she lived without rent or other domestic expenses was a month closer to having paid her debts.

None of their Cambridge friends knew how chaste their relationship was. Suzanne would never discuss such a matter with anyone, and Nick, who would generally tell anyone anything, kept quiet about this. He was starting to discover what Harrison Colt knew within three minutes of meeting her—people were easily intimidated by Suzanne Lawrence. Her quiet, beautifully dressed, blond presence at his side had saved him from innumerable entanglements, both professional and romantic.

Of course, living with Nick kept Suzanne from developing relationships with other men. But just like a career for herself, that too was on hold until she paid her debts.

Chapter Three

"These roads aren't the greatest, are they?"

This was from Carter Landau, and Patrick could not have agreed more. They weren't even at Nan and Ted's yet, and he was already regretting having come. Why had he ever let himself be talked into this?

The weather was terrible—an icy snow glazed the sidewalks with a glistening, treacherous beauty, and like a little old lady, Patrick had to worry about falling. No, not like a little old lady, he corrected himself, there was no one on the face of the earth more hardy and intrepid than Boston's formidable dowagers. They were probably out attending charity balls in full force tonight, utterly unperturbed by the weather.

New Englanders were supposed to scoff at the weather, treating their dreadful winters with magnificent disdain. At the moment, Patrick Britten was very conscious that he was letting the team down.

It wasn't just the weather. He was not particularly thrilled with the company he was in. Two summers ago he and Libby Wiley, Bunny Landau's sister, had sailed with another couple "down East" to Maine, stopping at the Isle of Shoals and Casco Bay. It had been fun, but now he remembered why he'd been relieved when it was over. Libby and Bunny were, at the moment, talking about the "outstanding tanning action" in The Bahamas, a pair of "really excellent" shoes, and an "ever so cute" boat. After a long, satisfying day spent writing, using words with a care that had damn well better please Miss Suzanne Lawrence on Monday, the lazy, imprecise, unvaried vocabulary of Libby, Carter, and Bunny irritated him.

Even at the best of times. Patrick didn't like big parties. He didn't like talking to people who bored him; he didn't like saying the same thing twenty times over; he didn't like having to dredge up the name of everyone he had gone to prep school with just to find out how many people he knew in common with this other person whom he did not know and whom he quite clearly did not *want* to know.

Above all, he didn't like the way women acted at big parties. They never looked like themselves. Their clothes were often strange, and as a man approached them, a hard, expectant look would glaze their eyes as they waited for admiration. That seemed to be the point of a party—not to have a good time, but to get compliments. Patrick felt sometimes like he was just functioning as a mirror, with women looking at him, waiting for him to react to their appearance. And there was simply nothing Patrick hated more than having people expect some sort of emotional reaction from him. It was something his family did continually.

Quite clearly, Patrick was not in a very festive mood. He didn't feel like celebrating, and he wished he had stayed home.

He hadn't seen Nan and Ted Montgomery since they had moved to their new condominium, and dutifully he kissed Nan's cheek when it came speeding in his direction, agreed that yes, yes, it had been much too long, and obediently admired both her dress and the silvery gray décor of the sweeping living room that he could see over her shoulder.

"Who's for champagne?" Carter asked as soon as they had gotten rid of their coats. "Libby? Bunny? No, no, Patrick, I'll get it for all of us. The room's too crowded for you to be lumbering around."

So Patrick had to wait with Bunny and Libby, pretending to listen to their chatter. He really wished he weren't here.

Suddenly Bunny interrupted her sister. "Suzanne!"

Suzanne? What was she doing here?

Patrick shook his head, grimacing at his response. What was wrong with him? There must be thousands of women in Boston named Suzanne. Why had he thought of Suzanne Lawrence? There wasn't a chance in hell that she'd be here.

And, to his surprise, that thought depressed him even more.

"Suzanne!" It was Bunny's voice again. "Suzanne, over here!"

And suddenly there she was, moving through the crowd, touching an arm apologetically, a blonde in a brown velvet suit, unmistakably Suzanne Lawrence.

"Hello, everyone, Patrick." Her voice was unhurried, as if she weren't surprised, as if it didn't startle her to see him here.

As usual, Bunny spoke in a rush, a hurl of words covering anything Patrick might say. "Oh, Suzanne, I was hoping you'd be here. I haven't seen you since Diana's wedding, not that any of us were worth seeing there; do you remember those awful dresses?"

"Don't remind me," Suzanne groaned, her brown eyes sparkling. "I'll never understand why Diana let her mother choose the dresses."

"At least you were maid of honor and didn't have to wear dentist's office green."

"It was mint, Bunny, mint." Suzanne laughed.

"Not on me, it wasn't."

What was this? Patrick wondered. Had Suzanne and Bunny worked the bridesmaids' circuit together?

Carter returned with the drinks. "Hello, Suzanne, you pretty thing." Once he got rid of all the drinks but his, he kissed her cheek noisily. "You look drop dead wonderful."

Silently Patrick agreed. She did. Many of the other women were dressed in the current fashion of taffeta and ruffles, making them look, he thought, like they were all in the same school play. Suzanne's velvet suit was quietly elegant, the brown turned her eyes chocolate and the lace on the high collar of her white blouse made her seem much more fragile and feminine than usual. She looked, his Grandmother Britten would have said, like a proper Boston lady.

"But skin, Suzanne," Carter continued cheerfully. "You never show enough skin. Always thought that about you. We'd like to see some flesh from you now and again."

He slid his hand along the velvet of her sleeve, resting it on her shoulder. Immediately Suzanne lifted her hand to smooth her hair, dislodging Carter's hand from her shoulder seemingly by accident. But Patrick guessed it was no accident.

She had done it so effortlessly that Carter hardly noticed; he scarcely paused. "By the way," he went on, "did Bunny think to introduce you to Patrick Britten?"

"Oh, we know each other." At last she turned her brown eyes to him and smiled. "I see you made it here safely, Patrick. How's the leg?"

Carter looked interested and Patrick decided even if he couldn't move, at least he could talk. "Suzanne and I work with one another."

"Patrick is being polite," she said immediately.

"There's no *with* about it. I am working *for* him at the moment."

"'At the moment' is probably right," Carter laughed. "Watch out, Britten, or before you know it, you'll be working for her. She probably makes more than you do."

"Don't be silly," Suzanne shook her head.

"But isn't it strange," Bunny put in, "that one of our old crowd is actually earning a living wage?" She turned to Patrick. "Suzanne Lawrence is the only girl in our class who is making money."

"Suzanne Lawrence," Suzanne returned, "is the only girl in our class who *had* to make money."

Patrick had to ask. "You were at Holyoke with Bunny? I thought you said you were at U. Mass." The University of Massachusetts was a good school but not nearly as expensive or prestigious as the "Seven Sisters."

"Why would she have said that?" Bunny asked blankly.

"I said I went to school *in* Massachusetts, not *at* Massachusetts." She smiled, as close to flirting as he could imagine her. "Watch your prepositions, Patrick, they'll get you every time."

With this as an exit line, she excused herself.

Well, damn it, he was intrigued. Who wouldn't be?

In a way, he should have guessed. He wasn't being a snob, at least he hoped he wasn't—he knew plenty of jerks and fools who summered in Nantucket and graduated from Harvard, but that background did give a person a certain air, a confidence. Suzanne Lawrence had it written all over her. That poised self-assurance of hers was the result of a privileged, comfortable world. No wonder she didn't quite fit in with the other secretaries at work.

In general, Patrick Britten was not a curious person.

He usually found that people volunteered much more information about themselves than he cared to hear. But not this lady.

She was full of surprises. Not only was she an extremely talented editor working as a secretary, hiding her credentials, but she was undoubtedly in conflict with every plan ever made for her, living with some guy she wasn't married to.

Patrick usually didn't speculate about the private lives of the people he worked with, but he couldn't help it now. Suzanne Lawrence and her lover would have, Patrick guessed, a very independent arrangement where neither one would cling or make demands. The man probably worked very hard and tended to be rather detached, even a little cool. In fact, Patrick reflected, he ought to meet this man who lived with Miss Suzanne Lawrence. He was probably a great deal like him.

The rest of the party was deadly. Patrick heard innumerable tales of other people's broken legs while his own started to ache in the most persistent way. Nan Montgomery, doing her duty as hostess quite credibly, did try to keep bores from trapping him for too long, but as the caterers carried out more and more cases of empty champagne bottles, she was gradually abdicating her responsibilities.

After midnight, he finally thought he was going to go mad, listening to a particularly windy complaint about how everyone else in Padnarum Harbor was buying fiberglass boats. "Wood," this snobbish boater was saying, "all wood, that's the only—"

"I'm sorry but that lady asked me to come get you," a cool voice interrupted him. It was Suzanne.

The yachtsman looked down at her blankly. "What lady?"

"The brunette." Suzanne pointed to the other side

of the room where a cluster of brown-haired women were gathered. Patrick could tell that she was lying. But the other man fell for it and excused himself.

As soon as he was gone, Patrick spoke. "If that was a rescue, I appreciate it. But you aren't on duty, you know." He hated the thought that she felt she had to look out after him on Saturday night just because during the week she worked for him.

She ignored him. "You look exhausted. Why don't you go home?"

She was right. He really wanted out of here. He ran a hand over his face. "I'd like to, but I hate causing a fuss." Bunny and Carter were clearly not at all interested in leaving, and the very unfestive notion of one guest leaving alone in a cab would set off all sorts of moans and drunken protests.

"I take it you don't mind leaving Libby Wiley behind."

"Not in the least," he said tactlessly. He hadn't seen Libby in several hours. He had undoubtedly served his purpose, and by now she would have found a better—or at least a healthier—escort.

"Then hoist yourself up," Suzanne ordered.

He assumed that she was just going to call a cab for him and in her best "you've got to be tough to work on the tenth floor" manner override any protests from the Landau-Montgomery "It's So Early" Committee.

But as they passed by their hostess who happened to be talking to Bunny, she said simply, "Patrick's leg is about to drop off so I'm going to take him home."

Her remark had such an air of calculated discretion, as if their leaving together had nothing at all to do with his leg, that no one dared comment.

It was a slick piece of work, and Patrick was impressed. "Is that how you get Harrison Colt out of meetings?" he asked as soon as the door closed behind him.

She smiled. "Not exactly."

"But, look, I didn't mean for you to have to leave too."

"I was just about to anyway," she answered, tilting back her head to watch the dial above the elevator record its progress. Her shoulder length hair floated down her back. "It's nearly one and we working girls need our sleep."

"But isn't your friend here?" he asked as the elevator door slid open.

"Friend?" She put her hand out to hold the door open. "Oh, Nick. No, he doesn't go to parties."

"He doesn't?" Patrick clumped into the elevator. "What an estimable man. How does he avoid them?"

"It's simple; he just doesn't go."

The sidewalks were slicker than ever and Suzanne insisted that he wait while she got the car. Of course she was right; it was foolish to object, but he wasn't happy about it.

"I feel like a teenage girl," he grumbled, after she had him safely installed in the passenger seat of her car, "who went out with the wrong sort of boy and had to be rescued."

She laughed. "It's good for you, Patrick; it will keep you humble."

She drove, even on these icy roads, with the same quiet competence with which she did everything. But her car, a little red Porsche, did surprise him. Good Lord, Patrick swore to himself, just how many times had she surprised him in the last two days?

"This is a nice car," he said, refusing to acknowledge his amazement openly. "Do you like the way it handles?"

"Actually I hate it. It's Nick's."

Thank God he'd been right about something.

"When Nick got his first advance," she continued, "he wandered into the Porsche dealer and said, 'I'll take the red one.'" Patrick stared at her, and she half-apologized. "It was not the most rational thing to do."

It certainly wasn't. Apparently he and this Nick character were not as alike as he had imagined. "An advance? What does he do?"

"He's a writer."

"Do you fix his verbs?"

"Good heavens, no."

But before he could ask why his question had made her laugh, she was pulling into a parking space that had suddenly materialized in front of his house. Oh, well, he sighed, Suzanne Lawrence seemed to have everything else up her velvet sleeve, why not a few parking spaces on Beacon Hill?

She followed him as he slowly lurched up the icy steps. "This makes lots of sense," he pointed out. "If I fall, I will knock you down and then we will end up with four broken legs instead of one."

"But think of all the work we would get done."

"Spoken like a true Yankee, Miss Lawrence."

Her key chain was still in her gloved hand and unthinkingly just as she had done every day this week, she opened his door. He felt like a very small child.

Some day, he vowed to himself, *I'll...*

He'd what? Drag her by the hair into a cave and show who was boss?

He had always prided himself on being able to deal with the woman he worked with in a sensible, rational manner, and here one of them was going out of her way to do him a favor and he was reacting like some gorilla off the bench of a Southern Conference football team.

Disgusted with himself, he sunk into one of the leather wing chairs and carefully raised his leg onto the footstool.

"Your leg hurts, doesn't it?" she asked gently.

He nodded. It did. And so did his back from standing and walking with one leg longer than the other.

"Is there anything I can do for you?"

"There is, but there's not a chance in hell that you'll do it."

Her eyes were liquid dark. "Try me," she said cautiously.

"You can stop feeling sorry for me."

She laughed. "You're right; I won't do that. But it is awful to be pitied, isn't it?"

"Are those the words of 'the only girl at Holyoke who had to make money'?"

She stiffened, but answered nonetheless. "Yes. Is there anything else I can do for you?"

"If you really don't mind, I could use a brandy."

She turned, moving toward the kitchen, where she now knew he kept his liquor.

His voice followed her. "But only if you will join me."

She obviously assumed that he was only being polite and shook her head.

"I wasn't just saying that. I wish you'd stay and talk for a while...Suzanne."

His unusual use of her name must have convinced her because she returned with the squat brandy bottle and two snifters on a brass tray. As she crossed the room, it occurred to him that Carter Landau had this evening probably said the wisest thing that he had said in his entire life. A little more skin would be nice. Patrick hadn't really noticed before, but she was lovely. Very lovely.

Suzanne set the tray on the butler's table between the two wing chairs. He gestured to her to go ahead and pour. She handed him a glass and then, sitting, cradled the glass in her hands, warming the brandy.

The room felt peaceful. Only the lamp between the two chairs was on so that his desk, her word processor, all the annoying signs of their work were just dark, shadowy shapes. Neither of them spoke, relishing the quiet after the noisy party. She had to be, he thought, the most peaceful woman he—

The hell she was.

"What does your father do?" His question was abrupt.

The dark eyes turned to him. "He's a longshoreman."

"Why are you lying?"

"Because you are being a snob."

"Perhaps," he acknowledged, "but I am also being a realist. You aren't the daughter of a longshoreman."

"Father was a curator of a small art museum as was my mother."

"Was?"

"Yes, they both died when I was in college."

"I'm sorry. Is that why you needed to make money?" Normally he was never this inquisitive, but somehow, tonight, perhaps it was the brandy... perhaps it was her.

In a few brief words, she explained about having college loans.

"A lot of people default on their student loans," he said conversationally.

"Not me."

Her voice was crisp, and he glanced over at her. The

government made little effort to collect these educational loans if a person did not have enough integrity to make his payments. But old-fashioned Yankee integrity was something Suzanne Lawrence seemed to have a great deal of.

Everything he found about her made him admire her the more.

"What are your plans once the loan is paid off?" He didn't doubt for a moment that she had plans. "Are you going back into the humanities?"

"No, I find that I rather enjoy making money so I plan on starting a typing and editing service."

That made sense. She was extraordinarily good at revision and editing, and she was quite clearly capable of running her own business.

Then Patrick decided as long as he was going to be nosey, he might as well go the whole way. "And your friend?" He was starting to sound a little strange, calling this man "your friend" all the time, but what else could he say? "You said he was a writer; will you start the business together?"

"Good heavens, no."

That was the second time she had used just that startled expression in reference to her lover. And Patrick was very curious indeed. "What kind of writing does he do?"

"Mostly fiction, a few reviews."

God, but she was being close-mouthed. He didn't know anyone this reticent—except of course himself.

Nonetheless, he persevered. "Has he published? I can't remember if you've told me his last name."

She took a breath. "It's Moretti."

"Mor—" Patrick sat up so abruptly that his leg nearly crashed off the footstool. "You don't mean Dominick Moretti, do you?"

"Yes."

He couldn't believe it. "You're living with Dominick Moretti?"

"Yes. Do you know his work?"

"Do I know—" He cursed. "I have every one of his books. He's the one author...I mean, I hardly have any time to read, but I buy his the minute they are released and..."

Suzanne Lawrence and Dominick Moretti. This poised, elegant person, her beautifully manicured hands curled around a brandy glass, the delicate gold bracelet swinging lightly at her wrist, the gleam of blond hair falling smoothly to her slight shoulders—she and Dominick Moretti.

It wasn't that Moretti's works were pornographic, not in the least, but there was an animal vitality about them, a dark and undeniably sexual energy, that seemed the exact opposite of Miss Lawrence's quiet poise.

Christ. Was he ever wrong in thinking that Suzanne's lover was probably a man a great deal like himself. If Moretti's works were any reflection of the man, there was an intensity, a spontaneity, a relish for emotion and turbulence, an openness that were entirely alien to Patrick's own character.

That was why he read Moretti so avidly; the books gave him a chance to warm himself at the flame missing in his own makeup.

So it was not Suzanne's lover he was a great deal like; it was Suzanne herself. They were cautious, disciplined, rational, but with a hunger for something, for an intensity they were probably incapable of. In that need, they both turned to Dominick Moretti.

But he just read the books; she went to bed with the man. He wondered which one had the best of it.

At the moment, it was clearly not Suzanne. She was sitting quietly as if she were still just relaxing after a party, but her lips were tight, and Patrick realized how uncomfortable she was.

She must have known what he was thinking; it must have happened to her before—people would find out that she lived with Moretti and then start to think and speculate about very intimate details. How he would hate that if he were in her shoes.

"Well," he said, desperately wishing he had not inflicted this on her, "when will his next book be released?" He hoped that his tone was even, that his question sounded casual.

"It will be out in the spring, late April, I believe." She stood. "Thank you for this lovely brandy, but I need to go. The streets are not getting any better."

He had driven her away. "It's not a night for driving a car you aren't comfortable with."

"I know, but Nick took my car this afternoon and managed to get it towed. Why a man who writes like he can can't read a parking sign I'll never know, but he certainly can't."

She was nearly chattering. It was so unusual for her to volunteer information like this; he must have upset her.

Patrick shifted his cast to the floor, and although he never bothered when she left during the week, he stood up. Her coat was lying across the back of the sofa. He picked it up and held it for her.

Silently she captured each velvet cuff with a hand so her suit sleeve would not ride up, and she slipped her arms into the coat. Her back was to him and as he drew the coat up her shoulders, he let his hands rest on her shoulders.

How delicate she felt. Even through the thick wool

of her coat, her shoulders seemed fragile. He felt his hands tighten.

Here she was, this person who was more like him than any other, the one person who would probably understand all that no one else seemed to, who would know what he felt like because she felt that way too, and she would know all this because they were so alike.

And yet they were not entirely alike. She was a woman, graceful and soft.

A thought gripped him. No, it was more than a thought, it was a knowledge, a certainty, rich, sable-colored, absolute. He and she should be together. In their alikeness they shared so much; their one difference, that merely physical fact of their sexes, was also something to be shared. Why else was she here, so very much like him? There was some reason for it— he believed that with an urgency transcending the sexual. Some force linking them, some bonding power, some—

What nonsense! Abruptly Patrick let go of her. What was wrong with him? He, of all people, to think such silly thoughts. "A bonding power"? What silliness.

They exchanged polite good nights but even after she had left, even after she had disappeared into the icy night, he couldn't stop thinking about what had happened when he helped her on with her coat.

He had never been one to dress sex up in pretty paper; he had always been careful not to confuse it with love, not to be led astray by the artificial intimacy its afterglow produced. Sex wasn't mystical, magical, mysterious. It just felt good, that was all.

So why had he been thinking like something out of a voodoo book that some mysterious force was drawing him to Suzanne Lawrence? He didn't believe that the world operated that way, with dark mystic powers urging people into irrational behavior. Only weak-minded people succumbed to such notions.

It had just been sex. He wanted her. What was the big deal about it anyway? It was hardly surprising; she was quite lovely.

And if he had been gripped by anything more than a sexual urge, it was undoubtedly just male ego, that fearfully destructive, shockingly immature commodity that Sally Britten had tried so hard to stamp out in her four sons. *Well, Mother,* Patrick thought, *I hope it worked better on the others because your oldest is acting like a Neanderthal.*

Surely his pride was just piqued because of the role reversal earlier in the evening—Suzanne driving, opening doors for him, generally looking after him. Moreover—and to his mind this was entirely unforgivable—she was suddenly Dominick Moretti's woman and that was a challenge.

Like the Puritans who adorned his family tree, Patrick Britten set high standards for himself. He knew that other people acted foolishly, on weird emotional impulses, but he believed that he did not. Belief in his own rationality was important to him; it was the central quality by which he understood and defined his own character: that he was at all times, whatever the provocation, capable of rational, sensible actions. And he chastised himself for what seemed to him irrational, overly emotional behavior.

But despite all these stern lectures, these cautioning reminders, he could not make himself pleased that he had let his hands drop off Suzanne Lawrence. He wished that they were still there.

Chapter Four

Are you getting a crush on him? Miss Lawrence asked herself sternly.

Oh, probably, Suzanne sighed in reply.

After all, there was a great deal to admire about Patrick Britten, his quick mind, his disciplined habits, his bright ambition that was tempered with a steady integrity, and, she admitted to herself honestly, his body.

She tried to explain the way she was noticing his physical presence, blaming it on his broken leg. His normal gait was probably lithe, so easy that no one would pay any attention to it especially when he was in a business suit. But now he walked with an awkward lurch that called attention to itself, and it was hard to look at his walk without noticing the rest of him.

She also blamed it on the way he dressed. She worked with men who wore only three-piece business suits, and Nick always wore baggy jeans. But Patrick, working at home, dressed in a casual but classic style she liked a great deal. His slacks were corduroy or flannel, perhaps pleated or cuffed, in grays, blues, or other very muted colors. He would wear a camel-colored sleeveless sweater over a tattersall shirt, a burgundy crewneck sweater, or a Pendleton plaid shirt over a navy turtleneck. He looked effortlessly attractive and quite masculine.

But what had happened Saturday night was more than just liking the way he looked.

She tried to tell herself that it was nothing—he had just helped her on with her coat, that's all. Yes, he had rested his hands on her shoulders for a moment and she thought she felt them tighten as if he were about to turn her to face him, but it was probably just that he lost his balance; that sometimes happened to him.

But the moment had nearly overwhelmed her; it had felt like... well, she wasn't sure.

Suzanne had read her Plato and she knew the parable in the *Symposium*, that man and woman were once one body, joined back to back and then were, like a hard-boiled egg, divided in half. The fable then defined love as each individual man and woman constantly searching for his other half. When found, the pair would desperately cling together, dazzled and comforted by the recognition of one another, trying through sexual embraces to achieve their lost unity, the oneness they had once shared.

That was how she had felt when Patrick had helped her with her coat. Standing there, close enough to feel him breathe, it was as though she had found something, the other half of herself, all that was needed to make her complete. If she would just turn, there he would be, waiting for her, also knowing that the two of them belonged together, that they were half of something that longed, that ached, to be whole.

But she had not turned and his hands had dropped. Those feelings were so silly, she told herself. It was just sex; there was no reason to puff it up into something mythopoetical. By doing so, she had just been trying to convince herself that it was all right to do something that was foolish.

Sleeping with him would be a mistake. There was

no doubt about that. She could never sneak around, catching furtive moments with a man, but an open affair with Patrick would not only make things impossible with Nick, but it would make her job a nightmare.

And that's all it would ever be with him, an affair. It might be a very pleasant one, but it would never be anything more because Suzanne couldn't imagine herself loving him.

She did respect him more than any man she knew; she was comfortable with him; she liked him. They were alike.

But all too often Suzanne thought that her caution, her reserve, made her overly fastidious, too precise, incapable of spontaneous delight or any true pleasure. In this, he was her mirror and she didn't always like the reflection.

Quite simply, Suzanne Lawrence did not like herself well enough to love Patrick Britten.

She had loved Nick Moretti for his undisciplined energy, for his sparkle and enthusiasm. Their differences had made their relationship impossible, but it had been those differences that she had envied and loved.

She supposed if she ever loved again, it would be another man like Nick, and she would be doomed to repeat the same pattern of failure. It was a shame; her life would be so much easier if she could love a man like Patrick Britten, someone who shared her habits, values, background, and temperament. But she couldn't.

That little shock of awareness on Saturday night changed things on Monday morning. They were each a little more careful. Suzanne was careful to walk around his desk rather than reach across him if she needed a folder that lay beyond his other arm, and he, in turn, was more careful about his balance when he was standing, no longer ever resting his hand on the back of her chair. And once when she was carrying a heavy box of paper for the printer and the pressure of the carton against her breasts opened the button of her blouse, he swiftly bent his head over his work, careful not to embarrass her by admiring the wisp of navy blue lace that molded her white curves.

There remained an unspoken consciousness, a tacit awareness that they were male and female that had not flickered between them before, but they tried to smother it, keeping it only a flicker, pale and faint, nearly without heat or light, never allowing it to smoulder into a blaze. They were coworkers and friends; they tried hard to forget that they were also man and woman.

But one morning, the steady routine was disrupted.

It was a windy, snowy day. Suzanne cut across the Boston Common where the drifts had covered the steps of the Soldier's Memorial, and the brick sidewalks on Patrick's street, which had been clear the night before, were ankle deep with new fallen snow.

Carefully she went up the steps of his house, holding on to the wrought iron railing. She let herself in.

She blinked. The front hall was not itself. A pile of down jackets, mufflers, and gray-flecked Norwegian sweaters were tossed over the bannister in a careless cascade. She opened the double doors that divided the living room from the hall. The room was dark and silent and cautiously she switched on a lamp.

The place was a mess. Beer cans crowded the end tables and flat pizza boxes lay open on the floor, their white cardboard soggy with red splotches of tomato sauce and strings of melted cheese. Patrick's usually neat desk was covered with papers and ledgers. This was odd, Suzanne thought, very odd. Normally his home was as neat as her own—or at least as her own would have been if Nick Moretti hadn't been living in it.

And then on the couch, she noticed the most surprising piece of clutter: a blue sleeping bag clearly swaddling a human form.

What an interesting thought—that in a drunken fit, Patrick Britten had emptied his front closet onto the hall stairs, dumped the contents of a file drawer across his desk, and then deposited his own person on the sofa in a sleeping bag. It was an interesting thought, but, Suzanne thought realistically, not very likely.

Then the form in the sleeping bag rolled over, exposing a swatch of bright, carrot-colored hair, and Suzanne had to relinquish the notion that it was Patrick sleeping there. She could not imagine any sequence of events that would result in him dyeing his hair.

She shrugged and sat down to work. Not surprisingly, Patrick had left no new pages of manuscript on her desk. Carrot-top, whoever he—or she—might be, had clearly been distracting. But Suzanne still had plenty to do.

The room remained silent, except for the few noises she made, the shuffle of paper and the scratch of her pen. She heard nothing from the back room where Patrick slept, or where he usually slept; she had absolutely no idea if he were there at the moment. Carrot-top started to snore.

Finally she heard a stirring from that direction.

"Hello." A puzzled voice made her turn. "You weren't here last night, were you?"

Carrot-top was a boy; well, he was probably eighteen or so, but still sleepy and confused, propped up against the arm of the sofa with the sleeping bag slipping down to expose a nearly hairless chest, he looked very young to Suzanne.

"No, I wasn't." Although she had to admit that she wished she had been. She was curious about the unexpected clutter in Patrick Britten's tidy life. "I'm Suzanne Lawrence," she introduced herself, hoping that that would produce some interesting tale about how this boy came to be sleeping on this sofa.

"Hi," he replied helpfully and then finally added, "Oh, I'm Andy."

He sounded like that was supposed to mean something to her; it didn't. "Would you like some coffee?" she asked. That seemed more polite than demanding "Who are you?"

"Coffee? That would be terrific." And when Suzanne returned from the kitchen having made some both for him and herself, he grinned, a quick flashing grin that somehow looked familiar. "Breakfast in bed," he crooned happily. "I'm going to have to come visit Pat more often." Then he laughed. "That should just thrill him no end."

Suzanne had never heard anyone call Patrick "Pat." Even David Stern, his closest friend, called him Patrick. Who was this person?

"Do you visit him often?" she ventured.

"Mid-terms and finals," he announced. "Two great times to come see big brother."

Brother! This boy was a decade younger than Patrick. "You and Patrick are brothers?"

"Sure. I'm sorry, I thought you knew."

Suzanne shook her head; she couldn't quite imagine Patrick with a kid brother. But apparently he had one, one who had spent the night on his sofa.

"By the way," Andy asked, "who are you? Don't be

insulted that I haven't heard of you. Pat never tells us one thing about his girl friends. I figure we're lucky that we know where he lives."

Suzanne glanced around at the mess in the room; she could understand why a visit from his little brother might not be Patrick's favorite occupation. "I'm not," she answered, "either insulted or his girl friend." She got up and while she explained the proposal she started to pick up the living room. As she was balancing the beer cans on the pizza boxes, a noise made her glance over at the double doors that led to the hall.

Patrick ambled in. His hair wasn't combed and he was wearing baggy chino pants and was still buttoning a faded flannel shirt.

"Patrick!" She couldn't help her gasp; to be this disheveled, it wasn't like him.

Indeed it wasn't. "No," the man said immediately. "I'm Ford, his brother."

Of course. Although this man looked so like Patrick that the first impression was unnerving, his hair was redder, his body slighter, and, of course, his leg wasn't broken.

"I *am* sorry," Suzanne apologized. She knew that many people hated to be called by their siblings' names—although Suzanne, a lonely only child, had always thought that being called by a sister's name would be a very small price to pay for having a sister.

"Don't worry about it," Ford shrugged. "It happens all the time. Everybody thinks I am him. I've been trying to get the I.R.S. to start sending me his income tax refund, but so far that hasn't worked."

A third man suddenly appeared behind Ford's shoulder; this one looked like no one and had perfectly ordinary brown hair. "The way you can tell the difference between Patrick and Ford," he said, "is that Pat generally manages to get dressed before he comes into the room. Ford is still working on that."

"Now, Brian, if I'd known Andy was going to have a visitor this early," Ford returned, "I'd have managed to get myself buttoned."

"Who are you? The cleaning lady?" The man named Brian glanced at the trash Suzanne was still holding. "Only Pat would manage to find a cleaning lady who wears a gray flannel suit."

Suzanne was not in a suit; she dressed more casually here than she did in the office. But she was wearing a gray wool skirt and a navy sweater over a gray and blue checked blouse. Once again, she explained who she was and, deciding that this was a crowd where sturdy Yankee bluntness would go a lot further than elegant indirection, asked Brian if he was another brother.

"Brian Britten—it's a dumb name, isn't it?" he returned. "Nonetheless, it's mine. I'm between Ford and Andrew, and I'm hungry. Is there any pizza left?"

"Pizza for breakfast?" Even Nick Moretti didn't eat cold pizza, all greasy and rubbery, in the morning.

"It's food, isn't it?" Brian pointed out.

"Not when it's cold."

And then without quite knowing how it happened, Suzanne, who was capable of saying no to anyone, who never did things during business hours that the firm wasn't paying her to do, found herself in the kitchen fixing breakfast for Patrick's three brothers.

As she worked, a few questions helped her sort them out. Ford had an antique shop, Brian was trying to become a writer, and Andy was a freshman in college, majoring in "being in college."

Suzanne's orderly mind noted that the four brothers were in reverse alphabetical order: Patrick, Ford, Brian, Andrew. She was sure Patrick was the oldest; he looked several years older than Ford; he acted several decades older than all of them.

"Incidentally what have you done with Patrick?" she asked as she carried a platter of French toast to the table. "He's usually up by now. He is here, isn't he?"

"No," Brian replied immediately. "We set him up on the street corner with a little cup and hung a sign around his neck, 'Help send this poor cripple back to Harvard Business School.'"

Suzanne had to laugh. Clearly Patrick's three brothers were enjoying his current disability. They must have teased him unendingly last night. It was probably very good for him, she thought heartlessly.

Ford transfered a piece of bacon directly from the platter to his mouth. "Maybe you better go check on him, Andy."

Andy, obviously used to having his older brothers tell him what to do, stuffed another piece of French toast in his mouth and went back to the study, opening the door without knocking.

"We're having French toast for breakfast," he mumbled, his mouth still busy eating. "Don't you want any?"

"Not if you made it," returned Patrick's voice.

Andy swallowed. "Are you kidding? Suzanne did."

"Su—" Then Patrick let out a startling curse and clumped into the dining room. "What are *you* doing here?" he demanded.

Brian immediately turned to Ford and deadpanned, "How come everyone is always telling us his manners are so much better than ours? That sounded pretty rude to me. Didn't it to you?"

"Yes, but what do we know?" Ford returned. "Maybe we should pay attention and see what we can learn." All three brothers abandoned their breakfasts and sat up straight, their hands folded, and their eyes wide and alert, pretending to be in class.

Brian elbowed Ford. "Can I borrow a pencil? I forgot to bring one."

Patrick ignored them, which Suzanne guessed was not at all an unusual occurrence. "Why are you here?" he repeated.

Brian instantly pretended to be taking notes. "Why... are... you—"

"This isn't going to be on the final, is it?" Andy interrupted.

"Don't worry," Ford whispered loudly. "The frat has last year's exam on file. We can cheat."

"What a relief." And Andy, experienced college student that he was, pretended to fall asleep.

Suzanne was trying so hard not to laugh that her hand shook as she poured Patrick some coffee. She handed the mug to him. "I had no way of knowing your brothers would be here," she pointed out.

"I called last night, but Mor—" He paused, glancing at his brother Brian, to whom the name Moretti would likely mean something. "But Nick said you were asleep; he said he would leave you a note."

This was hardly the first time Nick had failed to deliver a message. "Nick is very good at some things," she replied. "Phone messages isn't one of them. But it's all right; I don't mind."

And she didn't. The younger three Britten brothers had dropped out of Etiquette 101 and were back demolishing their breakfast. She thought them some of the most relaxed, engaging people she had ever met.

"Well, at least don't wait on them," Patrick replied. He looked at Ford, shaking his head. "Don't you know that you don't ask women to do stuff like this anymore?"

"How would we know?" Ford deposited some French toast on a plate for Patrick. "None of us have secretaries."

"Or are ever likely to," Brian continued. "In fact—"

"Now wait a minute," Andy interrupted. "We don't know that about me. I might end up president of Standard Oil—unless of course the president of Standard Oil needs to understand calculus. If so," he sighed, "I'm out of the running for that job."

Suzanne couldn't help laughing. Calculus or not, she couldn't quite see Andy Britten as the chief executive officer of a major oil company.

Patrick smiled too, and Suzanne realized why Andy's grin had seemed familiar. "You should ask Miss Lawrence if she understands calculus; she's the one in this room who could run Standard Oil."

Andy wrinkled his nose. "Do we have to call her 'Miss Lawrence'?"

"Yes," said Patrick.

"No," said Suzanne.

Patrick's three brothers not only made a lot of noise, but they seemed to take up an enormous quantity of space. When she came back into the living room after breakfast, everywhere Suzanne looked there was a brother. Andy was once again sprawled on the sofa, Brian was at her desk playing with her word processor, and Ford was in one wing chair, having swiveled around the other to put his feet on.

"They do change things," she commented to Patrick.

"More than you know," he returned and nearly fell over a shaving kit that was lying in the middle of the living room.

Suzanne grabbed his arm and felt his weight against her for a moment.

"Thanks," he said with a sigh. "I'm sorry to inflict them on you."

"Actually, I find them interesting."

"Interesting, that's a good word for them."

It turned out that Patrick did the books for Ford's antique shop and as Patrick was immobile, Ford had brought the books to him. Andy was getting help with calculus, and Brian had, he told her, come along to see if Patrick would let him sign his cast, a mission doomed from the start.

"I'm sorry, Suzanne," Patrick apologized again, "but as soon as I finish these books, they will go away."

"Why do you do the books?" she asked. "You aren't an accountant."

"No," Patrick replied. "But I'm sure more of one than he is."

That was clear. Ford obviously ran his business in the most relaxed fashion. He loved beautiful old things so he bought them and brought them to his shop. Selling them did not seem to be the point.

Suzanne sighed. She'd been like that, living in airy disregard of finances. A person had to be very sheltered to be that unrealistic, and for a moment Suzanne envied him—and wondered why he and Patrick were so different.

Indeed, Ford's method of bookkeeping seemed to be irritating his brother. "What's an 'S,R,T,S,colon,M, C,B'?" Patrick asked.

"I haven't a clue," Ford replied calmly.

"Ford!" Patrick was clearly exasperated. "It's your shop. Don't you—"

"Let me look at it," Suzanne interrupted. She was usually very good at figuring out other people's notes. It was a skill that had been in great demand during finals week at Mt. Holyoke.

She leaned over Patrick's shoulder and looked at the scrawled entry. She thought for a moment, although the distance between Patrick's shoulder and her breast did seem more interesting than anything in the ledger.

"If the 'R' is a 'D', then it could be 'silver dressing table set: mirror, comb, brush.'"

"That's it," Ford exclaimed. "I remember that. It was a dandy—an old Reed and Barton set; I hated to sell it."

"Did you find it a nice home?" Brian called over his shoulder. Apparently Ford's reluctance to sell things was a family joke.

Patrick glanced up at Suzanne respectfully. "How did you ever figure that out?"

She shrugged. "I don't know. I always look at them whenever I'm in antique stores."

"Do you like silver dressing table sets?" Ford asked.

She nodded. She loved them. To have a silver brush and mirror waiting for you each morning and night seemed like a very civilized way to live.

"I've got some beauties up at the shop," he said enthusiastically.

Suzanne shook her head. "I saw the price on that one. I can't possibly afford it," she said, although it was, of course, not clear if Ford actually wanted to sell them to her or just *show* them to her.

Patrick closed up the ledgers. "I am finished and if the weather reports are at all accurate, you three had better hit the road."

"Is this supposed to be a big snow?" Brian asked in surprise.

"Don't you look at the weather report?" Patrick groaned.

"Why? My knowing isn't going to change anything."

As the three were putting their coats on and gathering up their ledgers, calculus textbooks, sleeping bags, and other gear, Patrick was looking out the window. "Do you characters have enough cash in case you get stuck?"

"I certainly don't," Brian said proudly.

"Cash? Us?" Andy exclaimed. "What on earth would we be doing with cash? You're the only one in the entire family who doesn't have to fish up dimes from behind the car seats to pay tolls."

Patrick immediately pulled his wallet out of his back pocket and, almost as if he were his brother's father, handed Ford what was clearly several twenties. "When are you clowns ever going to grow up?"

"Not as long as you make it so easy for us not to," Ford replied, taking the money nonetheless.

"You're right," Patrick agreed. "Getting stranded on Route Two in a blizzard would probably teach you a thing or two."

"Nonsense," said Brian. "It happens to Mom all the time and she never changes. Why should we?"

Patrick was still standing at the window when they left, and over his shoulder, Suzanne saw his three brothers bound out into the snowy street, tossing snowballs at each other.

He turned abruptly, nearly losing his balance. "Let's get to work," he said crisply. "Those brothers of mine got me behind schedule."

But he seemed to have trouble concentrating. He must be getting very restless, Suzanne thought. His noisy brothers' comings and goings must have made his apartment seem like a prison in which he was trapped as much by the amount of work he had to do as by his broken leg.

So they worked silently as the snow fell outside.

When she got up for tea in the middle of the afternoon, Suzanne glanced out the window again and grew a little concerned about how she was going to get home. For a moment, she thought about leaving, but somehow it didn't seem fair to abandon Patrick. At least she didn't drive to work; the T would get her home.

So she worked on. The December dusk darkened the room, and the brass lamps cast friendly pools of warm yellow light across their desks, catching the golden glint of Patrick's pen and the delicate gold chain at Suzanne's wrist. The little green letters and numbers marched steadily across the screen of her word processor, and the only sound was the light click of the keys and the heavier thump of the space bar.

Suddenly the lights flickered, darkening for a moment and then flashing back on.

But Suzanne's little green letters didn't come back. "Oh, blast."

Patrick raised his head. "The power? How much did you lose?" When the electricity went off, the word processor lost everything that had not been stored onto the disc.

She flipped through the manuscript she had already typed. "Only five pages," she said in relief. She was generally careful to stop frequently and store on the disc what she had entered in the computer's memory. "It won't take long to redo." But as she started the machine up, the room went dark again and this time the light didn't return.

Suzanne went to the front window, opening the shutters all the way to let in the last bits of daylight. There was precious little of it. As they had worked, the snow had fallen heavily, turning the city street into a Christmas card. The parked cars were hidden under mounds of fresh snow whose icy whiteness glistened beneath the old-fashioned gas streetlamps that still lit Beacon Hill. The red brick of the townhouses glowed deep and rich against the white snow, and the black shutters up and down the street echoed the black lines of the wrought-iron railings that peeped out of the snowdrifts. It was a silent scene. No people tramped along the wide sidewalks; no cars ventured through the narrow street. It was all snow.

She heard Patrick opening his desk drawer and then a quick succession of voices and static as he apparently spun the dial on a transistor radio.

Still looking out the window, she listened. Twenty inches of snow lay on the ground, and the snow was still falling at the rate of two inches an hour. Plowing was almost pointless. The Southeast Expressway and Storrow Drive were like parking lots. The Red Line on the T was stopped because of problems on the Longfellow Bridge and the other lines were packed and completely behind schedule.

It takes a lot to shut down Boston. It's a hardy city full of rugged Yankees who refuse to pamper themselves. But this evening even the most stoic Bostonians were admitting that perhaps this storm was more than "a tad blustery." The mayor was asking people to stay where they were.

Suzanne couldn't get home, not with the Red Line down. "Patrick—"

He interrupted, making it easy for her. "Is it going to bother Moretti if you stay here?"

Suzanne turned. He was sitting, leaning back in his chair, his broken leg stretched out before him. He was in jeans and a black ribbed commando sweater with leather at the shoulders and elbows, having dressed more casually than usual that morning, not expecting her to come.

"Not if I call. But I do hate imposing on you."

"I'm sorry you feel that way because I don't mind."

"Even after your brothers were just here... ?"

He smiled quietly. "I may not be the most hospitable of men, but you can hardly be classed as the same sort of intrusion as them." He leaned forwad and tapped his gold pen on the desk for a moment. "And, Suzanne"—it was rare that he used her name—"I hope you know I would never impose myself on *you*."

"I know that," she said swiftly. "You didn't even have to say it."

"I didn't think I did."

And Suzanne knew that she, in turn, didn't have to say that she would rather not have to explain this night to people at work. He would never mention it, not even to his closest friend.

What a relief it was, to have all this awkwardness settled so easily. "Now," she said briskly, "I do hope you have some candles because the electricity seems to have abandoned us."

"Not only do I have candles, but I have a gas stove so that we can even eat. So what do you say we forget about work? I've got some decent wine; I think we should get drunk."

"What a splendid idea."

Of course Suzanne, after she had called Nick, had to do the bustling around—getting the candles, the wine, lighting an antique kerosene lamp with an etched glass chimney, and even, as long as they were playing pioneers, building a fire.

Perhaps it was the wine or the candlelight or the warmth of the fire, but the restlessness that had been gnawing Patrick all day eased and they sat quietly, relaxed.

"What would you like to talk about?" he said at last.

"Nothing," she answered. This was something about her which Nick had yet to understand; that she enjoyed quiet. "Except maybe dinner, that sounds interesting; I'm getting hungry."

He grimaced. "I am afraid that I don't have anything interesting to say about that—just the frozen stuff my mother brought down."

Suzanne knew that he was rather tired of eating the same thing again and again. "Do you have any canned tomatoes?"

He nodded and she stood up, "I haven't been living with an Italian for nothing. With tomatoes, I can do anything in a kitchen except wallpaper it."

Patrick's kitchen was small enough that three candles lit it; the yellow glow of their flames warmed the pale birch of the cabinets and pushed back the shadows that had darkened the terra-cotta tiles.

Lifting one of the candles, Suzanne began groping through the cabinets, taking out the red tomato cans, finding, almost by their shape, a squat can of clams and a long thin box of spaghetti.

"Don't set your hair on fire," Patrick cautioned. "By the time I'd get in there, you'd be in cinders."

His voice came from the shadows of the dining room. She set the candle down on the counter that divided the two rooms. He had arranged himself and his cast on a high stool, and with his chin in his hand, he was leaning against the counter, watching her work. The candlelight shone through his wine glass, glowing against the strength of his hand and the black sleeve of his ribbed sweater. In the half-light, in the intimacy of the warm shadows, it seemed as if she had always known him.

Suddenly she longed to say something, to tell him something about being here with him, the two of them together on this Boston night, the world outside soft with the falling snow and inside warm with the candles, the wine, and him. To tell him there was nowhere else she'd rather be, no one she'd rather be with.

"Do you have any garlic?" she asked instead.

"Sure. Next to the stove. First shelf."

"Then is linguini, or rather spaghetti since you don't have linguini, with red clam sauce all right? It's Nick's grandmother's recipe, although," Suzanne acknowledged sheepishly, "she doesn't use quite so many cans."

It was fine with him, and she set him to work opening cans; the electric can opener sat on the counter, ashamed and useless. As she pulled apart the garlic, the dried peels falling to the counter in white flakes, she heard him ask, "Do they like you? Moretti's family?"

"Of course they don't," she answered evenly, smashing the garlic with the broad side of the cleaver. "That's a great part of my charm—at least in his eyes—that I am so entirely unlike what was expected for him."

"Was he supposed to settle down with some nice Italian girl who would go to mass every day and have a baby every year?"

"Close. Except what Nick's family hasn't realized is that even the nice Italian girls don't want to do that anymore."

"Well, you can certainly understand that," Patrick agreed. "Given all the things you hear about how awful it is to have to stay home with kids, I'm surprised that anyone has them anymore."

"You probably only hear the bad," Suzanne pointed out. "People always complain. They don't talk about the good parts so much."

He looked at her interestedly. "I take it you plan on having children some day?"

She took the tomato can from him and quickly turned away. "No."

He said nothing.

"I don't know, Patrick...." The tomatoes splashed into the pan, soft red shapes floating in juices. Suzanne pushed at them with a wooden spoon.

Well, why not? He was hardly going to judge her; he was probably like this himself. "Actually, I do know." She broke into one of the tomatoes, its pulp separating underneath her spoon. "I don't think I would be much of a parent."

"Why?" Patrick asked as if she had said nothing more shocking than she didn't look good in red. "You are patient, you're generous, you're—"

"My mother was all that," Suzanne interrupted, "but that's not enough. I'm so rigid; I have to have everything just so; I can't stand noise or mess. If I had a child, I probably would never let it get dirty or leave its toys out, just like I was never allowed to." She was speaking very quickly now, the spoon dangling from her hand. "I don't even like it when a man takes my arm; I can't imagine having a child cling to me all the time, asking questions and needing so much. And, above all, I am no *fun.* I can't enter into things, do anything wholeheartedly. I'd be just like my mother, when she would try to play with me—even I knew how bored she was."

Patrick had picked up one of the candles and was tilting it, letting the wax run down its side. "It bothers you, doesn't it?"

"Well, sure." She was defensive. "I can't help thinking that it is the defects in my character that would keep me from being an adequate parent."

She couldn't even say the word. She couldn't even say, "I don't think I would be a good *mother.*"

"You're hardly alone on that one." And she knew what he was saying, that he too was like this, awkward and uncomfortable around children. "But," he continued, "you seem like you're good at everything you do."

"No, you said that before." She shook her head and set back to work. "I only do things that I am good at. If I think I will be bad at something, I don't do it."

She hated herself for this, for this caution, this unwillingness to risk making a fool of herself. She never played sports; she never sang or sketched; she avoided speaking French—she could read it but she didn't trust her accent. And above all, she was never going to have children. Failing at that would be much worse than letting a volley ball fall at her feet.

"How does Moretti feel about this?" Patrick asked.

"I'm not sure that he knows."

She heard his glass clink against the counter.

"Remember, we aren't married," she explained, keeping her voice light. "And if I can't imagine myself as a parent, I can even less see myself as an unwed one."

Patrick smiled. "I'm still having trouble seeing you living with someone."

"Put it down as the one act of rebellion against a too-strict upbringing."

"That makes sense," he acknowledged. He lifted his wine glass and suddenly grinned, a smile that was warm in the candlelight. "Except that by that token, given how liberal my parents have always been, I would be saving myself for my wedding night."

"And you're not?" Suzanne let her eyes widen in mock-surprise. She was glad they weren't talking about her anymore.

"Hard to believe, isn't it?" he returned dryly. "But we aren't all as rebellious as you, Miss Lawrence."

She laughed and carried the spaghetti over to the sink to drain in the colander. It was, she decided, his turn to be under the microscope. "I couldn't help noticing how much younger your brothers are than you," she remarked.

He didn't seem surprised at the abrupt change in subject. "I was six when Ford was born and ten when Andrew was."

"That must have taken some getting used to."

"It did. In fact," he said slowly, lacing his fingers around his glass, "I sometimes think that's part of the reason why I have so little interest in ever having children. I imagine I resented them a lot." He was leaning forward now. "I remember when each of them was born, how it disrupted everything. The nursery was next to my room, and Mother never really had any of them on regular schedule. Each time a baby would come into the house, I'd know there'd be another year of crying at night."

"Every older child must resent the younger ones some, especially after you had had your parents' full attention for so long."

"Attention?" Patrick shook his head. "Hardly."

"I don't understand."

"My parents were very young when I was born, not quite nineteen, and they weren't much in the way of parents—I'm not saying anything that they haven't said a hundred times—so in lots of ways Ford was the first child they raised, not me."

"Then why did they have you so early?"

"It wasn't exactly voluntary. I was born six months after they married."

"Oh," and then "*Oh*."

He looked at her curiously. "What is it?"

"You were an accident, a mistake?"

"Obviously." His answer was dry.

"But don't you see?" She turned to him, speaking quickly. "That explains it; it explains everything. I was too, a mistake, I mean; I wasn't planned either."

"You weren't? You were a mistake too?" Patrick looked stunned. And then suddenly, surprisingly, he looked a little pleased. "It does explain a lot, doesn't it?"

Of course they were alike. Suzanne had often wondered why they were; their families seemed so different. But now it was clear; neither of them had been planned; neither wanted; they were both mistakes.

They had been loved, but loved by people who did not know how to love children. Their physical needs had been attended to, but not their emotional needs. They had each had to sort out so much for themselves, deal with so much by themselves, in the oddly shaped world of a lonely child.

And so now they talked through dinner, and then afterward in the living room they talked. It was the first time for each of them that they had found another person to share their feelings with, knowing that what they would say would be understood, would not be mistaken for self-pity.

What it was like to be treated warily by adults who thought children to be strange mysterious beasts, what it was like to be alone so often. How Suzanne felt when after dinner, her parents would ask her politely if she was all right and then disappear into their studies; how long after she had stopped believing in Santa Claus, she was asking him to bring her a set of brothers like Patrick's. Or how Patrick felt when his mother would have her other sons piled in a deep chair with her, reading a book to them, a book that years before he had had to read to himself.

And they talked about how this had affected them, how they had learned not to need people, how they had learned to be self-reliant with an independence that other people misunderstood for coldness. They had both always worked hard as if they had to justify themselves, their places in a universe that hadn't expected them, as if by their work, they could purchase the right to an existence that was the result of carelessness and accident.

It was an unsettling notion, that you weren't supposed to be here, that you didn't quite belong, that you were a mistake, but it was an idea that was easier when it was shared.

They talked for a long time, late into the night, Patrick with his legs stretched out in front of him, his hands clasped behind his neck, while Suzanne sat with her legs curled beneath her, almost sidewards on the sofa, facing him.

At last they fell silent. The fire was just a heap of glowing embers and the candles had long since sputtered and died, leaving only the slender brass hurricane lamp burning on a low table nearby. But it didn't matter; the room didn't seem cold or dark, but more alive, more vibrantly warm, than any room that either of them had ever been in.

Patrick unlocked his hands, resting his arms on the back of the sofa. And Suzanne knew that it was time to stand up, time to ask about sheets and towels, time for this evening to be over.

But she did not move. She scarcely breathed.

Slowly he turned to look at her. The gray in his eyes blended into the shadows, leaving only the green, vivid and haunting.

She looked away—she had to—down at her hands, pale against her gray skirt. The gold chain around her wrist shimmered with the lamplight. Her eyes slid from the soft folds of her skirt to the denim next to her. The blue fabric took its shape from his leg, following, on the right, the swells and cords of his athletic body, while on the left, the jeans were a smooth column covering the hard cast. What was it like, there where the cast began, where the hair-roughened strength of his leg disappeared into the encircling prison of white plaster?

She felt a touch at her head, the lightest possible caress, just hovering at her hair, following the smooth fall of pale gold silk, slipping beneath it, until she felt his hand warm on her throat, lifting her face until she had to look into his eyes, now smouldering with a light she had to understand.

"We are not entirely alike, you and I." His voice was low.

How could she have ever thought they were? She was too aware of how his hand felt against her, a touch promising warmth, sweetness, glowing pleasures. How could she ever have been conscious of anything but that they were man and woman? The ribbed knit of his black sweater clung to him, to the sweep of his chest and shoulders, and she knew if she should touch it with her hand, her cheek, she would feel him breathe.

The hand at her neck curved around her face, urging her to him, and he bent his head to meet her.

His kiss was warm, just as she knew it would be. But it was cautious, giving her time, letting her decide if she should pull away, letting it be, if she should so choose, nothing more than a kiss of affection, a gesture that pledged only friendship and promised no passion.

But how could she move away, how could she draw back from him? He who was her other half, everything she was, except he was male, strong where she was soft, thrusting where she was welcoming, man where she was woman.

His hands moved on her shoulders, caressing against her sweater, his palms learning the softness of her upper arms, his thumbs following the delicacy of her collarbone. The feel of his mouth changed, the tip of his tongue easing her lips apart, his kiss still soft, but searching now, silken and deep.

And the pale flicker that they had both banked so carefully under the ice of their New England upbringing now flamed, bringing warmth to this snowy night, light to this dark room.

She wanted him. Those delicious sensations, which she thought had been driven from her body forever by the silent, secret reaction of chemical and hormone, were with her again. The melting richness, the willing pressures, all rose with her now, blossoming at his touch.

It felt so right, his arms now moving to encircle her in the embrace that she had longed for, pulling navy sweater against black. It felt so right, so natural, so inevitable.

No.

No, it wasn't right. It was stupid, a mistake. There was Nick. And work. And arrangements of whens and wheres, questions of openness and concealment... bitter stones of grating, gray practicality.

Suzanne was no tease and instantly she drew back.

"I know," Patrick sighed, still holding her, but staying the hand that had been slipping down her body, searching for the softness muffled within her navy sweater. "It's probably a terrible idea."

Suzanne knew that she didn't have to explain or apologize. He understood.

"Anyway," he went on, clearly trying to fight off the passion that still swirled through them both, "with this blasted cast, I'd probably break your leg too."

Suzanne went faint at the thought of their legs tangled together, of....

"So," Patrick continued, "perhaps you had better take advantage of the fact that you can defend your virtue simply by going upstairs. I can't possibly get to you up there."

Shakily, she stood up and asked all her questions about sheets and towels.

The sheets on his bed were clean since Ford had just put his sleeping bag on top of it last night and there were new toothbrushes and fresh soap in the medicine cabinet.

"You're prepared," she said. And then it occurred to her that that was hardly a tactful thing to say. There were probably very good reasons why he kept extra toothbrushes around—for women he didn't work with, for women whose lives weren't complicated by other men, for women who weren't so stupidly cautious.

But he just smiled and answered, "With brothers like mine, you have to be. One or the other is perpetually crashing here, and they're never prepared. Now do you have everything you need?"

She nodded and wishing him a soft good night, took the lamp, leaving him the one flashlight.

She'd never been up to his bedroom, but there was nothing that surprised. It was simply decorated, with walnut antiques he had probably coaxed out of his brother Ford. The quilt was navy, there were a few engravings on the ivory walls, and a reading lamp on only one side of the bed.

When she was undressed, Suzanne set her lamp down on the other nightstand, getting into that side of the bed, as if she were leaving room for him to sleep in his usual spot, as if she were waiting for him to join her.

And for a moment, she was willing to risk her home, her peace of mind, her job, even her legbone, to be with him.

Stop it, she ordered herself. She was being weak-minded and romantic. Snowdrifts, wine, and firelight might send other women to a man's arms, but not her. She was too sensible to be carried away by an impulse, and he was too. They were both very rational people who weren't about to make a mistake.

Chapter Five

The first flicker of awareness between Patrick and Suzanne, that night following the Christmas party when Patrick had let his hands linger on Suzanne's shoulders, had left the two of them a little uncomfortable, a little awkward and constrained. Surprisingly, the flare of openly acknowledged passion on this snowy night had the opposite effect.

Matters had been dealt with. They admitted that they were attracted to each other, that they wanted to sleep together, but it was decided that they weren't going to, they couldn't, it would be foolish, stupid, impulsive, irrational; they wouldn't do it.

And it wasn't too hard. They were from Boston and Bostonians did not indulge themselves; they didn't give in to the body's clamors. Just as Bostonians went about all winter defiant of the cold outside, so too were they able to disdain the warmth inside. Wayward passion was a problem for people from lesser cities.

Having everything settled and clearly understood made for an ease. One morning when she picked up another box of paper, Patrick eyed her interestedly and then noting her slate blue turtleneck, turned back to his work. "Buttons, Suzanne, buttons," he muttered with an exaggerated sigh, "they're good things."

Although they had not set out to be friends, Suzanne felt there was no one who understood her as well as Patrick did, simply because given what he knew of himself, there was so little that he needed to learn about her. They had no more late-night, heart-to-heart talks, but they didn't need to; the quickest phrase told each more than a lengthy conversation with another might have.

Probably the only thing he didn't understand about her was her relationship with Nick. But out of loyalty to the man she had once loved, she would never discuss him with Patrick. Too much of Nick envied men like Patrick. He would writhe if someone like Patrick knew about the failure of his relationship with Suzanne.

So she never spoke about Nick, saying only, for example, that she would like to leave early on the day before Christmas.

"Are you going away?" he had asked.

"Just to New York for a day or so."

Patrick's eyes went gray. She didn't have to say more. He understood that New York meant Brooklyn and Christmas with Nick's family.

The afternoon of the twenty-fourth, as she stood up from her desk to get her coat, Patrick pulled open his drawer and took out a flat package wrapped in red paper. "This is for you," he said quietly.

It was a Christmas present. She wished he hadn't. She desperately wished he hadn't.

Yes, she had done an excellent job on the proposal, doing work far beyond what any other secretary could have done, and yes, she had done him innumerable personal favors, the sort that Patrick would certainly never expect a secretary to do. A Christmas gift was an entirely appropriate way to thank a secretary.

But she didn't feel like his secretary, and she didn't

want the usual secretary's gift of perfume or lotion. It would cheapen everything. She hadn't bought him aspirin or picked up the latest *Sports Illustrated* because she wanted a gift.

She had done them because she considered herself his friend.

She hated the thought that he had felt obligated to do this, that he had had to worry about what to get her. She was hard to buy gifts for; she knew that. Nick always gave her books, which she loved, but she read so much and owned so many that only he, who knew what was in her library, dared buy her a book. Harrison Colt, who understood exactly why she was working for him, broke every rule of etiquette and gave her a check. She hated to think of Patrick fretting because he felt like he had to buy her something but didn't know what.

"Patrick, you didn't have to do this."

"I know that. I wanted to."

He didn't sound like he was only being polite.

Gingerly, she slit through the tape holding the red paper, hoping that she would not have to lie to him about liking what was inside.

The box was white, unmarked, the kind where the lid and the bottom are the same size and difficult to open. She tugged them apart and then folded back the tissue paper.

Gleaming on a bed of white were a silver brush, comb, and mirror. Delicate etchings of vines and flowers scrolled up the handles and across the silver backs, circling her initials.

She lifted the mirror, turning it over, looking at it, unbelieving. It was so very lovely. "Patrick," she breathed. "They're perfect." They were exactly what she would have chosen for herself.

"Do you like them?" His voice was warm.

"I love them." She could hardly believe that these beautiful things were actually hers.

"I am glad of that." There was a trace of relief in his voice. "I really wanted to give you something, but I decided it had to be something special or nothing at all. Then I remembered your talking to Ford, and I called him and he had these in his shop."

He had gotten up and was now standing behind her shoulder. She could see him in the mirror, his eyes warm and green. He was clearly pleased that she liked the set; an almost boyish enthusiasm lit his face.

"Ford had them re-engraved," Patrick continued, "and put new bristles on the brush. He claims that that may lessen their value, but I couldn't see you using a hairbrush you didn't know the history of."

How did he know that? It was so true. If the brush had been old and worn, it would have taken Suzanne a while to overcome a certain reluctant squeamishness about using it.

She traced the graceful vine that scrolled around the edge of the mirror. She had taken this assignment for the overtime; she had wanted the money. She had never expected these lovely things... or him.

Then it was all over. After the usual difficult visit with Nick's family, she returned to Boston, working with Patrick for a few more days, but after the New Year's holiday, she had to be back at her usual place in Harrison Colt's outer office.

Working with Patrick now seemed like an idyllic dream. They had worked very hard, but it had been unstressed and uninterrupted. Now the phone on her desk rang continually; it sometimes took Suzanne three-quarters of an hour to get to the ladies' room and back, she was stopped so often by people with questions. And she could never completely concentrate on one thing: As if she were the mother of a toddler, she always had to have part of her mind alert for Mr. Colt, where he was, who he was talking to, who he was supposed to be talking to, what he was scheduled to do next. It was exhausting, demanding, and what they paid her for.

One day toward the end of January was particularly trying. She was trying to set up a meeting Harrison Colt was going to have with some Arab businessmen, and it seemed as though the entire firm had decided that this was the day to waste Colt's time. When they found themselves unable to do that, each one of them decided that wasting her time would be almost as much fun.

When she heard one more person at her door, she refused to look up with her usual cool smile.

"How come your office is bigger than mine?"

She knew that voice instantly. "Patrick!" she exclaimed, rising in delight. "When did you get back to work?"

"Just today."

How wonderful, how welcome, he looked standing there in the doorway and—

Standing... he was standing like any normal human being, evenly balanced on both legs. "You can stand," she laughed. "Can you walk too? Or did someone just prop you there?"

"Watch this." He walked across her office and back. "Was that impressive or not?"

"It takes my breath away."

His walk was a lithe, easy gait. His suit coat was off, and his navy vest and slacks were carefully tailored, fitting him well. When Suzanne said watching him move took her breath away, she was not exaggerating.

"Knees, Suzanne, they're wonderful things."

"As wonderful as buttons?"

It had just slipped out, but he remembered. "Well, I don't know. If you show me yours, I'll decide."

She thought she had better change the subject. "Have you heard anything about the India proposal?" She had kept track of the proposal, glancing at it when it was completed, sensing that it was very good indeed.

"Not a word," he replied, "but I don't want to talk about that. I want to talk about when I am going to get to buy you dinner."

She sank back down in her chair and sighed his name.

"Come on, Suzanne, I'm not trying to put a move on you, you know that. Let's just celebrate my having two working knees. Make it lunch if that makes things easier with Moretti."

"No, it's not Nick. It's this place; you know how gossipy it is."

"It's just lunch."

Suzanne shook her head. "How many people have already asked you what it was like working with me?"

He grimaced, not needing to answer. "You spook a lot of people."

"That's the point, Patrick; that's why Mr. Colt can get some work done once in a while. People believe me when I say he's busy."

He understood.

So they did not see each other on a regular basis. Days would pass, and then suddenly she would step on a crowded elevator and hear a voice, low with a teasing undercurrent. "Hello, Miss Lawrence."

It would be him and they would smile and he

wouldn't get off at the fourth floor, and at the tenth, when the elevator was empty, he would hold the door open with his hand, and they would talk for a bit.

But even if she only saw him infrequently, she knew he was there. She knew if something happened, if she needed someone, she could always go to him. Whatever it was she needed or wanted, he would do for her. She knew that as surely as she knew that she would do the same for him.

One day in February, she was in the outer office of William Southard, the company president, conferring with his secretary. The door opened and one of the vice-presidents, Edward Laughlin, stepped in. Then Patrick followed his boss into the president's suite.

Both men seemed to be suppressing a certain jubilation, and Suzanne looked at Patrick with her eyebrows raised. Under the guise of reaching into the breast pocket of his suit, he gave her a quick thumbs up.

They had won the India contract.

She was careful not to react, but she was thrilled for him and longed for a chance to tell him. Forty-five minutes later, just as she hoped, an auburn head peered around her door.

"Close the door, Mr. Britten," she ordered with mock sternness and came around from behind her desk.

"Yes, Miss Lawrence," he said obediently, and as she stood on tiptoe to kiss his cheek, he circled her waist with a firm arm.

"Patrick, this is really wonderful. I'm so happy for you. Are they going to let you manage it?"

He nodded, his eyes shining, and Suzanne knew exactly what an opportunity this was for him.

"Now will you have dinner with me?"

How could she refuse? With him so happy, so exhilarated by his success, with his arm around her waist, with his eyes smiling green, how could she say no? "Of course. Tonight, if you want."

But as soon as she had hung up from telling Nick that she wouldn't be home for dinner, her phone rang. It was Edward Laughlin's secretary. Mr. Laughlin was understandably proud that one of his people had pulled off a contract when another vice-president had nearly ruined the proposal. He was taking everyone even remotely involved out for a drink after work. Could she come?

Naturally she agreed, thinking that she and Patrick could go out afterward.

But everyone was so cheerful, ordering so many drinks, staying so late, that when the waiter waved some menus invitingly, people took them, and drinks became dinner.

As they were all filing out of the restaurant and were exchanging farewells on the sidewalk, Suzanne felt a warm, quick grip on her arm. So when the others hailed cabs or started back to the office for their cars, she waited and in a moment she found herself alone on the dark sidewalk with Patrick.

Wordlessly they started walking—she didn't know where and she didn't care.

The night was clear and cold. The shops were all closed but their windows put out a bright white light that mingled with the softer yellow glow of the street lamps.

"It's odd walking with you," she said softly. "I suppose I still think of you as having a broken leg."

"I could put my arm around you and pretend to be leaning on you if that would make you feel better."

"Actually," she smiled, "that would probably make me feel very good indeed."

But they both knew perfectly well that Patrick was too much the proper New Englander to ever embrace anyone, especially her, in the middle of Tremont Street.

They turned down School Street and in a moment, Patrick was holding open one of the heavy brass doors of the Parker House, one of Boston's old, classic hotels.

As she stepped into the richly paneled lobby, Suzanne looked at him quizzically.

"Don't get your hopes up," he laughed softly. "They just have a quiet lounge here."

They stopped at the cloak room and Patrick helped her off with her coat and then took off his.

"Do you realize we are dressed alike?" Suzanne said as they climbed up the short flight of burgundy-carpeted stairs to the bar that was tucked in the corner of the lobby.

They were both in vested gray suits and white shirts. Patrick's tie was navy, and Suzanne's blouse, which had a wide stock she tied at her throat, had a fine stripe of a similar dark blue.

"No, we aren't. You're in a skirt. I am not brazenly flaunting my great legs for the whole world to see like you are." He pointedly looked down at her legs as she slid into the curving banquette.

She smiled. "How are they? Those great legs of yours?" He had complained to her before that those weeks in a cast had left him a little out of shape.

"They are doing better, thank you. Stern hasn't stopped laughing at me, but that probably won't happen for another century or so."

When the drinks came, the waitress put them down

wrong and they each reached to switch them, their hands brushing together. Neither pulled away, and their hands lay on the table, close but not touching.

"You always wear that bracelet, don't you?" Patrick asked in a moment. "Did Moretti give it to you?"

How quick he was to get Nick's name in the conversation. Was he telling her that he hadn't forgotten about him?

"No," she answered. "My parents gave it to me when I turned eighteen." The bracelet was her only piece of good jewelry. If her parents had lived, there would have been a string of pearls when she graduated from college, but of course that hadn't happened.

Patrick lifted her hand, looking at the bracelet. "It is a very unusual chain."

"Yes, the links are S's and L's, my initials. They had it made for me." She tilted her wrist so that he could make out the letters; the scrolling links were so intricate that few people realized they were from the alphabet.

"Oh, I do see that now. That's very unusual."

Suzanne knew that he didn't really care about the chain; he wanted to touch her, holding her hand if that was all he could do.

His touch was warm and she let her fingers curl around his. Slowly he bent his head and she felt his lips press against her hand.

He was going away. At the end of June, he would be going away. For two years he would be in India, halfway around the world. Two years. That was twenty-four months; a hundred and four weeks; seven hundred and thirty days.

How was she going to stand it?

"Oh, Patrick," she breathed, almost in tears. "I'm going to miss you so."

He nodded. "I just wish..." He stopped and abruptly released her hand. "I don't know what I wish."

"For things to be different?" That was what she wished.

"Yes, but I'm not sure what... if we didn't work together, if I weren't going to India, if you weren't with Moretti. That's a lot of 'if's' and even so..." His voice trailed off.

"We don't love each other," she finished for him. There seemed no point in not being honest. "And we aren't likely to."

He blinked.

"Patrick, this can't surprise you. You must know it."

"Yes, yes, I do, but I don't understand it." He turned to face her, putting his arm across the back of the banquette. "Explain it to me. My God, Suzanne, if I were ever to draw up a list of what I thought I would want in a woman, you'd be everything on it. Your habits and values are like mine. Your mind... I mean, you aren't only bright, but you are sensible. So many very intelligent people don't have a lot of common sense, they aren't practical, but you are."

"I haven't always been; I learned to be practical."

"That just makes me admire you all the more. I've always thought that living with another person would be very difficult, there'd be so many sacrifices of privacy—"

"Tell me about it," Suzanne murmured under her breath.

"—but I could live with you easily. So I say all this, but still... I don't know, during that last week we were working together, I kept asking myself why am I not falling in love with this person?"

Suzanne swallowed; she could hardly speak. "Don't

read too much in being able to live with me. I live with Nick Moretti; I could live with anyone.''

"Don't be flip.''

"It's that or cry.''

Patrick took her hand again and murmured her name. "Why don't I love you?''

And he really seemed to want an answer, an answer that seemed very clear and obvious to her. "Patrick, I think it is really simple. We are so alike; in so many ways, we are mirrors of each other, and honestly, how much do you like yourself?''

"What does that—?'' And then he stopped, understanding. His eyes darkened. "Oh, I see. Of course.'' He paused. "It's the same for you, isn't it?''

"Doesn't a part of you,'' she asked gently, "long for a woman who could teach you to be different, to be less cautious, to be more spontaneous, less reserved?''

He shrugged. "That's not going to happen.'' But he couldn't deny that that was what he wanted.

"We wear too much gray, you and I,'' she said sadly.

There were so many colors in the world, vibrant reds and deep rich golds like the carpets of this hotel, but when she and Patrick had crossed the lobby, the two of them had been dressed in gray.

Suzanne knew that there was another side of him, a green side, some vitality, some intensity that came out only when he played sports. He needed help, he needed someone to show him how to reach the green fire that occasionally lit his eyes. But Suzanne couldn't give him that help; she too knew nothing about emerald laughter. When he was with her, his eyes were often flat and gray.

They each had the same needs, for warmth, for

color, and so neither had much of life's rich glow to offer the other.

"Where does that leave us?" he asked slowly.

"As friends."

He shook his head. "That doesn't sound right. There's more than that, and I don't just mean sex."

Suzanne thought of that Saturday night when she had felt for a brief blinding moment that somehow she and this man were a part of some powerful current, as if some destiny wanted them to be together. "Well, 'friend' is the only word we have for it."

"But if we are friends who just happen not to be lovers, why is this all so sad then?"

She didn't know. He was right. Something was sad; she felt a tight knot of forlorn longing. Was it that there could be more between them and they just didn't know how to reach it? Was the deliberate rationality that they both prided themselves on blocking a path that led to something they could have cherished?

There was no way of knowing. At the moment, they both wished that they were different, that they were the sort of people who could ignore everything and, not worrying about consequences or outcomes, cheerfully trundle off to bed together. But they weren't like that. They just weren't.

So there was nothing to be done; nothing could be changed even if she left her job and Nick. Those were just minor obstacles; this, their alikeness, was the real barrier. They just had to accept it.

Suzanne smiled, trying to break the somber mood. After all, this was supposed to be a celebration. "Do you think we might be identical twins who were separated at birth? That would explain the way we feel about one another."

"It certainly would," he answered immediately,

clearly understanding what she was trying to do. "And it's possible too. My mother was entirely capable of having twins and leaving one of them at the grocery store by mistake—although how do you explain the fact that you are two years younger than me and had a pink baby bracelet if we are supposed to be identical?"

"Environment, Patrick, don't you know that environment is as important a factor in development as heredity?"

But it was a very feeble joke, and they both knew it.

Chapter Six

As winter became spring, Suzanne knew that even if there was nothing to be done about her feelings for Patrick, she had to do something about Nick. His publisher had decided to send him on a book tour when his next book came out in late April. It was his first publicity tour, and the thought of all the places he would have to be on time, of all the tickets and schedules he would have to keep track of made him nervous and distraught.

He wanted Suzanne to go with him, but she refused, giving as her excuse that Mr. Colt needed her in Washington the first week of May. She had never refused to do something for him before, and he instantly sensed that she was getting closer to leaving him.

Her denial was halfhearted, and he protested, insisting that he couldn't work without her, but there was less fear in his protest than ever before. Surprisingly he then tried to make love to her. He didn't beg as she might have expected. Instead he put his arms around her firmly, almost with a hint of force, and Suzanne knew that he was subconsciously rebelling against the way their relationship worked, trying to reclaim a more dominant role, a role that his traditional upbringing had told him a man should have.

But of course she refused him. This was not time to

complicate their relationship, and even more important, Suzanne had no way of protecting herself. She knew Nick Moretti, she knew him very well, and he was the last man she would trust when it came to details like birth control.

Leaving him became a real possibility when in March she took her income tax refund and made the final payments on her loan.

But the bond with Nick was hard to break. They'd been together so long; she still was trying to save money as she was planning to start her editing service next year; and, she thought ruefully, Nick was probably the closest thing to a child that she would ever have; whatever ragged scraps of maternal instinct her character had kept her with him.

So he left for his book tour at the end of April, and then she for Washington the next week without her having made any definite plans to move out.

Harrison Colt was testifying in front of a Senate subcommittee investigating the federal government's use of consultants. The committee was generally hostile, and Colt wanted Suzanne in Washington in case there were any surprises. She could monitor other people's testimony and do some quick research if their answers seemed inaccurate; she could even write press releases and speeches if she had to.

They were staying in the Mayflower, a big, old hotel that all Southard-Colt people used when they were in Washington. In fact, the firm had enough people down in Washington working on federal government contracts—just the kind Colt was defending to the Senate—that Suzanne started feeling it was almost like being in the office. It seemed as though every Boston accent in the coffee shop in the morning belonged to a face she recognized.

But still Harrison Colt was keeping her busy enough

that she hardly had time to do more than nod to them so she was very surprised the second morning when the elevator opened to disgorge not Mr. Colt as she had expected but Patrick Britten.

He noticed her immediately, and breaking away from a few other Southard-Colt employees, he made his way to her side.

Of course, he couldn't touch her, not with all the people they knew milling around the lobby, but his smile was enough—at least it almost was. "This is a surprise," he said, carefully lowering his voice.

"I don't know why," she heard herself answer lightly as if seeing him hadn't made her mouth go dry. "I think half the firm is here. Why are you down?"

"Kevin Tolliver and I are talking to some people at the Defense Department to see if we can take a look at the software that the U.S. Navy uses for its computerized supply systems."

"Is it working?"

"Who knows?" He shrugged and smiled. "We're getting a colossal runaround, but that's to be expected. But why are you here? Has the President asked you to take over?"

She smiled and explained. "Mr. Colt leaves on Thursday, but I'll be here until Friday monitoring the rest of the hearings."

"Me too." And there was a gleam in the gray-green of his eyes as if he were hoping that something interesting might come of this.

But it made no difference, absolutely none, that they were both in Washington, both staying in the same hotel. They could hardly sneak into each other's rooms; they didn't even feel that they could go out to dinner together. Suzanne was with the man she worked for while Patrick was with a man who worked for him.

By Friday afternoon Suzanne was very ready to go back to Boston. The thrill of seeing the senators in person had long since evaporated, and she was growing impatient with some of the pompous posturing. One of the networks had sent a film crew and the glare of bright television lights had hurt her eyes.

So it was with relief that she filed out of the committee room, dodging the cameras that the newsmen had slung over their shoulders, threading her way through the clusters of people that had engulfed the senators.

The hall was bustling—several other hearings were getting out at the same time—and Suzanne was politely maneuvering herself through the crowd when she felt a touch on her arm.

She stiffened, but the voice that spoke her name was familiar for much more than its Boston accent.

"Patrick! What are you doing here?"

"Waiting for you."

How strange. Why was he waiting for her? Unless he wanted to share a cab to the airport. But surely the pleasures of sitting in rush hour traffic together would not justify the trouble he must have gone to in order to find out where the subcommittee was meeting and when the hearing was likely to be finished.

Nonetheless his next words suggested that a trip to the airport was exactly what he had in mind. "Your luggage is still at the hotel, isn't it?"

"Yes."

"Shall we get a cab or would you like to try the subway? It's new and quite spectacular."

"The T is fine; I'd like to see it." They were talking as if they were strangers. Patrick didn't even smile when he corrected her, telling her that Washington called its subway the "Metro."

It was a quick walk through the May sunshine to the big blue M that marked the subway stop. They spoke only of work, of the hearings she'd been to, of his meetings at Defense. Suzanne knew that Patrick couldn't care less about this conversation; he was thinking of something else, planning something, but she had no idea what it might be.

A set of steep escalators took them down to the subway station, and Suzanne looked around with a curiosity that gradually gave way to an odd sort of awe.

The world beneath the nation's capital was quietly cool. The trains swept into the station almost silently and the light was muted and even, giving it an almost unearthly feel that was nothing like the harsh glare and screeching clang of the subways of New York and Boston. And the gray concrete walls, cast in honeycomb forms, swept upward in vaulting arches, carving out stretches of space that kept the stations from feeling dank or claustrophic.

Patrick showed her how the walls curved outward from far beneath the tiled platforms, making it impossible for anyone to reach them and write graffiti on them. Indeed, these underground caverns were strikingly clean almost as if they had no past, as if they had never been used before.

At last Patrick spoke. "I saw in the paper that Moretti's on a tour."

Suzanne nodded.

"How is it going? Do you hear from him often?"

"It's going very well, but I only know that from the clippings; Nick doesn't call." She spoke carefully, answering both Patrick's questions. She knew that they hadn't been polite little pleasantries, that at least one of the questions had had some point, but she didn't know what it was.

"So you've no one to answer to if you don't go back to Boston this weekend."

"Patrick!" She stared at him. Not go back to Boston this weekend. That could mean only one thing. That she would stay here. With him.

He was standing quietly, one hand lightly gripping the handle of his attaché case, the other thrust in his pocket. Anyone might have thought he had just commented on the weather, but Suzanne saw the pulse beating in his throat and knew differently. This was why he had come to the Capitol, he wanted to ask her to spend the weekend with him.

He cleared his throat. "Is it that you don't want to, or that you think you can't?" She hadn't had to say anything; he had already sensed all the complicated questions, all the doubts and reservations that had flooded through her.

"You know the answer to that."

"Then it may not be as impossible as you think. Everyone from the firm is clearing out this afternoon. I am sure of that. So there is no way that anyone in Boston would hear about anything that happens this weekend; at least they won't from me."

And by "anyone in Boston," they both knew that he was talking mostly about Nick.

"Suzanne," he went on, "I'm leaving for India at the end of next month, and this is our one chance to spend sometime together. We can see the sights, go to museums and such, just the two of us, without other people, without any work to do. It would just be for this weekend. It doesn't have to mess up your life. When we go back to Boston, I won't get in your way."

Just the two of us, without other people, without any work to do. How wonderful that sounded. And how impossible.

But wait. Maybe he was right. Maybe it was possible. What was there to stop them? She had just reacted with the automatic reflex of a Massachusetts Puritan—that if something sounds wonderful, it must be either impossible or wicked.

"But you aren't talking just about playing tourist together, are you?" she asked carefully.

"If that's how you want it," he said instantly, "then of course. We don't have to share a room; we really don't. I just want to be with you, and if it's only in the daytime, then that's better than nothing. It's entirely your decision; you're the one whose life is complicated, not me."

And ever after, Suzanne wondered if her answer would have been different if she had been in any other city besides Washington.

She knew it wasn't fair, but she thought of Washington as a city of faceless bureaucrats mingled with politicians who came and went every four years. It seemed like a rootless, anonymous city, full of people who hadn't grown up there, who were planning to leave some day.

It was so unlike the Boston she knew. In Boston there were roots, ties that bound a person to the city and all that it represented. Boston was a place where the past still mattered, where standards of propriety were more rigorous than in the rest of the country, where ideals still counted for more.

But Washington was a political city, a practical city. It had to be. This was where ideals had to be hammered into reality's shape. Promises had to be broken; compromises had to be made; that was how the city worked.

So maybe it was possible to come to Washington and do things that you couldn't do back in Boston.

She looked at Patrick, at his thick auburn hair, his gray-green eyes. Once again she felt that inexplicable tug, the idea—no, it was more of a sensation than an idea—that there was something between them, some destiny that could not be explained by rational categories.

But that made no sense. But what did make sense was that she too wanted to be with him, and this, this one little weekend, was probably their only chance.

"I imagine," she said with quiet realism, "that however we start, we will end up in the same room anyway."

"Then you'll stay?" His voice was as even as if she had offered to work late.

"Yes."

The row of lights imbedded in the edge of the platform started to flash on, indicating that the train was about to arrive. Patrick stepped forward.

Wait a minute, Suzanne thought frantically. Wasn't there supposed to be more? They had just decided to start sleeping together as calmly, as bloodlessly, as if they were deciding where to open a joint checking account.

Didn't there have to be something more than a quiet discussion at a subway stop? Some romance, some passion that was not merely physical, some mystery that couldn't be explained in the manuals and magazine articles?

Had they been too rational, too sensible? Suzanne couldn't imagine herself ever asking such a question, but now she wondered if by being so careful and calm, by acting as if what they were about to share were routine and unimportant, they had taken all the magic out of it.

No, she told herself, *how can you be too rational?*

Other people may get carried away with passion and they might actually enjoy their impulsive moments more than Patrick and she were capable of enjoying anything, but then neither she nor he were ever likely to end up with strange diseases or—

That reminded her.

She touched Patrick's arm. "Let's take the next train." She had something to say, something she couldn't say on a crowded subway car.

In a moment, the platform was nearly empty, all the people having gotten on the train, which was now disappearing into the dark tunnel.

"Patrick, I didn't come expecting a weekend romance."

"I didn't think that you did." He clearly did not understand her point.

This was much too important to let embarrassment stop her. "So I didn't come prepared." A light emphasis on the last word told him exactly what she meant.

"You're not on the Pill?" he asked.

"No," she answered, briefly thinking of what misery taking birth control pills had caused her. "But that means precaution has to be your responsibility."

"That's fine; I don't mind."

"Patrick, listen," she spoke firmly, wanting to be sure he wasn't agreeing too glibly. "I mean this, no games, no shortcuts, no 'just this once.' I'm sorry if this sounds crude and unromantic, but it's just too important to me."

He looked down at her, his face unsmiling but gentle. "Suzanne, remember who you're talking to. If my feelings on this subject aren't as strong as yours, then they're as close as a man's can be." Suddenly he pulled his hand from his pocket and lightly touched her cheek. "I don't think you sound crude; you sound like a very sensible woman."

Suzanne sighed in relief. Other women must have this conversation all the time, sometimes with near strangers, men they had known only for an evening or two. She, with her New England primness, could not imagine speaking like this with anyone but him.

They did understand each other. Whatever was wrong with her was wrong with him too. Whatever magic was missing from her character was missing from his too. There might be insurmountable barriers to any kind of richly fulfilling relationship for the two of them, but they could talk. She could be more honest with him, she could communicate with him more easily than she could with Nick, the man she had loved.

He had been terse and abrupt not because this weekend was unimportant to him, but because it was important. He didn't know how to be gushingly enthusiastic and he hid his feelings behind this calm mask. She understood that; she understood because she was the same way herself.

If a physical relationship mirrored that closeness, wouldn't there be some magic in that?

They stopped and had a drink before returning to the hotel, wanting to be sure that all the other Southard-Colt people had left. They picked up Suzanne's suitcase from the check room, and it was not until they were on the elevator that Suzanne again succumbed to misgivings.

This time it was simple, old-fashioned nervousness.

What if being with Patrick would be like it had always been with Nick? What if she just had to lie there and wait until it was all over?

It's not going to be like that, she tried to reassure herself. *You were on the Pill then; that was the problem. There's nothing wrong with you.*

Patrick must have sensed that something was bothering her for as soon as he set down her suitcase on the luggage stand in his room, he picked up the restaurant guide the hotel supplied and said, "Where shall we go to dinner?" Suzanne knew that he was giving her time to change her mind about sharing his room. He would never reproach her if she did.

Suzanne wished that she could depend on herself to be wonderful in bed. She wished that she were skilled and experienced enough to give him more pleasure than he had ever known. She wished that she could avoid all the awkwardness and apologies that were bound to occur if she were unresponsive.

But suddenly she realized that as agreeable as all that would be, none of it really mattered. Patrick liked her; he respected and admired her; nothing that happened this weekend could possibly spoil their friendship.

She took the restaurant guide from him with a smile. "I think we should go to an Indian restaurant and choose the things that have the strangest spelling. You need to get used to weird food."

"Well, Miss Lawrence," he teased, "when did you get to be so adventurous?"

"At about four forty-five this afternoon," she replied dryly, and she sat down at the table to look for an Indian restaurant.

He came and stood behind her, and resting one hand on the table next to hers, leaned over, looking at the guide with her. "These places all seem pretty casual," he said in a moment. "You choose while I get out of this suit."

How had he been able to read the entries? The printing had been a black blur to her. She hadn't been able to concentrate on anything except the shape of his hand on the table and the brush of his chest against her hair as he leaned over her.

But without him in the room, she managed to talk her eyes into focusing. She chose a restaurant and went over to the phone, sitting down on one of the two double beds while she called to make a reservation. The restaurant didn't seem particularly interested in answering its phone so she waited patiently.

The bathroom door opened. "I would have done that," she heard Patrick say.

"I don't mind. It's the secretary—" She stopped.

She had never even seen him in a short sleeve shirt and here he was now, shirtless, without shoes, just in a pair of well-fitting jeans and a wide leather belt.

She couldn't help the comparison. Nick was pale and slight, with black hair that was stark against his fair skin. But Patrick was colored with warm tones, as if he had been fashioned on a summer day, when the sun was hot and the earth rich and welcoming. His skin was a honey brown and the tangle of hair on his chest and arms glowed with mahogany lights.

For once in her life, she didn't hide what she felt, and he had to know. She saw him swallow, but when he spoke, his voice was even. "I assume you've seen men without shirts before."

"Yes," she answered, meeting his gaze. "But not you."

He dropped his shirt and moved toward her, but just then the Indian restaurant answered its phone.

She bent her head. "I'd like to make reservations for a party of two for seven o'clock please."

She felt Patrick sit down on the bed next to her.

She listened to the host flipping through his reserva tion book, agreed that seven fifteen would do as well, gave him a name, and tried to hang up the phone. Patrick took the receiver from her trembling hand and hung it up for her.

"Why did you give Colt's name?" he asked, soft laughter warming his voice.

"I did?" Suzanne didn't remember doing that. "I guess I'm so used to making reservations for him; I just wasn't thinking, it was automatic...."

It was as if the greens and grays of his eyes were blinding her, leaving her able to see only him. Her other senses gave the moment shape—the low hum of the air conditioner, the cool feel of her blouse against her arm and her breast, the faint scent of her own cologne. She reached out, her gold bracelet slipping down her wrist, tangling with the dark green cuff of her blouse. She reached out until she touched him, her hand flattening against the warmth, the strength that was his chest, touching him for the first time.

The window's white curtain stirred gently in the drift of air from the air conditioner, and Suzanne's hand moved across Patrick's chest, ivory against bronze. All else was still, except the curtain, her hand and the rise and fall of their quickening breath.

Patrick trapped her hand against him and cleared his throat. "Now, look here, Suzanne, I was willing to pretend that we were interested in seeing Washington, but you aren't making it easy."

She wriggled her hand out of his grasp and slid it up his shoulder and round his neck. "What is it you really want to see?" she whispered.

His laugh was soft. "What do you think?" He leaned forward slowly and tilting his head, he kissed her.

The kiss was gentle, moving lightly across her mouth, but without the questions, the necessary hesitations, of last December. There were no questions now, just a wash of rose-colored beauty. And she felt his arm, an arm stronger and warmer than any arm she had known, close about her shoulders, and his kiss trailed down her cheek to bury itself in the warm fragrance of her neck. This ordinary room in a big businessman's hotel swirled with an enchanted loveliness.

His hand moved slowly down her back, following the curve of her waist, treasuring through the whisper of her blouse the shape of her body. A silken glow spread through her, a willingness, a blossoming longing, a sweet sensation that she once thought was forever lost.

She bent her head to watch as his fingers opened the buttons of her blouse. How right it was that today she was in green, not in the gray of the office world, but green, the color of freshness and spring.

The blouse slipped to the floor, followed by her skirt and stockings.

She was apricot and ivory, the blushing wisp of her lingerie, the pale curves of her shape. His hands moved to caress her, following a curving line, and he whispered, "I've wondered what you looked like."

"You've seen women before," she said softly.

"Not you."

His head bent to follow the path of his hand, and whatever words he now spoke were muffled against her leg and thigh. She slipped down among the pillows, stretching out, and now he was lying down beside her, kissing her deeply, one hand moving down her shoulder to her breast, the other one lying unmoving on her stomach. Even as he curved his hand around her breast, even as his breath warmed her, even as his lips tantalized her, she was conscious of the weight of his other hand, flat against her.

She'd seen this hand so often, tapping a gold pen against a walnut desk or flipping through the white pages of a manuscript. Now that same hand, Patrick's hand, lay on her, waiting, promising.

It was really him, not Nick, not some faceless fantasy, but it was Patrick who lay here beside her, Patrick whose jeans were warm against her leg, Patrick, the man she cared for, felt achingly close to, the man she would have loved if she could. It was his hand that lay on her.

She touched his arm, whispering his name, knowing that in this as in everything she need say no more. He would understand. He would understand her body as intimately as he did her mind. As her legs shifted, his hand slid down beneath the apricot gossamer.

His touch was more experienced, more confident than any she had known, and a glowing, golden warmth blossomed in her. She felt as if, for years, she had been a bud, curled around herself, tight and hard. But now all was different. Patrick was with her, touching her, warming her, as if he were coaxing a rose into blooming. Now that it was Patrick who was with her, the lush petals opened, soft and moist, ready for him.

She turned to him, fumbling for the clasp of his belt, the snap of his jeans. As impatient as she, he brushed her fingers aside, and standing, he pulled off his jeans, readying himself for her.

His body cast a shadow across hers, and then the shadow became warmth, longing became substance, and the vigor of his body became hers.

What had burned quickly in Nick, building so sharply to a fever-hot pitch that as it consumed him, its flames left her cool and untouched—that too was different in Patrick. The rhythm of his body had grace and control; he didn't journey to a place where she couldn't follow, a place of weltering, dark confusions, of panting spasms.

Patrick's passion did not invade or violate. Instead it joined them, this age-old act, dissolving the separateness of man and woman, uniting, perhaps reuniting, the two into one. And for this man and this woman who shared so much in mind and in heart, passion created, if only for a moment or so, a physical bond that mirrored all others.

Chapter Seven

Although all they saw of Washington that night was the room service waiter's uniform, they did better on Saturday. It proved to be a lovely day, a little spot of time that the two of them carved out of their busy, complicated lives. It was only one day, but it was as if they had no lives outside that day, as if there were not a past in which Suzanne had lived with another man or future in which Patrick would go off to India. There was nothing but the present.

They did the museums. At the National Gallery, they admired the breathtaking lines of the new east wing more than any of the modern art in it. The movie at the Space Museum made them dizzy, and at the Museum of American History, Suzanne was patient while Patrick explored an exhibit of early computers, and in turn, he put up with the First Ladies' gowns. They certainly didn't see everything, and at times they would pass through rooms without seeing anything so absorbed were they in each other.

In the late afternoon, they went back to rest before dinner. Suzanne got out her book, slipped off her khaki skirt and navy sweater, and clad in a white turtleneck, navy kneesocks and pale blue underwear, propped herself up against the pillows.

Patrick lifted his attaché case onto the table and opened it up. He reached in it as if he too were about to take out a book, and Suzanne looked over curiously. She always liked to know what people were reading.

He caught her eye and suddenly closed the case, clicking the latches shut. "I think I'll go down and get a paper."

"What's wrong?" she smiled. "Are you reading some dirty book you are ashamed to have me see?"

"No." And then he came over and sat next to her on the bed. She scooted over to make more room for him, but not so far that his leg was not still against hers. "Actually, it's Moretti's latest."

Suzanne immediately moved farther over.

"I reread all his books this winter."

She wished she had gotten under the covers so she could pull up the sheet, hide herself.

He went on. "I hadn't ever paid a lot of attention to the female characters; the men are so compelling that I guess I ignored the women."

But not this time, she thought unhappily. Everyone did it. If they found out she was living with Nick Moretti, they reread his books, curious to see if there were any portraits of her.

And in every book, every single one of them, at least one female character had shoulder-length blond hair.

Patrick continued. "He does seem to have an awfully adolescent view of women."

"The feminist critics have been saying that since his first book," she acknowledged stiffly.

"Women are so distant and incomprehensible to him, as if they belonged to an entirely different species. He doesn't quite see them as people." And suddenly Patrick's eyes turned toward her. "Isn't that very diffi cult to live with?"

Suzanne stiffened. She did not want to talk about this. She really, really didn't.

She had a standard line, a line she used whenever people asked about Nick. "I'm sorry," she'd say politely, "but since he has become something of a cult figure, I don't dare talk about him." She had said that even to her closest friends.

But Patrick had moved himself beyond the closest friend category.

She spoke carefully. "Surely you realize that if everything were perfect between Nick and me, I would hardly be here with you."

"No, I suppose you wouldn't be." He swung around, now sitting cross-legged at the foot of the bed, facing her. "Is it just a bad patch, or are you going to leave him?"

"I don't know," she said miserably. "I just don't know."

Of course, part of her did know, did know that the reason she was here with Patrick, having this very out-of-character weekend romance, was that it was the easiest way to break with Nick. In fact, she was probably using Patrick, although she suspected that he would not mind in the least.

But acting as much like Scarlett O'Hara as upright New England-bred Suzanne ever would, she just wasn't going to think about that until tomorrow.

Patrick gathered up her hands in his. "If you need a place to go, you can come live with me. I hope you know that."

"For a month, Patrick?" She pulled her hands free. "What would be the point?"

Of course she was right, he knew that. He was going to India at the end of June. Even if he wanted to, he could make no commitments or promises. They just had this weekend; that was the arrangement, just this weekend, and then back to their usual lives.

Except that Patrick didn't want Suzanne to go back to her usual life. He didn't at all.

He'd vacationed with women before; sailing with Libby Wiley, skiing with Brooke Mitchell, innumerable autumn weekends in Maine or Vermont admiring the changing leaves. It had never bothered him that these trips hadn't involved any sort of permanence. He hadn't been at all threatened by the knowledge that on Monday morning, these women would resume their routines quite unchanged by their pleasant days with him.

But this time it was different. This time he was with Suzanne Lawrence and he did not want her to go back to Dominick Moretti.

Saturday night he felt his hands tighten on her, gripping her waist, her thigh, with more force than he had ever used on a woman before. "Patrick, you're hurting me," she had cried out, and appalled at himself, he wondered if he had done it deliberately, if he had been trying to mark her, giving her bruises she would not be able to explain to Moretti.

He told himself that he wasn't being a possessive male, the kind his mother had taught him to despise. It wasn't, he tried to convince himself, that he felt like he owned her, that he was jealous, that he didn't want her with another man. It was just that he cared enough about her to want her happy.

Surely she wasn't happy with Moretti. He had seen a side of her that he had never seen before, and he suspected that she didn't see it too often either. She had always said that she wasn't fun, that she wasn't capable of much enthusiasm or spontaneous emotion. But she was. She had been a joy to see the museums with; she had had such a good time. It was a side of her that she must repress and hide in the same way a part of his character emerged only when he played sports.

And it was more than just psychological; her life in Boston was limited in physical ways as well. She had said nothing about it, but she didn't have to; he could tell. Her body's capacity for pleasure astonished her. Whatever sexual exuberance ran through Dominick Moretti's writings, he had not known how to please this woman.

But each time Patrick had touched her, she had gasped and her eyes shone as she discovered new ways of being pleased.

He shrugged, trying not to puff up with pride about her pleasure. Was it really any different than teaching her to shoot baskets? Apparently she wasn't any good at that either.

But another voice, a voice he had never heard from himself, told him that sex, making love, was fundamentally, profoundly different from shooting baskets.

In recent years, sex had come to seem very matter-of-fact to Patrick. It was as much a part of dating now as kissing had been in high school.

"What's the point?" she had asked. He didn't know, but he wanted there to be one. He hungered to have this weekend mean something. He wanted what had happened to bind them together, to link them, to unite them for much longer than a few moments.

As she lay sleeping Sunday morning, he found himself propped up on an elbow, watching her, her slender graceful body, and a vision flashed through him—Suzanne changed, changed by him, her body blossoming and swelling, he having possessed her in the only way a man can truly make a woman his.

He was horrified, horrified that he could have such a

thought. No, it wasn't even a thought, but something more primitive, more physical, than thought. These were urges, instinct, powerful and dark, as inexplicable as magic.

But at least, he thought as he flung out of bed, heading for the shower, at least he would never act on these promptings. Rational man had civilized these primitive instincts out of himself. At least the rational man of Boston had. Acting on instinct—that was what Southerners did.

Yet as Suzanne woke and dressed that Sunday morning, his eye was drawn to a slight change in her body. Her breasts were a little fuller than they had been, and when he had brushed against her, she had winced as if they were swollen and tender. He knew that his caresses of the night before had not hurt her; this change was caused by the workings of her own body, by the lunar rhythm entirely alien to men. Perhaps in this at least, Dominick Moretti was right; there was a mystery in women.

His feminist mother had drilled it into him. *Don't treat women as if they are different; they aren't; they are just as capable, just as intelligent as men.*

Certainly Suzanne Lawrence was more capable, more competent, more intelligent, than almost any man he knew. But still she wasn't a man. Women's minds might be the same as men's, but their bodies were different, designed for different purposes. There was no getting around that.

What he found most lovely in her, most feminine, was the shape of her, the soft fullness of her breasts, the flare of her hips. But if there was a scheme behind the workings of the universe, she was not shaped like this for his pleasure. In fact, the desire she aroused in him, the intense desire, much fiercer than anything he had felt for any other woman, that desire was simply a means to an end—nature's way of luring him to her so that her body could fulfill its function.

The reproductive aspect of sex had never interested Patrick except as a nuisance to be avoided. But today, as they went to Sunday brunch in Georgetown, on the last day they would perhaps ever have together, he was keenly aware that reproduction, the creation of another life, was, for some people, the purpose of sex.

Was it different for them, he wondered, men who loved the women they slept with? Was it different for a man who left part of himself in the woman he loved, a part of him that her body would treasure and nurture?

He had no answer; these were questions he had never thought about before, and soon they returned to the Mayflower to pack and check out. Their time was over.

As she packed, Suzanne was talking about how lovely Washington had been, the masses of lavender azaleas, the white magnolias, the beds of scarlet and yellow tulips. "Some time," she said, "we'll have to come down earlier in the spring and see the cherry blossoms."

He supposed the "we" had been unconscious, but it had sounded very right, the idea of Suzanne and him doing things together in the spring.

Spring. The time of life. Of birth.

None of this made sense; he was acting irrationally, he told himself, but he moved to her, letting his hand tighten on her shoulder, coaxing her to him. Wordlessly, she turned and slipped her arms around him, standing on tiptoe to nestle her head in his neck.

He felt a gentle breeze. She was slender in his arms, slender, soft, and very much a woman.

He held her tight against him, one hand flat against

the small of her back, letting his body speak for him. And hers answered; with leisured grace, she pressed herself to him, moving slowly, the fabric of her skirt against his jeans. And her hands floated down, touching him with confidence, with ardor. Denim, heated by the warmth of her hands, rubbed against skin, an arousing, erotic irritant.

Her kiss was melting, open and yielding. Her breasts were full against his chest, her hips liquid. A hunger surged in him, a hunger scarlet and demanding.

"Shall we take a later plane?" His voice sounded deep, not quite like himself. "I'm not ready to leave yet."

She tilted her head back. "I'm not either." Her face, her throat, glowed with a willing flush; her eyes shone with a light as bright as springtime. "I want you now."

She wanted him—her words echoed as he eased her shirt over the lustrous pearl of her shoulders, as her skirt drifted to the floor. She wanted him.

But no, he thought as he moved with her to the bed, no. If she wanted him, she would, this time, have to take all of him.

She was a woman, and he knew with a certainty that was beyond the rational, he knew with a dark and primitive conviction, the sort he had always scoffed at before, that this time he was not going to protect her from the consequences of that.

And he wanted her to know. He wanted her to understand that this time was different. So with his hands on either side of her, as he felt the warmth of her body rising to meet his, as her hands slid up his arms, around his shoulders, he poised over her for a moment, waiting, waiting for her to understand.

In a moment, she did. "No, Patrick," she gasped, "wait, you haven't . . ."

He sank into her.

She went stiff with tension, a deep shock rippling through her, gripping her, and she struggled beneath him, her hands pushing at his shoulders, her legs fighting against his. "Patrick, no, you promised." Her body felt like warm silk against him. "What are you doing?"

Gently, trying to keep his weight off her, he brushed a strand of hair from her face. "Nothing, love, nothing that we don't want."

He was stronger than she, he was already deep within her; if he wanted, he would need only capture her wrists and in a few quick moments, finish what had already so clearly begun.

But he knew that it need not happen that way. There need be no force. She would want this too. He believed with a faith surer than knowledge, that this instinct, this force, whatever it was, surpassed his own physical strength. She could not fail to feel it; she could not fail to understand that their craving for each other, their thirst for some kind of bond that would mirror the closeness they felt, was now fulfilled by this embrace. She would give in to that force just as he had. He was certain of that. He would wait for her.

He bent his head and kissed her, a long, tender kiss that sought the velvety warmth of her mouth, kissing her until her writhing protests stilled.

"Patrick, please..." she whispered, "please don't do this."

"I won't, love, not if you don't want." His voice too was low. "But this is the way it's supposed to be." He slipped his hand between their bodies, touching her breast, her belly, reminding her why she was made as she was, why they were man and woman.

Her body softened under his hand, the tension easing, giving way to something else, a quivering vibration, silvery ripples. "Listen to your body, Suzanne. It wants this."

Her eyes were full and dark, and gently he kissed them closed. His lips close to her ear, he spoke to her once more. "Listen to your body, not your mind. Let me give this to you."

And for the first time in her life, Suzanne listened to something other than the careful workings of her orderly mind, listening to, responding to, heart, body, feeling, instinct. And it was at last she who moved, who stirred beneath him, finding for them the dark surging rhythm of the moon, the steady beat of tide upon shore that would not end until the magic wave crested and broke and he had thrust his seed into the fertile depths of her.

For a moment, neither moved; their minds were dazed; their breaths now aching shudders, and their hearts pounding hard in exhausted passion.

Suddenly Suzanne gasped, and pushing Patrick's weight from her, she rolled over, burying her flushed face in the cool white of the pillow. Her hand convulsed, gripping the sheet. "What have you done? What *have* you done?"

Patrick lay on his back, his arm over his eyes.

She turned toward him angrily. "Do you know what you've done?"

He eased himself upright, leaning back against the wall. A stricken, exhausted look on his face, he nodded.

"You said you wouldn't." Her voice was bitter, accusing. "I thought we were friends. *Friends* don't do that to one another."

"Suzanne...I—I've never done anything like that before."

"Do you think that makes it all right, that it—" The anger, the bitterness, suddenly faded into misery, her voice now a whimper of heavy, sodden misery. "Oh, Patrick, why me? Of all the women you've ever been with, why *me?* You know me, you know how I feel about this. And you said you wouldn't mess up my life. How could you?"

"I don't know." His voice was thick. "I just don't know."

"I thought I was safe with you. You promised me that wouldn't happen. You *promised.*"

"I know. I know I did." He swallowed and cleared his throat. "Suzanne, I can't begin to explain what happened. There's never been anything I haven't been able to control rationally, until this. But some instinct kept telling me that I had to do this, and God help me, I did it, consciously and deliberately."

"Instinct? Patrick, what are you talking about?"

He spoke carefully. "Perhaps the animal instinct to—to reproduce is sometimes stronger than reason."

"No. Maybe in other people. But not in you, not in—" Suzanne buried her face in her hands, her blond hair falling forward. Her voice came out as a strangled moan. "I could have stopped you. You would have stopped, wouldn't you?"

He didn't answer; he didn't have to. He smoothed her tangled hair and pulled her to him.

"It was just as much my fault," Suzanne moaned.

And lying there, Patrick holding Suzanne to his chest, they had to acknowledge the lesson of the last hour. Everything they understood about themselves, everything they had prided themselves in, had just been exposed as false. That the calmness, the careful rationality that directed every move was only a veneer. In them as in every human creature, reason was the force that balanced the confused welter of passion and instinct. Patrick and Suzanne, believing so in the power of reason, had denied that the dark tangle existed at all, that they had impulses and urges too powerful for reason to control, but they had been wrong, terribly wrong.

It was two shaken and humble people who boarded the shuttle back to Boston. The beauty of their time together faded, its memory wilting beneath their bewildered terror. As desperately difficult as it was for them to accept what they had done, to understand why they had done it, one idea was even more blankly incomprehensible—that there weren't two of them flying back to Boston, but three.

Chapter Eight

Suzanne tried to remind herself of the conversations she had heard at baby showers or among the married secretaries in the ladies' room. It was hard to get pregnant.

"The doctors won't even talk to you until you've been trying for a year," they all said.

It was true that she and Patrick had made love on the worst possible day of the month—in fact, Suzanne now wondered if that moment of fertility had prompted her behavior as if her body were trying to get pregnant—but these were women who were trying with their minds as well, taking their temperatures every day, having intercourse at scheduled times and in strange positions, and it took them three months, six months, two years, to conceive.

Maybe it hadn't happened to her.

But she knew it had; she knew she was pregnant. Once she had stopped taking birth control pills, she and her body had gotten along quite well. She took care of it, and it didn't pull any surprises on her.

But since coming home from Washington, the body was not living up to its end of the bargain. She was fatigued; her breasts were tender, often painful; her appetite was irregular.

She tried not to read too much into these signs. She reminded herself how often this had happened in the dorm during her college days: Girls were so worried about being pregnant that they developed—or started noticing—many of pregnancy's symptoms. There wasn't any reason why that wouldn't be happening to her too.

But when her period was one day late, it was all she could do to stop herself from rushing into a drug store to buy a home pregnancy testing kit.

Obediently she waited for ten days and went to her doctor and then there was no doubt at all.

As she drove home from his office, she was surprised at how simple everything seemed, how clear the options were, how easy the decisions. She had deliberately decided to postpone all such considerations, but her subconscious must have been working, if not as deliberately and as orderly as her conscious mind would have tackled the problem, probably more productively. She knew what she was going to do.

At work the next day, she picked up a random folder and went down to the fourth floor.

Katie Bowers's desk sat in an alcove outside Patrick's office.

"Is he free?" Suzanne asked, gesturing to her folder as if that explained her very unusual visit. She had decided that the less explaining she did, the less interest this would arouse.

Katie looked at her blankly. "Mr. Britten," Suzanne reminded her, "is he free?"

"Patrick?"

Suzanne briefly wondered if it were possible for a secretary not to know her boss's last name.

"Sure," Katie continued. "Go on in."

Nonetheless Suzanne knocked and at Patrick's "Come in," opened the door.

Patrick instantly stood up.

David Stern, casually draped across a chair, looked at Patrick curiously. Standing up when a secretary came into an office was not a part of the routine at Southard-Colt.

Suzanne was so disconcerted to see David that she couldn't think of what to say.

David broke the silence. "Hello, Miss Lawrence."

"Hello, David," she replied unthinkingly.

David straightened in his chair, now clearly intrigued, and Suzanne cursed herself for the careless use of his first name. But she had gotten so used to hearing Patrick talk about his friend that she thought of him as "David." Well, it couldn't be helped now.

"I'm sorry," she apologized to Patrick, unable to call him Mr. Britten, "your secretary said you weren't busy. I will come back."

With a quick jerk of his eyes, Patrick silently told David to leave.

"He's not the least busy." David stood up. "We were just sitting here, complaining about the real estate market." Although clearly curious, he left, carefully closing the door behind him.

Patrick moved toward her. "Suzanne—"

There was no way Suzanne was going to talk about this at the office and she interrupted him. "Are you going to be home this evening?"

"I can be."

"Then I would like to come by about eight if I may," she said much too formally.

"Of course.," His tone was like hers, but then his eyes flashed and he spoke abruptly. "For heaven's sake, at least let me take you out to dinner."

"No," she refused. "We aren't exactly celebrating."

Suzanne felt miserably awkward that evening, stepping into his living room and finding it just a living room. If the word processor and stacks of file folders were still there, she probably would have felt more comfortable. Instead the sofa and two leather wing chairs were arranged precisely on either side of the fireplace, and Patrick moved around easily, coming to the door, taking her coat, with none of the awkward movements his cast had forced on him.

Seeing his home back in order underscored how completely that part of their lives—working together on that proposal—was over. All traces of her time here were gone, and if that was the way he wanted things, she was willing to have them be that way.

"Would you like a drink?" he was asking. "Sherry or white wine?" By now, he knew her preferences.

"No, thank you." And this seemed as good a way as any. "I'm going to be on the wagon for the next eight months."

Patrick went still. Very still.

"I'm not having an abortion."

They were both standing awkwardly. And in a moment, Patrick gestured to the chairs. "Sit down. Please sit down."

She folded her hands in her lap almost primly. She had no idea what he was thinking.

"I'm sorry." She tried to keep her voice even and clear. "I thought I could; it never occurred to me that I couldn't. It does seem like the sensible thing to do, but I just can't."

"I think," he said slowly, "that we both need to accept the fact that we don't know ourselves nearly as well as we thought we did."

He reached across the arms of their separate chairs

and took her hand. The warm strength of his touch made her next words come out in a rush.

"Maybe I am doing my mother a terrible disservice, but I honestly think that if abortion had been legal twenty-eight years ago, I wouldn't be here. And"—she looked at him directly—"you might not be either."

In the light from the brass lamp, his eyes seemed a flat, dull gray. "I'm sure that you're right."

He clearly found the thought just as chilling as she did.

"And, Patrick, I know that this isn't rational, but somehow that seems to make a difference. We were both mistakes; we weren't supposed to be here, but we are. And"—the next two words were very hard to say—"our child is a mistake too, and it somehow seems that, more than most people, we have an obligation to make the best of it. I'm sorry, but that's how I feel."

"Suzanne," he said softly, "this is nothing you need to apologize for."

"I feel like it is," she replied. "You had every reason to expect that I would have an abortion; certainly that's what I expected. And since the decision is entirely mine, since I'm not even giving you a chance to change my mind, you have every right to have nothing to do with all this."

"I don't agree," he said flatly. "I will do absolutely anything you want me to. I decided that a long time ago." He took a breath and almost as if he were talking to a client, said, "I suppose you've given the problem some thought. Why don't you tell me?"

Suzanne was very reassured at the prospect of some orderly, organized analysis. She had told Nick last night, and the conversation had been a disjointed nightmare.

"Quite simply," she began, "this could not have

happened at a worse time for me. I have no money at all. Last month I had a great deal, but I used it all to make the final payment on my college loans." She spoke in a firm, forthright tone. She was not asking for pity. "And I simply won't be comfortable staying on at Southard-Colt. I would find the kind of talk this would cause to be simply intolerable."

Southard-Colt was not a progressive firm. The senior management would have put pregnant women on unpaid maternity leave in their third month if they thought the government would let them get away with it. And for the one unmarried executive secretary to be pregnant would have caused simply unending gossip.

"So this seems like the time for me to start my own business. It should work out very well since this is one business you can run out of your home, and I guess that will start being important."

The reason that that would be important—that she would have a small child to take care of—seemed absolutely incomprehensible.

"The major cost," she continued quickly, eager to get back on more familiar territory, "would be a very good small computer with word processing software. I am sure I can arrange financing for that. I don't want to be in debt again, but I could do it. As for living expenses and such, I could go back and live with Nick. That way—"

"Back?" Patrick interrupted.

"I have been staying with friends ever since ̲ ̲ ̲ ̲ back from his tour," she said crisply, still r ̲ ̲ ̲ ̲ talk about Nick with him. "I talked to h ̲ ̲ ̲ ̲ and he says I can stay with him until ̲ ̲ ̲ ̲ financially."

"Does he think the child is ̲ ̲ ̲ ̲

Suzanne stiffened. "Nic ̲ ̲ ̲ ̲

but he understands enough biology to work this one out. Anyway, my point is that I can make it without your help.''

Patrick's lips tightened. "I can understand how knowing that is important to you, but to my mind, it's unacceptable. I know your emotional ties to Moretti must be much stronger than any feelings you have for me, but still this is my responsibility, not his."

Suzanne hoped that he didn't resent that she had told Nick first. She had dreaded that conversation so much more than this one. She knew that Nick, in his total self-absorption, would see this situation as being about him, as if Suzanne's very difficult position was unimportant compared to the intensity of his own feelings. And indeed, Nick had taken her pregnancy as a reflection on himself, as a criticism of him, believing that it was her way of telling him that he was not good enough for her. By the end of the conversation, he had convinced himself that he had always known that this would happen, that, as he put it, she would leave him for a *Gentlemen's Quarterly* ad.

Not that the conversation with Patrick was going particularly well either. They were both so constrained, speaking so awkwardly and formally.

Patrick must have felt the same way because he cleared his throat and when he spoke again, he was obviously trying to make his voice lighter. "Now was that Plan A—what to do if Britten won't help?"

She nodded.

"Then what's Plan B? And the answer to your first question," he added, "is yes, I have money in the bank, but no, I am not going to lend it to you; I am a great deal more likely to *give* it to you if you need it to your business."

that had been Plan B, to have him help

her some financially. It did make it easier that he had perceived it himself. Well, she thought, it should be no surprise. His problem-solving skill, his ability to see alternative solutions quickly, was what earned him his very comfortable living.

"No," she answered gratefully. "I would much prefer borrowing it, but if it doesn't strap you too badly, I'd rather not legally commit myself to starting payments for a couple of years. I just don't know how much work I will get done when I am also—" She faltered, again utterly unable to envision herself looking after a baby. "The other thing I may need help with is health insurance. I'll lose mine when I quit work, and although I haven't looked into it yet, I rather imagine it's expensive to get a new policy when you are already pregnant." And that reminded her of an even more urgent question. "What's your blood type?"

He looked surprised but answered. "B positive." When she sighed, he went on, "Is that a problem?"

"A little. I'm O negative."

"Exactly what does that mean? I've forgotten."

She explained how, during delivery, the baby's blood cells enter the mother's blood stream. If the mother was Rh negative, as Suzanne was, and the baby Rh positive, as Patrick's child was likely to be, then the baby's blood cells would cause the production of Rh antibodies in the mother which could create problems in later pregnancies. Fortunately there was a shot that had been developed which would prevent those later difficulties.

As she finished her explanation, Suzanne shivered. This discussion of their blood types seemed, beneath its surface impersonality, shockingly intimate. The genes and chromosomes that had made each of them themselves, that had given her blond hair and brown eyes and him auburn and gray-green, that had given both of them clear, orderly minds, and ten fingers and ten toes, had already joined and were now, at this moment, rapidly dividing and reforming into a third human being. Another mistake.

She saw Patrick's glance flicker to her lap, suggesting that he was thinking similar thoughts. Almost embarrassed, she continued quickly. "Anyway if you will help me with health insurance and the like, then in return I will do whatever you like about the birth certificate."

"I'm not sure I understand," he said politely.

"I can put your name on it and we can go to court and have visitation rights and all sorts of things spelled out for you if that's what you want. Or I can"—and Suzanne prayed that he would not realize how very difficult this would be for her—"just list the father as unknown."

"That seems a little extreme," he said immediately. "And it does seem like there is a Plan C. Now tell me, do you *want* to try and work things out with Moretti? Is that what you want?"

She shook her head.

"Are you sure?" he asked.

She met his gaze. "Very."

"Then wouldn't it all be a lot easier if we got married?"

"*What?*"

Patrick leaned back in his chair easily. "Why are you surprised? It is the usual thing to do in such situations. And think of the problems it solves—the health insurance, for one. To say nothing of the fact that the child won't be illegitimate, and I do recall your once saying that you couldn't quite see yourself as an unwed mother."

"As I recall," Suzanne pointed out, "I first said I couldn't see myself as a mother at all, and I still can't."

"But you seem like you have it all under control."

"Oh, no." Suzanne sighed. "Why do you think I'm so obsessed with organizing the money? That seems like the easy part. The actual mothering—I still can't imagine myself as being anything but very stiff and awkward."

He frowned, obviously wishing he could say something comforting, reassuring, but he knew of nothing. "Well, being married isn't going to change your personality, but it's bound to make some things easier."

"Well, for *me,* yes," she acknowledged. "But what about you? You don't want to be around a baby; you haven't changed your mind about that, have you?" She remembered all he had said that one night last December: how intrusive, how disruptive, he found children to be.

"Well, no," he answered. "But I wouldn't be—wait, let's get one thing clear. You've said nothing about the fact I am currently planning on going to India for two years."

"Oh, that's right. Then I guess you don't have to worry about being awakened in the middle of the night. No baby cries that loud." She tried to smile.

He ignored her pleasantry. "Suzanne, don't you realize that you have the right to keep me from going?"

"Patrick!" She knew how much the India project meant to him. "I would never, never do that."

"Are you sure? I will give it up, you know."

He would, he really would. She shook her head. "No, you don't need to."

"Then if I am going away, we could be married and not be in each other's way at all."

As usual, he was making a great deal of sense. "But what about when you get back?"

"Well, let's be realistic. We both know marriages aren't for keeps anymore. When I get back we can tell everyone that our being separated so long was a terrible mistake, that we had grown apart, etcetera, etcetera, and then we can get divorced like sensible people."

Suzanne was too much of a realist not to see the many advantages of his plan.

"The only possible downside," he continued, "is that we will probably have to live together for a few weeks before I go, but I don't imagine that that will be a particular hardship."

"Good heavens, no."

"Then is it settled?"

"I guess."

And after a few quick words about going in for blood tests and such, Patrick spoke again. "Now I have some questions about Moretti. You told him. How did he take it?"

"Badly."

"Suzanne!" He was clearly impatient with her terse answer. "I understand that you don't want to talk about him, but, look, I'm sorry to be so crude here, but I did get the man's mistress pregnant; if he thinks that gives him a right to shoot me, I'd like to know about it."

Suzanne went white. "I hardly think you need to worry about that," she said stiffly.

"Oh, Suzanne, I *am* sorry," he apologized immediately. "Are you very unhappy that things are over with him?"

Suzanne was touched by the sympathy in his voice. "No," she said honestly. "I think I am more relieved."

The situation—her leaving Nick to marry Patrick—was, in truth, a great deal less complex than Patrick probably thought it. She was not leaving one lover for another.

"Patrick, I don't think you quite understand—"

"I'm sure I don't," he interrupted. "On one hand, it seems like you don't love him anymore; while on the other you are willing to go live with him, while you are taking care of a child that isn't his. I don't understand that; it doesn't sound like you. You aren't the sort who uses people, but that arrangement does seem to take advantage of him. I feel like I am snooping into things that are none of my business, but I can't help thinking that this would all be a lot easier if I understood. But don't tell me anything you don't want to," he added hastily.

"I haven't slept with Nick in over two years."

Patrick stared at her. "But—"

"But I have *not* been using him." This was important to her; that Patrick not think she had been living on Nick's charity. "True, he did support me, but I did more for him and his career than any wife or agent or editor."

Almost defensively, she explained about the manuscripts she had typed, the galleys she had proofed, the speeches she had revised, the phone calls she had made, in addition to all the other ways a woman takes care of a man.

"He must be devastated to lose you," Patrick reflected at last.

"He is—rather he thinks he is. I think that in the long run, he will be better off without being so dependent on one person. But, anyway, my leaving him is a lot more like my leaving Harrison Colt than it probably seems." She smiled, trying to change the subject. "Now, it is Mr. Colt you need to worry about shooting you, not Nick."

Patrick wasn't interested in changing the subject. "Why did you do all that for Moretti? You aren't a user, but you aren't a doormat either."

"No, I'm certainly not." Suzanne could be emphatic on that point. "He was paying the bills so it felt like a business relationship especially as..." She faltered.

"Especially as you weren't sleeping together," Patrick finished for her. When she started to speak, he held up his hand. "You don't have to explain that. I am sorry if this embarrasses you, but the one thing I could tell about your relationship with Moretti was that that part of your life together was very unsatisfying. I didn't know that it was nonexistent, but I can't say that this news is entirely surprising."

"I was that bad?" Suzanne sighed.

"No, that unsure," he corrected. "I just wish..."

"Wish what, Patrick?" If she could be honest, so could he.

"Well, I know that your relationship with him hasn't one thing to do with me." Patrick spoke like the son of his progressive parents. "And I also know that the two of you must have both been pretty unhappy if you stopped sleeping together. I know I ought to feel sorry that the relationship deteriorated so badly instead of..."

"Instead of?" she prompted.

"Instead of being so damned pleased."

Chapter Nine

After Suzanne left that evening, it occurred to Patrick that this marriage would not only solve some problems for her and the child, it would also solve the one thing that had bothered him the most about leaving the United States for two years.

He owned no property. He certainly had the money for it; in fact, every year at tax time, he swore that he would buy something soon, but he was so busy and so comfortable in his townhouse apartment that he had never gotten around to it. But it did make him nervous to leave without having gotten a start in the real estate market. He had spoken to a realtor last February, but the man told him there wasn't mortgage money for rental properties; it would be better if he were buying a principal residence.

But he realized now if he bought a house and Suzanne lived in it, then it would probably qualify as his principal residence.

What a strange thing marriage was. He and Suzanne were about to become a legal unit. It was rather frightening.

To say nothing of being time-consuming. They were getting married Saturday morning, and so not only was

Patrick trying to get his affairs organized so he could leave the country for two years, but they were having to get blood tests, buy a license and a ring, meet with realtors, and see a lawyer about some sort of prenuptial agreement.

Suzanne had insisted on that, and as usual she was right. They would almost certainly get divorced sooner or later, so why not straighten everything out in advance?

But they had trouble agreeing as each was primarily interested in protecting the other. Suzanne wanted him to have no obligations besides the child's educational expenses, and he of course wanted to do a great deal more. But when he mentioned the word "alimony," the lawyer looked at him as if he were a visitor from the Stone Age, so they compromised. In the event of divorce, Patrick would pay monthly child support and school tuition. They also devised a plan whereby Suzanne could buy out Patrick's equity in the house if she wanted and could afford to.

Then they had to tell people. Patrick called his family, and in the abrupt way he had learned was the best way to deal with them, announced that he was getting married on Saturday and then just held the receiver away from his ear for a good five minutes while they squealed. He refused to let them come to the ceremony, but did agree to bring Suzanne up to Concord afterwards.

Suzanne said that she had told the people she worked with, but the news had not filtered down to the rest of the firm—the tenth floor was very good at keeping what it knew to itself. The lower floors were clearly Patrick's responsibility.

But he found it hard to tell people. He finally decided that the easiest thing to do would be to tell David and let him take it from there. David wasn't a particular gossip, but he would have the sense to realize that Patrick would want him to spread the news.

But what David didn't realize was that he first needed to go up to Patrick and say, "By the way, Britten, are you getting married before you go to India?"—because Patrick was not having the least bit of luck bringing the matter up during any of their usual conversations about work, the American League East, and German white wines. He almost managed it when they were talking about tax deductions; he almost managed to say, "Well, it looks like I'll have a few more deductions next year."

But the thought that a squalling infant was going to figure on his tax return, or in any other part of his life, was so appalling that he couldn't get it out.

Finally on Friday afternoon when David stuck his head in his office, casually asking, "What are you up to this weekend?" Patrick answered.

"I'm getting married."

"You're *what*?"

Patrick grinned. Now that it was out, he was rather pleased with the effect of this news. "You heard me. I'm getting married."

David sank into a chair, stunned. "I don't believe it."

"I'm grieved, David, truly grieved. I thought we trusted one another."

"Trust? Hell," David cursed. "You're a fine one to talk about trust when out of the blue, you are suddenly talking about getting married."

Patrick just raised his eyebrows. He was enjoying this more than he thought he would.

"Who is it? You are getting married *to* someone, aren't you?" David asked. "I know you think you don't need people, but for this one, if my memory serves, you need at least one other person. Who is she?"

"Would you believe Suzanne Lawrence?"

"No," David said bluntly. "Try again."

"Thank you, no. I had enough trouble persuading her," Patrick said with what he thought was a nice piece of uncharacteristic gallantry. "I don't care to try again."

David tilted his dark head. "You're serious, aren't you?"

"Yes."

"I should have known your sense of humor wasn't good enough to make this one up." David sighed and then as the news began to sink in, his tone changed. "I didn't even know that you knew her," he marveled.

"We worked together last winter, you knew that, and then we've been away on a few weekends together." Patrick decided that "a few" sounded better than "one."

"You've been away together?" David was astonished. "I had no idea."

"We kept quiet about it; we didn't want people talking about us."

"Well, they will now," David returned. Then he shook his head, still surprised by the news. "But it's so sudden; you and Miss Lawrence—I hardly know what to say."

"I think you are supposed to congratulate me," Patrick pointed out.

"Oh, I do," responded his friend. "Not only is she as pretty as they come, but she's just frighteningly competent. With her along, you'll probably get the India project done in one year instead of two."

"She's not coming to India."

David looked surprised. "I don't understand. Why not? Presumably you like her."

"I like her a great deal, but she's pregnant and—"

"Oh," said David.

It was a very knowing "Oh" as if David felt he now understood everything, and suddenly Patrick felt what he never had before, what he had assumed that as a man of his generation he would never feel—a desire to protect a woman. He had been told over and over that these days women can take care of themselves. But now he was suddenly conscious that he and she were in a different position. She was more vulnerable than he to gossip, to comment and rumor, and he found himself wanting, even needing, to make her way easier for her.

He loathed explaining himself and his doings to people. He didn't care what people thought of him, but he discovered he minded very much what people thought of Suzanne.

"There's no 'oh' about it, David," he said crisply. "We're hardly ignorant kids. We wanted a child together; we were trying." The last was true enough. "The timing is a little imperfect but that's because Suzanne needs to be with American doctors through the whole pregnancy," he improvised. "She's Rh negative and she wants to be in an American hospital for her delivery."

"Then she'll come out to India?"

"Probably," Patrick lied. "It will depend on the health of the infant." How strange it seemed to be talking about deliveries and infants as if they were actually factors in his life.

David found it equally strange. "*You* wanted a baby? But I thought you hated little kids. You always swore you didn't want children."

Patrick wished he hadn't been quite so emphatic about that. "I didn't," he replied, "but that was before I had met Suzanne."

And, to Patrick's complete surprise, David seemed to find that remark not only sensible and convincing, but really rather touching.

"I hope a colonial is all right with you."

There was a fair amount of traffic on Route 2 Saturday morning, and it was a moment before Patrick could glance over at the woman who was now his wife. Very typically, she had a folder open on her lap. Whatever other couples talk about in their first hour of married life, she and he were discussing real estate.

He wasn't surprised that Suzanne was drawn to colonials: They were the most formal of houses, with balanced floor plans and traditionally proportioned rooms. That was why he liked them too.

She had found several in Belmont, an older, settled suburb next to Cambridge, where many people from the faculties of Harvard and M.I.T. lived. Belmont was a pleasant, wooded town without any of the stretches of identical houses so often associated with suburbs.

But it was entirely up to her, and he told her so. He doubted that he'd ever be living in the house; it was just an investment so he didn't care a great deal what it was like. In fact as the even, competent tones of Suzanne's light voice continued, as she discussed assumable mortgages and waterproofed basements, his attention wavered.

He wished she were happy. They had just gotten married; they should be celebrating. Instead of so calmly discussing the real estate market, she should be giggling and chattering. Well, maybe not giggling and chattering, but at least not so very businesslike.

Not that he had any right to complain. He was acting just exactly as she was. Neither one of them were any good at celebrating.

That was the point she had once made. They were too much alike. Each of them needed a person who was looser, lighter, livelier. Another man would have told her to toss her folder in the backseat, forget about all the hundreds of things that they had to do in the next two weeks, and have some fun. Another woman would never have brought a carefully organized folder to her wedding. A different partner could have helped each of them to enjoy this day.

But Suzanne *was* capable of delight, he had seen that in Washington. She had been happy there, cheerful, enthusiastic, a charming and enchanting companion. She hadn't had any responsibilities while she was there; without Harrison Colt or Nick Moretti to worry about, she had been able, probably for the first time in years, to enjoy herself.

Patrick's lips tightened in guilt. It was Suzanne's burdens, as much as anything in her character, that forced her to be so cautious and organized all the time. Her responsibilities kept her from relaxing, from being happy. So what had he done? Just when she had paid her college loans, just when she was about to break free from Moretti, he had, in an impulsive, impassioned moment that he still did not fully understand, given her a greater burden than she had ever had before.

She didn't seem the least excited about having a child. It was a responsibility, a duty, and she was prepared to do her best. She was trying to find a house with a fenced-in backyard on a quiet, safe street; she was looking at the test scores of local elementary schools. She was planning and preparing because she felt that she had to, not because she wanted to.

No wonder her dark eyes weren't sparkling as they had in Washington. What was there for them to sparkle about? She had just married him, a man who would add nothing to her life, no warmth, no happiness, just a measure of social respectability and financial security; she was faced with an eighteen-year-long responsibility that she dreaded, that she felt herself entirely unsuited for.

What had he done to her?

The least he could do was make her stop talking about real estate. He interrupted her. "I like your dress; it's pretty."

It was. He had been a little surprised by the dress. Had he thought about it in advance, which of course he did not, he would have guessed that she'd be wearing business clothes, a skirt and a blazer, the quiet grays that she wore to work. But she was in a dress and it was prettier, more feminine than the things she usually wore. It wasn't white, but some pale, natural color for which Patrick supposed women had a word but he certainly did not. The dress left her shoulders bare to the spring sunshine, a wide, lace edged flounce drifted over her arms and the bodice of the dress.

Suzanne colored a little at his compliment and obviously felt that she had to explain. "The Colts gave it to me. Mrs. Colt came to the office Thursday and insisted on taking me shopping." She touched the lace at her shoulder apologetically. "That's why it looks so much like a wedding dress. If she had had her way, it would have been white satin."

She had touched her dress with her left hand, and Patrick noticed the gleam of the wide gold ring she now wore. "Well, there's nothing wrong in that," he pointed out, sorry that she was embarrassed. "You did just get married."

She deserved better than this, he thought. Not the flowers and the bridesmaids so much, as just someone who would make her happy. He would never make her unhappy; he would never make her life complicated or difficult, but he couldn't make her happy. He was too much like her.

And then it occurred to Patrick that if the Colts were giving her a wedding present, he should have too. She didn't seem to have much jewelry, just that gold bracelet she always wore. She didn't even have her watch on today; it was a leather-strapped business watch, and she had probably thought it would look wrong with the dress. He could have given her a gold wristwatch.

It was, after all, their wedding day, and even if he didn't exactly love her, he cared more for her than he had ever cared for a woman. She probably didn't know that; he hadn't told her.

A good watch, maybe a string of pearls, or something. He wished that he had thought about it earlier.

Oh well, he reflected with a shrug of self-knowledge, he just wasn't good at that sort of thing—thinking of the right thing to do at the right time. The silver mirror set he had given her at Christmas was probably his lifetime quotient of perfect gestures.

At least, thank God, she didn't expect him to have done anything.

He glanced at her affectionately. How delicate she was. It was easy to forget, in light of her inordinate, unflinching competence, that her skin was fair, easily bruised, that her shoulders were slight, the clean line of her collarbone fragile under the satin skin.

Suddenly, it seemed very unfair to force her to have anything to do with his family. They were so overpoweringly boisterous, so eager and affectionate, and there were just so many of them, three brothers, two parents, two dogs, and an unpredictable number of foreign exchange students, friends, and friends' dogs.

"About my family—" he began.

"I've met your brothers," she interrupted. "I liked them a lot."

"Don't be polite. It's not going to hurt my feelings if you don't like them. They drive me crazy. My parents too. They're just as bad as my brothers."

Suzanne was silent for a moment and then asked slowly, "Do your parents know I'm pregnant?"

"Yes." Then when he saw her bite her lip, he added quickly, "You've nothing to worry about. They are probably the most baby-mad collection of people outside an obstetric ward. They adore little kids, even Andy does. My parents have probably already started calling each other 'Grandma' and 'Grandpa.'"

"But..."

"The timing?" He was hardly surprised that at heart Suzanne was a great deal more conventional than she was professing to be last week. "Remember, Suzanne, my parents are the last ones who would ever judge anyone for that. Anyway, they don't really know that it was a mistake." He told her what he had told David, a refined version of which he had passed on to his parents last night.

Suzanne seemed relieved. "That was very nice of you," she said softly.

He shrugged. "It was nothing."

"No. It makes a big difference to me. I'd hate to have them think I trapped you."

Trapped him. What an old-fashioned expression that was, a relic of her elderly parents, no doubt. He took his eyes off the road for a moment to smile at her. "As I recall, it was quite completely the other way around."

Patrick circled Concord, heading out to the north side of town where he had grown up. His parents lived near the Old North Bridge and the battleground where "the shot heard round the world" had been fired, beginning the American Revolution.

At a low stone wall, he turned, following the drive as it curved back through stands of slender-trunked trees—sugar maples, butternuts, ashes, and elms—whose leaves would flame yellow and red in the autumn until falling into rustling amber piles.

The Brittens lived in a comfortable buff-colored house. It was quite old, having once been a tidy little Cape Cod cottage, but generations of owners had added rooms and wings so that the house sprawled across the wooded lot, its irregular roof line softened by the drooping limbs of the overhanging trees.

"Is this your house?" Suzanne breathed. "It's lovely. What a perfect place to grow up."

Patrick glanced at her, surprised. The irregular charm of this place had little in common with the formal colonial she was looking at for herself. "Well, imagine being the one whose turn it was to rake the leaves," he said, keeping his voice nonchalant. "It didn't seem so perfect then."

The front door opened and they heard a shout: "They're here; they're here!" Two large Irish setters, their mahogany coats gleaming in the sun, bounded down the front steps and came running to the drive, barking and leaping.

Patrick felt Suzanne gasp and fumble for his arm. She had never done that before. He glanced down at her. She was afraid of dogs.

"Hoover, Bissell, down!" he commanded and instantly the dogs dropped to their haunches and looked up at the humans eagerly, their pink tongues out and their feathery tails sweeping across the grass in excitement.

Patrick put a light arm around Suzanne's shoulders. "They won't bite," he said reassuringly. "In fact, they're better trained than anyone else in the family."

She was clearly a little embarrassed. "I was just surprised that's all," she explained. "I've never been around dogs."

"It doesn't matter." In fact, he rather liked the way she reached for him. The idea of Suzanne frightened and turning to him for protection—well, he hoped his mother never found out how old-fashioned he was getting, but he did like it.

By now the rest of the family had tumbled out of the house: Ford, Brian, and Andy, all tall and healthy; Sally a wiry package of energy; and his father Nat, a tall, lean man, whose brown hair was just starting to fade.

"We didn't expect you for another..."

"... Suzanne, we are so glad..."

"... Andy hasn't even finished mowing the back..."

"Hoover, don't jump on her."

"Good heavens, call me Sally; everyone..."

"Oh, Pat, what a stuffy tie; where on earth..."

The voices jumbled in a blur of happy, confused noise. Suzanne looked overwhelmed, and Patrick started to shove Brian away from his tie, but his father reached her first.

"There are quite a few of us," Nat smiled, and took her arm, leading her to the house. "People who meet Patrick first always threaten to take us to court for violating the truth-in-advertising laws. I am afraid he doesn't give you a very accurate picture of what the rest of us are like."

"Yeah," Andy chimed in tactlessly. "We always

worried about Patrick getting married. Who on earth would be able to stand both him and us?"

Two hours later, Patrick stopped Suzanne as she passed through the hall on the way to the kitchen to help Sally get the food on the table. "Are you changing your mind about Belmont?"

She looked at him blankly. "No. Should I be?"

"Belmont's closer to Concord. Do you want to make it any easier for them to drop in on you?"

A funny expression came into her eyes. "Patrick, I like them," she said softly. "A lot."

"Well, they like you." It had never occurred to him to wonder if his family would like her; it didn't matter one way or another to him. But they clearly did.

"You know," she went on, "I can't help thinking what it would be like if it were reversed and you were meeting my parents. We would all sit around the living room, staring at each other. It would have been awkward, very proper and boring."

He laughed a little ironically. "No one has ever called my family proper and boring."

"I can see why they get to you," Suzanne acknowledged very softly. "But you don't know what the alternative is like."

The menu had a distinct ring of Easter to it—ham, fresh asparagus, and homemade hot cross buns. It turned out that Sally Britten had, in her usual fashion, read the calendar wrong this spring and had been very surprised in church one Sunday morning when the rest of the congregation seemed to think it was Easter. When she and Nat got home, Andy and Ford were sitting on the front porch expecting Easter dinner. She had had to feed them creamed dried beef on toast and was now trying to make amends.

After Nat told this story, Sally just sighed and put down her napkin wistfully. "Well, it's harder now. Holidays don't seem the same without children." Then suddenly she looked at Suzanne happily. "I can't wait until next year. It will be so lovely to have a baby in the family again."

Suzanne blushed, and Nat covered her hand. "I hope you know how happy you are making all of us," he said to her. "We've always worried that Patrick would never be able to have the sort of loving marriage that he ought because of—"

"Dad," Patrick interrupted, "we don't need to go into all that." It would only embarrass Suzanne to have them talk about how this "loving marriage" was somehow rescuing him from the emotional sterility that his parents considered their own fault.

"Speaking of marriages, Dad..." Ford was obviously trying to remind his father of something.

"Oh, that's right," Nat nodded. "I'd forgotten."

"What's up?" Patrick asked suspiciously, much too familiar with the ways of his family to trust the sudden silence.

Ford leaned back and reached over his head to get a slim package off the buffet. His chair would have crashed had not Andy grabbed it.

He slid the package, wrapped in what was clearly left-over Christmas paper, to Nat who in turn handed it to Suzanne.

"What's this?" she said in surprise.

Patrick cursed himself. He hadn't thought. Of course, his family would have a present for her, and more than likely, it would be something dreadful; she might not even know what it was. He should have warned her.

He watched as she carefully slit the tape on the green paper; her hands, normally so quick and competent, were moving slowly, the only sign of her embarrassment.

"Oh, come on," Andy urged impatiently. "Tear the paper."

"If she's the sort of person who tears wrapping paper," Brian pointed out, "she's not going to like what's inside."

"Shut up," Ford ordered.

She unfolded the paper, revealing a worn case of navy leather that looked vaguely familiar to Patrick, but he couldn't remember where he had seen it. Well, the family never remembered to get gift boxes when they bought things; they always had to make do with whatever was lying around the house.

Curiously he watched Suzanne as she eased open the hinged case.

Her hand flew to her mouth, stifling a gasp. Her eyes shot to his, pleading, and he had to shrug helplessly. He didn't know what was in the box, just that for some reason she didn't want it.

If they were lucky, he thought, it would be something from L.L. Bean and they could return it. That was possible. Like many New Englanders, his father loved buying things from the Bean catalogue.

Suzanne was shaking her head. "They're just beautiful," she breathed, "but I can't take them; it's too much."

"We want you to have them," Sally said immediately.

"And you are the logical person to get them," Nat pointed out. "Sally certainly doesn't want them, and you are the first bride in the family."

Bride! Well, yes, he supposed she was. "What is it?" he asked. "If Mother doesn't want it, maybe Suzanne doesn't either." That struck him as quite possible. Suzanne's taste was probably a great deal nicer than his mother's.

"You make this sound like a rummage sale," his mother accused, "and we're just trying to do the right thing, giving Suzanne Grandmother's pearls."

Grandmother's pearls. Patrick sat up. No wonder Suzanne was upset.

He had only seen the pearls once or twice; most of the time, they lived in the safe deposit box. They were a long perfectly matched natural strand that his great-grandfather had bought in Paris. The diamond clasp alone was going to require a special rider on his insurance policy.

Not only were they very expensive, but they were family heirlooms and Suzanne certainly would not feel that this morning's brief ceremony entitled her to family heirlooms.

But the rest of the family would think so. Anyway, Sally was hardly the sort of person who would wear pearls, and Suzanne clearly was. They might as well make the best of it.

"You know, I had completely forgotten about them," he said calmly, hoping that his matter-of-factness would help Suzanne. "Send them down here; I'd like to take a look at them."

Suzanne immediately handed the case to Ford who, instead of passing it to Patrick, took the pearls out. "Let's see how they look on." And with the kind of easy, utterly unselfconscious gesture that Patrick rather envied, Ford stood up and started to fasten them around her neck. "Do you want them looped a couple of times?" As an antique dealer, Ford knew more about how women wear jewelry than did the rest of the family, which wasn't saying much.

"Please," Suzanne said softly.

Ford wound the pearls around her, arranging the sparkling clasp off to the side. "The dress is just perfect for them."

Patrick supposed his brother was right; Ford knew about things like that, but he would have said that it was Suzanne, not her dress, who was perfect for the pearls.

"Come on," Sally held out her hand, "there's a mirror in the hall."

They all gathered around, admiring the lustrous gleam of the pearls against Suzanne's warm skin, and suddenly Suzanne looked as if she were going to cry.

Sally immediately hugged her. "We're so glad you like them, but don't cry. It's really nothing."

"What do you mean, nothing?" Nat gently teased. "For you and me to hold onto something for fifteen years without losing it, Sal, is something indeed. But they are just things, Suzanne," he said as he pulled her out of his wife's embrace to enfold her in his own. "They're nothing compared to what you are giving all of us."

She'd never had this, Patrick thought to himself. Maybe it did irritate him, all this gushing emotionalism, but she had never been with people who had the Brittens' capacity for such unreserved affection. Her parents hadn't had it, and Moretti had probably been too self-absorbed. Undoubtedly she needed more love than she had ever gotten—or would ever get, considering the husband she had ended up with.

"And now," Nat said briskly, "let's take some pictures."

"Oh, Dad," Patrick groaned.

Nathaniel Britten loved art. He collected eighteenth-century engravings and one of the many things that he liked about this new daughter-in-law was that her parents had been curators of an art museum and she could hold her own in a discussion of Hogarth and Rowlandson.

But for a man with his taste for line and color, Nat was a simply dreadful photographer. His idea of a well-composed picture was his family lined up in front of some building. At twenty-nine, Patrick felt he had outgrown standing in front of the house and having his picture taken as it were the first day of school.

"Well, of course, we want pictures," his father said. He turned to Suzanne. "You don't mind, do you?"

"No, of course not."

But what else could she say?

So they all trooped outside and automatically the four brothers lined up on the porch in order of age just as they had done at every family holiday since Andy could stand up on his own.

"Where should we put Suzanne?" Sally wondered. The newest member of the family was standing quietly on the grass, her pale dress gleaming in the green shade.

"Don't you want a picture just of them?" she asked immediately.

"Not at all," Sally assured her. "You're just as much a part of the family as any of them, and you certainly look better. Go stand next to Patrick."

Obediently she came over to stand next to him.

"Now I only have half of Andy," Nat announced from behind his tripod.

"Who would want any more?" Ford called back. "Half of Andy should be quite enough."

Patrick touched Suzanne's back, moving her and her pearls to stand in front of him.

"That's nice, I like that," Sally announced. "And

then when the rest of you get married, we can put all your wives in the front row and still get everyone in the picture.''

That idea clearly thrilled Sally, but Patrick wouldn't have been surprised if Suzanne fainted at the thought. He hoped she realized that he didn't expect her to spend the rest of her life standing in front of him in family portraits.

"What if one of us marries an Amazon?" Brian asked. "Ford's wife might be so tall that you couldn't see him."

"Or Brian's might be so wide there wouldn't be room for mine," Ford returned.

Suzanne giggled, and encouraged by her laugh, Ford and Brian continued, adding some pointed descriptions of what she was going to look like in the rather near future.

Finally he couldn't stand them anymore. "Will you guys shut up so we can get this over with?"

Surprisingly, they did and with as much efficiency as that thoroughly disorganized family was capable of, went through an endless combination of people and poses. Patrick was amazed that Suzanne seemed to be enjoying it all.

And in the car that evening on the way back to Boston, she did seem to be more relaxed. She didn't open her folder, simply resting her cheek against the head rest and murmuring how much she liked his family.

"But it looks like they wore you out," he said. She did look sleepy; she was rubbing her eyes and blinking.

"Oh, I don't think it's your family who's making me tired." She stifled a yawn. "It's this business of being pregnant."

Well, Patrick thought suddenly, wasn't that still a case of his family making her tired?

Being married was nothing like what Patrick had ever expected it to be. Suzanne didn't leave clutter in the bathroom or insist that he rearrange his schedule to accommodate her. She didn't go through his belongings or look at his mail. She didn't even move many of her things to his apartment. Why bother? she had said. She would just have to move them to the house. Patrick wasn't thrilled at the idea that most of her possessions were still with Moretti, but she was right, it was silly to move them twice in one month.

In fact, except for her silver mirror shining on top of his dresser or the curl of her soft body next to his every morning, she was more like a secretary than a wife. They were always discussing practical details, settlement on the house, his getting a power of attorney drawn up before he left the country, her selecting a micro-computer for her new business.

The one thing they never spoke about was the baby, and most of the time he just pushed it out of his mind, not wanting to think about it, not knowing what to think about it.

But at nights, when he would feel her next to him, his body would remember, and without deciding on it, without choosing to, he would act differently. He was more gentle than he had ever been with a woman, more tender than he thought himself capable of being, and sometimes he'd wonder if he were falling in love with her.

At last, one night just before he was to leave, as he eased himself from her, he kissed her smooth, still flat stomach, and then with his hand warm against her, heard himself asking, "Will you come to India with me?"

He felt her sigh in the dark. "No, Patrick," she whispered, and he thought he heard regret in her voice. "I just can't leave the U.S. until the baby is born. I want to be in an American hospital."

"Then afterward? Will you come?"

"If you ask me again, yes," she breathed. "Yes, I will. But you'll have to ask again."

But as things turned out, he never asked.

Chapter Ten

January 28
Dear Patrick,

Well, I have done my duty as best friend and hauled myself out to Belmont to see this week-old tax deduction of yours. She is red, Britten, red. They may not be telling you, but it's true. It's not just her hair, but her skin too—all wrinkled and red. She looks a lot like a scarlet prune—a very nice scarlet prune, I am sure, but still if I were a female infant and had a mother who looked the way this female infant's mother does, I think I would prefer to resemble Mama as opposed to something from the vegetable kingdom.

But your mother, who, by the way, persists in refusing to run off with me, says that this prunedom is temporary. Apparently Caesarean babies are the only pretty ones at this very advanced age—they didn't get so squashed during their entrance routine—so we are, I guess, to be grateful that you are blessed with such an ugly offspring.

She—your mother, that is—is, of course, simply thrilled that the baby is being called "Sarah" after her.

Your brother Ford—who does look astonishingly like you as I imagine you know—is apparently the hero of the hour. He turned up at the hospital and, by virtue of simply calling himself "Mr. Britten," let all the nurses think he was you. So he was with Suzanne all through her labor although he skipped the last half hour in the delivery room. It was a long haul for her, and I guess she was glad he was there. Apparently toward the end, she got confused and started calling him by your name, a fact which your family seems to get great delight in teasing her about.

Your whole family was there when I showed up. I couldn't quite figure out who was staying and who was just visiting and I am not sure that any of them knew either. Is that the way your clan usually operates? If so, where did you come from?

David

P.S. You owe me a great debt. I have saved you thousands and thousands of dollars in medical, psychiatric, and perhaps even dental bills by refusing, despite considerable urging from the new grandparents, to hold your daughter. Who knows what permanent damage I might have done to her?

April 10
Dear Patrick,

I lied. She isn't red, wrinkled or ugly, not in the least. She's a fair-skinned strawberry blonde with eyes that are on their way to being chocolate brown like her mother's. Your brother, Uncle Ford, as he is now known, points out that she may end up with the coloring of a golden retriever. But this girl is no dog; I would instead recommend that you think of her as a particularly delectable ice cream sundae.

She can do all kinds of swell things—follow an object with her eyes, maneuver her thumb into her mouth by herself, smile, and wave her little arms about. Of course, there are a few things she can't do, like run up a big bill at Lord and Taylor or write for the Harvard *Crimson,* but give her time.

She's cute, Patrick, really cute. It's a shame you aren't around.

David

December 15
Dear Patrick,

I suppose you have heard the big news already—that Miss Sarah Britten has started to walk. Don't believe what they tell you; she's no good at it. She wavers and sways, and she falls. A lot. The Red Sox are trying to draft her; she can only improve their outfield.

But she's bright. She's figured out that the one thing that always brings Suzanne rushing to her in concern is when she falls on her head so even when she lands squarely on her well-diapered bottom, she pats her strawberry curls, trying to get some sympathy.

I had no idea little kids were such a treat. Almost makes me want one of my own—only almost though.

David

That was easy for him to say, Patrick thought as he closed the folder of David's letters wearily and tightened his seat belt in preparation for landing at Boston's Logan Airport. It was one thing for Stern to think she was cute; he wasn't going to have to live with her and her ear infections, her diapers and her car seat.

What he had always sworn to avoid was going to happen: For at least a month or so, he was going to be living with a small child. Of course, he was biologically responsible for her existence, but he didn't imagine that that was going to make her any less noisy, smelly, and sticky.

What were seventeen-month-olds like? Did they wake up in the night, screaming? Could they feed themselves or did their suppers have to be shoveled into them? Could they talk yet? Patrick simply did not know.

Certainly he had seen plenty of pictures of her. His parents had sent dozens to Calcutta, and every month or so, Suzanne would send a replacement for the small walnut frame that sat on the credenza behind his desk. He assumed that she sent the portraits because men were supposed to have pictures of their families in their offices; surely she didn't imagine him to be mooning over them soulfully. But he trusted her sense of what was appropriate and so he had dutifully put in each new picture, hardly even glancing at it.

He hadn't been that way at first. When he had arrived in India, he found, to his surprise, that he missed Suzanne and was concerned, even anxious, about her well-being. Although his father's photographic techniques were not improving in the least, Patrick felt a surge of pleasure when he got an envelope marked "Photographs: Do Not Bend." He knew the pictures would be of Suzanne.

She had, he thought, grown pregnant in a pretty sort of way. She always seemed happy and relaxed, and sometimes looking at the pictures, he would long to be with her, even to the point of thinking that he might have been very wrong to leave her alone. And although he had always considered himself the most contemporary of men, he found that he was doing as much as he could for the few pregnant women he encountered, carrying things for them, making sure that they were comfortable. Such old-fashioned gallantry was entirely out of character, yet he couldn't help thinking of Suzanne. If she were tired, he hoped that some man somewhere was giving her his chair.

But by the time Sarah was born, his life in India was much fuller and far more satisfying, and he had trouble relating to laughing pictures of the redheaded baby that everyone else found so adorable.

He had never seen the child. Plans had been made last winter for him to meet his parents, Suzanne, and Sarah in Europe for ten days, but apparently Sarah had had one ear infection after another and her pediatrician advised against taking her on an airplane. So only his parents had come.

He was surprised at how close Suzanne seemed to be to his family. She had named the baby after his mother, and she spent a lot of time in Concord. She went up there far more frequently than he had ever done, at least a weekend or two a month, and she had spent both of her summer vacations with them, even in the second year when she could clearly afford to take a real vacation.

Her business, he knew from their joint income tax return, was doing astonishingly well. She had two editors and a number of typists working for her, and they were all as busy as they wanted to be.

Apparently all her employees were mothers who, like Suzanne herself, wanted to work at home with very flexible hours. She provided the business and the word-processors, and they typed or edited during school hours or naptime. It had proved to be a very successful arrangement.

Well, that really wasn't a surprise. Of course, Suzanne's business was successful. She was running it, wasn't she?

It would be nice to see her, he thought with a sudden memory of the affection he had once felt. Of course right now he was so tired, so exhausted from this long journey from Calcutta, that he just wanted to be alone for a while. But unless she had changed a lot, being with Suzanne was almost as good as being alone.

The airport was crowded and busy. Just as in New York, he was struck by how fair-skinned so many people were, and how extraordinary it was to hear absolutely everyone speaking English. Suddenly very weary, he walked slowly up the concourse, not really seeing much, but forcing himself to listen to the public address system just in case Suzanne had left a message for him. He had written her, asking if he could stay with her, pointing out that he had no key.

"There he is! Patrick! Pat!"

It was not the hollow tones of the P.A. system, but, Patrick realized sickeningly, the equally loud voice of his youngest brother.

He looked beyond the ropes of the security system to a cluster of red and auburn heads. His whole family was here, parents, brothers, and undoubtedly dogs.

He did not need this. Not at all.

But he hardly had a choice and the stream of passengers pulled him out of the anonymous safety of the concourse and into a smothering mass of hands, hugs, and voices, welcoming him, engulfing him, exhausting him.

Finally he lifted his head and over his mother's shoulder, he saw her. Suzanne. Quiet, peaceful, safe amid all this weltering storm of confusion and noise.

Firmly he put his mother aside and moved toward Suzanne. He meant only to kiss her cheek, but some movement in the crowd jostled her off balance, and automatically his arms had gone around her, steadying her.

"Patrick"—her voice was warm and low—"welcome home."

She felt good in his arms, soft curves and fresh scents. He had been hearing for two years how competent she was, what a shrewd businesswoman she was, he had forgotten how very feminine she felt. He bent his head and kissed her, his mouth suddenly opening at the feel of hers.

Abruptly he let go of her. He hadn't meant to kiss her that way, not in a crowded airport, not at all.

She stepped away, a little confusion showing in her brown eyes, and put her hand on the stroller she had been standing next to....

A stroller.

Involuntarily Patrick glanced down, seeing only a confused image of a small white dress and golden-red curls. Suzanne knelt down to the sleeping child and Patrick abruptly turned away.

You knew this would happen. You knew it would.

Suzanne carefully lifted Sarah out of her stroller and started fastening her into her carseat. She looked over to where Patrick was helping his brothers load his luggage into the family station wagon.

She had tried to prepare herself for Patrick's reception of Sarah. He wouldn't go into raptures, she had told herself repeatedly. With his family there watching him, he would feel too much pressure; he would feel like they expected too much of him, too much interest, too much enthusiasm, too much love, and knowing he could not react to Sarah with all the emotion they wanted from him, he might not even try; he might ignore her completely. Suzanne had predicted it all.

But it had still hurt terribly when he had turned away. *Oh, Patrick,* she wanted to cry. *We were so wrong. She's wonderful, and she can make us that way too.*

Suzanne's doubts about her ability to mother had long since vanished. Although she had felt very inept at first, those feelings had faded in a week or two. Sarah never bored her; she never found herself awkward and self-conscious about being with her; the tenderness, the little games, playing peek-a-boo, kissing her fingers and toes, it all came easily, naturally, and, for the first time in Suzanne's life, spontaneously. She loved Sarah more than she thought she was capable of loving.

At first, she had tried to rationalize her feelings. The survival of the species required, she told herself, that a mother feel this way about her young, especially when there was only one offspring per litter.

But how irrelevant her explanations, her rationalizations, started to seem. She loved her child; their place in the scheme of human evolution did not matter.

She had changed so much from being Sarah's mother; she was more relaxed, more open, more loving. She was no longer afraid of feeling things. She no longer tried to explain her feelings away; she no longer hid from them. She knew that Patrick could grow just as she had, if only he would let himself love Sarah.

At the moment, he looked particularly blank. When he had been walking up the concourse, Suzanne had thought he looked wonderful, he was so tan from the bright Indian sun, but up close, it was obvious how very tired he was. He was clearly finding his family's enthusiasm a strain; undoubtedly he was dreading the weekend ahead.

When everyone started to move around to the doors of the station wagon, Suzanne spoke.

"Patrick, I was hoping you would ride up with Sarah and me."

No one could possibly question the appropriateness of that arrangement, and Suzanne was pleased to note a brief flicker of relief cross Patrick's face as he came over to her car.

"Would you like to drive?" she asked.

"I think my license has expired," he answered.

"Oh." Suzanne pointed to an envelope resting on the dash. "I brought your new one just in case."

He looked at her, shaking his head. "How did you think of that? You're a marvel."

Suzanne blinked back a quick, hot tear, stunned at how much this praise mattered. "No, I am not," she said lightly. "I'm a criminal. I forged your signature on the renewal application."

He smiled and said no, he was probably too tired to be driving.

He said nothing as Suzanne maneuvered out of the tangle of airport traffic, and in the sickly artificial light of the Sumner Tunnel they spoke only of inconsequentials, saying nothing at all about the only thing that mattered to Suzanne, the small child sleeping in the backseat.

At last he spoke of something besides the weather. "Moretti has a new book out, I see."

"Yes, it's been nominated for several awards. I imagine he's thrilled."

"Imagine?" he asked.

"Oh, didn't I tell you? He moved back to New York." In their very brief time together two years ago, Suzanne had learned to be careful about how often she mentioned Nick to Patrick. It wasn't precisely that Patrick was jealous, but... well, Suzanne had never been sure what it was. His tightening face, his steady persistence in referring to Nick by his last name, all seemed to point to jealousy, but that seemed so out of character for Patrick. "I haven't seen him in over a year though he sometimes calls and has sent Sarah some presents."

Suzanne winced. Why did she say that? She didn't want Patrick to think she was reproaching him. He had never sent Sarah anything, neither at Christmas nor on her first, and so far only, birthday. It certainly hadn't hurt Sarah who had had more than enough presents on both occasions, so many it had bewildered her in fact, but it had been hard for Suzanne to explain it to his parents without telling them what she was sure was the truth—that it simply had never occurred to him.

But he was unperturbed and in a moment asked her if she had much contact with people in the firm.

"Oh, yes," she had answered, feeling on safe ground. "I do a lot of work for them, and of course, I am invited to all the parties."

"You are?" he said in surprise.

Wasn't there anything safe to talk about?

Probably when he was in India, Patrick would go for weeks at a time without thinking of her or their marriage, but it had been very different for her. She was surrounded with reminders, the ring she wore, the name she used, to say nothing of the daughter she was raising. She was invited to Southard-Colt parties not because she was a former employee, not because she did editing for them now, but because she was Patrick's wife.

And that's why she had always gone. Certainly she liked many of the people there, but there were nights when the last thing she wanted to do was find a babysitter and a pair of pantyhose and go and listen to people talk about the proposals they were writing.

But she understood exactly why Patrick was in India; he wanted to be made a vice-president as quickly as possible, and so he was gambling that this project was the fastest route to that goal, with one of the risks being the reduced visibility the absence would bring.

So Suzanne was visible for him, going to every party she was invited to, taking Sarah to every company picnic. Of course, her pleasant conversations with the Management Committee, whom she knew better than she did Patrick's friends, weren't going to win a promotion for him, but they weren't hurting either.

Was Patrick going to be surprised, she wondered, by the way he would find things? They had married somehow with the notion that it wouldn't change much, that it would just give Suzanne better health insurance, but they had been wrong. However they might feel, to the rest of the world they were a couple, now a family, a permanent, fixed unit. It had happened slowly to Suzanne; she had had time to adjust to this new role, but Patrick was going to be hit full-force with people expecting him to be a husband and a father when undoubtedly he had no intention of being either.

When Suzanne turned into the drive that curved back to the Brittens' house, their station wagon hadn't arrived yet. She was by now much too familiar with their erratic habits, their tendency to stop or take short-cuts, for her to have bothered keeping track of their car on the road. She had a key to the house, which she handed to Patrick, saying "I think I'll wait out here and see how much longer Sarah will sleep, but you can go on in."

How silly. As if he needed her invitation to enter the

house he grew up in. But she now felt very much at home there and had spoken unthinkingly.

"No, I don't mind," he answered politely. "I'll wait with you."

Was that a singular "you" or a plural "you"?

But she didn't dare ask. "Then let's at least let out the dogs. They'll go mad if we don't."

He looked at her curiously. "I thought you were afraid of dogs."

"Not anymore."

So Patrick opened the front door, which someone had apparently forgotten to lock, and let out the two Irish setters, Hoover and Bissell. They knew him instantly and crashed into him, wriggling, waggling, and barking in shameless ecstasy.

"Well, I'm glad to see you too," he laughed, trying to keep them from licking his face. The two animals danced around him as he petted and scratched them— or at least to the extent that two whirling, squirming dogs can be petted and scratched. He seemed happier to see them than he had been to see her or his family.

The three of them then went around to the backyard, with Patrick looking at the house and the yard, and the dogs, their dark red coats gleaming, looking at Patrick.

Slowly Suzanne got out of the car. The soft mass of green trees shaded the buff-colored house, and the late tulips peered out from the beds of darker ivy. This was just how the house had looked when she had first seen it, two years ago last week, on the day she had married Patrick.

Did he ever think of June 5 as his wedding anniversary? Or did it just come and go like any other day?

Patrick reappeared around the corner of the house and came over to where she was leaning against the car. "The place looks good," he said.

Suzanne didn't know what to say. The condition of the house and the yard seemed so entirely unimportant compared to their child, but Patrick seemed intent on ignoring her.

So she said nothing, not moving until, in a moment, she heard Sarah stirring.

She turned and opened the back door of the car, sliding into the seat. She tried to act naturally, talking to Sarah as she always did, unbuckling the straps of the carseat, lifting her out, checking her diaper. But as she did these familiar tasks, she was thinking of Patrick and she wished she could watch him to see if he were watching Sarah.

How she longed to put Sarah in Patrick's arms. She ached to see his face soften with love for his daughter.

But she knew what would happen if she handed Sarah to him. He would stiffen and his eyes would go tense and gray. He didn't want to hold this child. So Suzanne put her down, letting her toddle around in the grass, moving only to stand between her and the quiet street.

Sarah looked so perfect; her little dress shone white against the green lawn, her arms and legs were warm honey, and the red-gold of her hair gave her a slightly elfin quality as if she were on a visit from the fairy world. How could anyone not notice how exquisite she was?

Sarah squatted down in front of the now sleeping Bissell and tugged at his ear until he rolled open an eye. He ignored her; both dogs had long since learned that if they weren't calm around Sarah, if they didn't let her roll on them and pull their tails, they spent the weekend in the basement.

At last Patrick spoke. "That's a pretty dress she has on."

Not that *she* was pretty, but only her dress. Well, it was a start.

"Your father bought it for her."

"Dad?" Patrick's eyebrows shot up in surprise. "Dad buys her clothes? I don't think he ever bought clothes for any of us."

Suzanne smiled. "One granddaughter is a different matter than four sons." And there was something she had to say; she didn't know if he cared, but she had to say it. "Patrick, your family's been wonderful. I simply don't know how I would have managed without them."

It was so true. Although mothering was possible when she had expected that it would be impossible, it had still been hard. There were times when she had been exhausted, had felt at the end of her patience and energy. She did use babysitters, but she herself had been left with a babysitter all day every day, and she didn't want Sarah turning out as she had.

But unlike many other women raising children alone, Suzanne had a safety net under her—Concord. Whenever she wanted some help, whenever she wanted to be able to spend an afternoon reading a book or catching up on some work, she could go to Concord and know that Sarah was being cared for by people who loved her, who cherished and treasured her just as much as her mother did.

The Brittens were thrilled that she came so often. They adored all babies, and they were wild about this one. Taking such an active part in Sarah's upbringing was important to Nat and Sally. It was as if they were somehow trying to compensate Patrick for all they had failed to give him by giving it to his daughter.

Suzanne thought that these visits were also very good for Sarah. Her Belmont house was quiet and Suzanne wanted Sarah to know about noise and confusion. Her three uncles and their dogs provided plenty of that. Sarah was turning into an active, adventuresome little girl, quite unlike Suzanne had been, and Suzanne was pleased, very pleased.

But Patrick said nothing in response to her remark about his family. Nothing at all. Was it just that he was tired?

She asked herself the same question again several hours later. He had spent the afternoon patiently answering everyone's questions about India, but he seemed to be so distant, so removed. Was he just numb with exhaustion or had he always been like this? Perhaps he had been, and she just hadn't noticed it before because she had been like that too.

As the afternoon turned into evening, as Patrick sat in the living room answering questions and she moved about the house, taking care of Sarah, helping with dinner, it almost seemed as if she were more a part of the family than he was, as if he were the in-law, not she.

In fact, after dinner that night, when Suzanne and the brothers were heading upstairs for bed—Nat and Sally's room was on the first floor—a quick conversation seemed to confirm it.

As they rounded the landing, Ford touched Suzanne's arm and spoke to her softly. "Is Sarah asleep?"

"She'd better be," Suzanne answered, smiling at him. She truly liked Ford; she had started doing the books for his shop as soon as Patrick had left, and then a very strong bond had grown between them during the long hours when he had held her hand in the labor room. At first she had found it unsettling to look at him because he looked so much like Patrick; but several times this afternoon, she had caught herself looking at

Patrick in surprise, thinking how much he looked like Ford, rather than the reverse.

Ford now grimaced. "I should have offered to have her crib in my room; I wish I had thought about it earlier."

Suzanne realized what he was saying; that on their first night together in two years, few husbands and wives would want to share their room with a seventeen-month-old daughter. She smiled at him, touched by his consideration. "That's all right, Ford, we'll be home soon enough."

It was, she reflected as she crossed the hall, the sort of conversation that should have been between brother and brother, not between brother and sister-in-law.

And, she also reflected, she too wished that Ford had thought about it a little earlier.

Patrick opened the door to his room, going in without waiting for her as if perhaps he didn't quite realize that she too slept there now. He reached out his hand to flick on the light.

She quickly touched his arm, stopping him. "Please don't," she said softly, "you might wake Sarah." She moved over to the bed, turning on the reading lamps whose soft glow would not shine into the crib.

"She sleeps in here?" he asked blankly.

And Suzanne knew that he was not thinking the thoughts that Ford had been. Patrick didn't want to be alone with Suzanne; he just wanted to be alone.

Suzanne had slept in this room several times a month for nearly two years, and she had come to understand how important the room had been to Patrick growing up. Even now the family made jokes about it, about how no one was allowed in Patrick's room, how no one could touch his things or open his drawers. She understood, remembering how relieved she had felt when she had gotten her own room, safe from Nick Moretti's clutter and curiosity. And she too had on occasions been glad of the sanctuary that this room had provided from the noisy, loving confusion of the Brittens.

But how Patrick must feel, entering this room, exhausted, weary, oddly tense, to find it invaded, changed, belonging as much to these two females as it did to him.

Of course, it was neat and orderly, and the pictures of his Little League team still hung on the wall; his Soap Box Derby trophy still sat on the shelf. But on the top of the dresser were a hairbrush, a jar of moisturizer and a small vial of perfume. Women's clothes hung in the closet; Suzanne's blouses and Sarah's little overalls, and in the corner a bright mobile danced over a crib. It wasn't *his* room anymore.

Suzanne longed to seize her child and run away, leaving him the solitude he obviously craved. "I'm sorry, Patrick," she faltered. She felt like she had to say something. "Sarah and I have been using this room. The guest room is so small, and, well, to your parents, she and I are your family...."

"No, no, it's fine," he interrupted. "I just wasn't thinking, that's all."

But it wasn't fine. He hated it.

Patrick, no, she wanted to plead. *Don't you remember? It's me, Suzanne. I won't intrude; I won't push you; I won't ask questions. Remember, we're alike.*

But Suzanne knew that they weren't alike anymore. She wasn't the careful Miss Lawrence. She was now more of a Britten than he was, more comfortable, more at ease, more a part of things. All the things she hadn't done before, she did now. She sang lullabies to Sarah, knowing that Sarah didn't care how good her voice was.

She drew pictures for Sarah; Sarah was no art critic. She had let Andy try to teach her to play tennis, no longer caring that she was terrible. She was a good mother; she didn't mind that she was bad at other things.

Wordlessly they got ready for bed. Patrick was very careful not to look at her as she undressed.

"You can leave the light on if you want to read," he said politely. "It won't bother me."

She understood what he was saying and so pretending as much as possible that they were in two twin beds not in one double, they got in bed, Suzanne sitting up against the pillows to read, Patrick almost immediately falling asleep.

Except she didn't read. She watched him. The glare from her reading lamp softened before it reached him and he slept in a pool of dim light and gentle shadows. And suddenly he seemed very, very dear.

Did she love him? How could she? She hadn't seen him in two years, and she certainly hadn't loved him then.

It was just warmhearted compassion, she told herself. And not even for him as he was now, but for the boy he had been.

Over the last two years, she had slowly come to realize how unhappy and lonely Patrick had been as a child. One wall downstairs was filled with family photos, and except for the routine poses of the four boys lined up on the porch, the rest were of Nat, Sally, and their three sons—the fourth son, their first son, hadn't been in the group; Patrick had been the one behind the camera, taking the picture. He was the outsider.

And once when she had opened a drawer, trying to find a place to store the sweaters she was leaving in Concord, she had found his baseball card collection. Although she almost never pried, she looked at it—at least she had until she worried that her tears might spot some of the cards.

He had created the most elaborate indexing system she had seen outside a computer program. The cards themselves were arranged by year and then by team; in a loose-leaf notebook were his indexes and statistics. He had kept track of batting records, of no-hitters and earned run averages, of assists and errors. He had cross-referenced every Red Sox player, tracing where they were from, where they had been traded to. It was a remarkable effort.

But no boy should have had the time to do that. Suzanne's heart had ached at the thought of him coming up to his room to work on his indexes, while his parents romped and played with the babies. No wonder he found it so hard to deal with his family now.

Very gently Suzanne brushed a lock of the thick, silky auburn hair off his forehead. Anyone, she told herself, would feel a tug of compassion for him.

No. She stopped herself. This was how she used to be, always trying to explain her feelings as if she had to rationalize and justify them to herself. Maybe she was falling in love with her husband. But what on earth was the harm in that?

She clicked off the lamp and snuggled down in the pillows. How lovely it was to be sleeping beside someone again, to feel the warmth of his body seeping over to her. Even the weight of the blankets felt different, no longer molding themselves around her body, but rather, on the left side, dipping just a little until they swept upward supported by Patrick's larger body. His breathing was low and even, and his shape familiar.

He was home.

Chapter Eleven

Hands. Hands that were warm in the dark.

Suzanne stirred slowly, sleepily, luxuriating in the imagined caress, not wanting to wake up from this dream of a man's touch. It had been so long, so achingly long, since she had felt all this, the way a man lets his hand follow the line of your body, the way his kiss lingers at your breast, the curve of your waist, the way his leg moves against yours.

And as she turned to him, feeling the hot, hard wonders of a man's body, she knew it was him, no dream, no imagined man, but Patrick, her friend, her husband. She moved, responding, letting his silky hair flow across her fingers, sliding her hands along his shoulders, down his chest, gasping when she felt him easing her nightgown up over her thighs and his body moving over hers.

He wanted her. After all the misery of the day, after the tension and strain, there was still this: The two of them and the mysterious wonders of physical love, the two of them alone, sharing—

But we aren't alone.

"Patrick, no," she gasped, pushing him away. "We can't, not with . . . not while Sarah's in the room."

He stared down at her blankly.

"I'm sorry," she faltered. "But—"

"Suzanne?" His voice was empty, confused. And then suddenly he cursed and rolled away from her.

Had she been too prudish? Was she wrong to stop him? Desperately she tried to explain. "If we...if Sarah wakes up, it takes her forever to get back to sleep and tomorrow—"

"No," he interrupted, his voice tight with tension. "I'm sorry. I didn't mean...I didn't realize..."

Sickened, Suzanne understood. She understood why he had said her name so blankly.

He hadn't realized it was her. He must have turned in his sleep, and discovering a warm female form in his bed, he had, unconsciously, not even entirely waking up, begun to caress her, just some vague anonymous "her."

Suzanne was mortified.

And he was embarrassed. "I'm sorry," he muttered, apologizing once more. "It won't happen again."

What did that mean? For her part, Suzanne devoutly hoped that once they were home, it would happen again. And often.

Sunday turned into as difficult a day as Suzanne could imagine. She just didn't know what was wrong with Patrick.

Of course, he was still tired. He hadn't gone back to sleep; she had felt him twist and turn at her side a few times before he finally got up. Pretending to sleep, she listened to him dress; she knew he would refuse any offers of coffee, breakfast, or company—so what was the point of offering?

All morning he had buried himself in the Sunday papers, only smiling politely when his father asked if he had missed American newspapers.

By the middle of the afternoon, it was clear that he was restless and didn't know what to do with himself. There was nowhere for him to escape to. Sarah was taking her nap in what was once his room.

The family tried—asking him all about India, wanting to know what he had missed the most. And they would talk about Sarah, thinking to please him by calling him her "Daddy," a word that made his eyes go gray with a chill that froze Suzanne's heart. It was poisoning the day for everyone.

As soon as she brought Sarah down from her nap, Patrick immediately spoke to his mother. "Is it all right if I go lie down for a while? I'm afraid I've still got a bad case of jet lag." Without waiting for Sally's "Of course," he started upstairs.

"Suzanne, go to him," Sally pleaded. "See what you can do. I'll watch Sarah."

Patrick was sitting on the edge of his bed, staring down at his folded hands. Suzanne sat down next to him. She said nothing.

"God, they never change, do they?"

No, they don't, Suzanne wanted to say. *No, and who would want them to?*

Suzanne loved the Britten family. Yes, they were disorganized; their lives were constant chaos, but they were wonderfully generous and spontaneous.

But this was hardly the time to defend his family.

"Patrick," she spoke gently, "I know you feel a lot of pressure about Sarah, that people expect you to suddenly start loving her. But remember that I don't. I know it will take you time."

He rubbed the back of his neck. "It almost sounds like you understand."

"I do," she answered although she wasn't entirely sure that she did. "And more important, Sarah doesn't expect anything of you. In fact, I'm not sure that she fully realizes that you aren't Ford.''

He laughed softly, a shiver of irony chilling the sound. "I never thought looking so much like him would prove such a benefit."

That seemed so sad, that he should be relieved that his child couldn't tell the difference between her father and her uncle.

Suzanne pitied him. How isolated he was. She had been that isolated once, and she knew how much fuller, richer, life could be.

Unthinkingly she touched his neck, massaging it as he had been doing a minute ago. At his little grunt of pleasure, she stood up and began to rub his neck and shoulders.

Deftly she slipped open a few buttons of his shirt so that she could slide her hands beneath the fabric. He was warm, his skin warm and his muscles firm. Suzanne could feel his strength as she kneaded his muscles, and she remembered how strong those arms had been around her last night, how they had pulled her to him. Her hands moved over his shoulders to his chest, at first just tracing the line of his collar bone and then gliding lower, pressing against his chest, gently urging him to lean back against her.

At the touch of his back against her, Suzanne felt weak, breathless, waiting, expectant. Conscious of his breath quickening, of the feel of his heartbeat against her hand, she bent her head and kissed his neck, feeling the warmth of him against her lips and the brush of his thick hair against her cheek.

His hand came up and for a moment, she was sure, very sure, that he was about to caress her, to encourage her, that he would weave his fingers through her hair, directing her kisses, until he would finally turn, taking her in his arms, and in the soft light of this spring afternoon, once again share with her the rapture that she, at least, had missed so terribly.

But instead he straightened so abruptly that her hands fell from him. "I'm sorry," he said stiffly, "but I'm very tired."

The rejection stung her; it surprised her, and she glanced down.

He was lying.

They left after supper on Sunday, Patrick following Suzanne in his car that had been in Concord for the last two years, and she suspected that he was probably very relieved to be alone. This drive along the dark, empty highway was probably the first time he had felt at ease since he had returned to American soil.

She wished she knew what was tormenting him. She had to believe that it was more than just the usual difficulties he had with his family. Was it Sarah? Was it herself?

The two pairs of headlights sliced paths of white light across the cream-colored brick of the Belmont house. Then the two motors switched off, the lights died and the house was quiet and dark, the formal shapes of the carefully pruned boxwood just shadowy masses in the moonlight.

Suzanne carefully extricated her sleeping child from the straps of the carseat, hoping to get her in bed without her waking up.

Patrick was waiting for her at the steps. "Come in and make yourself at home," she said softly. "I'll be down as soon as I get rid of this child."

Our child, she thought to herself, and as she laid

Sarah in her crib, she allowed herself the luxury of whispering into the red-gold curls, "Sweetheart, your daddy's home."

Downstairs Patrick was standing in the center of the living room, looking around. It was as if he were a guest, waiting to be asked to sit down.

She felt like a hostess. "May I get you a drink? Or something to eat?" she asked politely.

"No, I'll just go and get my stuff out of the car."

Suzanne went out with him, carrying one of the smaller cases upstairs, opening and closing the baby gates that were across the stairs, but as she moved to her room, Patrick spoke her name.

She turned and looked at him questioningly.

"Suzanne, we have to talk."

"Can't it wait until morning?"

"No, I am afraid it can't." He set down his suitcases outside the door of what he must have guessed was the guest room. "Shall we go downstairs?"

Suzanne was confused. Of course, she knew perfectly well that when they married, one option was that they would divorce as soon as he returned from India, but the other option was at least to try living together for a while. When he had written, asking if he could stay in Belmont, she assumed that he wanted to try.

Two years ago, the two of them making any sort of permanent commitment to one another would have been an admission of failure, making that commitment because each had given up hopes for love and joy, settling instead for respect and affection.

But the woman who had read that letter was a very different woman than the one Patrick Britten had married. She no longer disliked herself; she no longer hungered to love a man different than herself. And seeing him this weekend, she no longer felt as though she were looking in a mirror that reflected a too cautious, too fastidious person without sparkle, life, or enthusiasm. She had grown enough, she had changed enough, that she believed she could now love him.

But his setting his suitcases outside the door to the guest room was not a promising start.

He was right; they probably did have to talk.

Suzanne unlatched the baby gate at the top of the stairs and unthinkingly led the way down to the kitchen, sitting at the long trestle table where she and her friends, the women who worked for her and the mothers of other young children, shared coffee and complaints.

Patrick took a chair opposite her. He picked up the pewter salt shaker that sat on the table, turning it around in his sun-browned hand, as if he had never seen one before. He set it down and looked across the table to where her hands were clasped.

"You aren't wearing your bracelet anymore."

Surely they weren't down here to talk about jewelry. But she answered. "Sarah broke it."

"That's too bad."

"No, it isn't." When the unexpected strength of Sarah's soft baby hand had pulled on the chain, it had been like another chain had been broken, the chain that had linked Suzanne to her own mother whose influence had made her so rigid and fastidiously precise. Suzanne Britten could not wear a fragile chain at her wrist; her life was so much more robust, so much fuller and richer, than Suzanne Lawrence's had ever been.

But she didn't expect Patrick to understand that, not yet. "It doesn't matter," she told him instead. "I had it repaired. Anyway," she ventured, "my initials aren't S.L. anymore."

He picked up the salt shaker again. "No, I guess they

aren't," he said slowly. And then he spoke quickly. "Are you all right? I mean, money and friends and Sarah? Are you busy, happy?"

"Everything's fine. Sarah had ear problems this winter but that's nothing too unusual. The business is—" He knew all this; she had written him every week, and they had filed a joint income tax return. He knew all about Sarah's health and the success of her business. "Patrick, why are you asking this?"

He set the salt shaker down, arranging it neatly by the pepper grinder. "Suzanne—" His eyes, now glinting green, met hers; perhaps for the first time since he had been home, he really looked at her. "Suzanne, while I was in India, I met someone."

She looked at him blankly. Well, of course, he had met someone. He must have met lots of people. India was full of people. What on earth was he talking about?

Then she knew.

"A woman?" The voice seemed faint, drowned in some swirling, ringing fog, and she could barely recognize it as her own.

"Oh, yes, and she's just wonderful." His voice was low, urgent. "She's the most vibrant, most alive person I've ever met. She has such a capacity for delight—I've never known anyone like her."

Suzanne watched him as he talked. He seemed very far away, very distant—and very different. Never before had he seemed this animated, never before had his smile seemed so unforced, had his eyes sparkled this green. The gray that dulled them when he looked at her, at their child, vanished when he spoke of this other woman.

A leaden weight crushed her, pushing down on her lungs, her chest, her heart; she could hardly breathe.

"And you love her," she heard herself say.

"More than I ever thought possible. I want to spend the rest of my life with her."

The legs of a ladder-backed chair scraped against the floor, and Suzanne found herself at the counter, fumbling automatically for the coffeepot, which was only a metallic glitter through the thick haze of tears now blurring her sight.

She struggled to keep her voice even. "I'm very glad for you."

She wasn't. Not at all.

But she should be; she truly should be. He had found what they had both thought impossible for themselves, rapturous, ecstatic love. She had never seen him like this. She didn't know he was capable of being like this. He probably hadn't been before. Not until he had met this other woman.

Carefully Suzanne filled the percolator with water and measured the coffee into the basket. They would never drink that much coffee, not even if they sat and talked all night.

But what did wasted coffee matter when Patrick had fallen in love with someone else?

She plugged the black cord into one of the wall outlets and sat back down.

"Is she Indian?" Suzanne asked politely.

"No, not at all. Her father is with I.B.M.; he was in India supervising the installation of the hardware for the new navy system."

"Yes, I knew that I.B.M. was providing the hardware."

Suzanne longed to talk about this, computers, hardware, software, I.B.M., macrosystems, microsystems, anything but the woman Patrick had fallen in love with.

But she had to know more. "Is she"—Suzanne didn't even know her name—"with I.B.M. too?"

"Kim?" Patrick smiled. *How could he smile, how could he possibly smile?* "Kim work with computers? She's hardly the type."

As opposed to his wife, who kept track of everything, from her business receipts to her child's immunization records on the floppy diskettes of her home computer.

"Then what was—" Suzanne broke off. *Kim.* Her name was Kim. What a pretty, modern sort of name. Nothing like Suzanne, cold, old-fashioned.

She tried again. "Then what was she doing in India?"

"She was there with her parents."

"Doing what?" Suzanne had no idea why it was so important to find out about Kim's occupation. But it felt terribly important. "What was her job?"

"Oh, she wasn't working," he said casually as if having a job were a very unusual way to spend one's days. "She didn't much like college so when her parents—"

"College?" Suzanne interrupted. "Wait a minute, Patrick, how old is this person?"

"She's nineteen."

"Nineteen!" She stared at him. "Are you joking? Nineteen?"

Last summer Sarah had had some babysitters who were home from college. They were nineteen, and very pleasant girls they were, warm, lively, friendly—and unformed and uncertain, more interesting for their potential, for their dreams, than for anything they had done or any ideas they had thought.

Suzanne couldn't imagine adult men—and Patrick was now thirty-one—being genuinely interested in such girls, except for... well, Suzanne thought, maybe that was it. Nineteen-year-olds looked wonderful; their skin was fresh and taut; their stomachs were flat and their legs lithe. And they thought of themselves as women.

The orange-red light on the coffeepot glowed and Suzanne got up. She took two mugs off their hooks underneath the cabinet and, without asking Patrick if he wanted any, poured the coffee.

"Well," she said stiffly as she watched the arc of dark, steaming liquid fill the cups, "this has all been planned for. I mean, that was the point of that contract we signed, to make a divorce very easy."

She wasn't even going to have a chance. She too was more fun than she had been, less constrained, less rigid; his daughter had made her that way. But she wasn't going to have a chance.

She carried the cups back to the table and sat down in front of hers, watching it miserably, wondering why he wasn't agreeing, why he wasn't talking about child support and equity in the house.

"Wait a minute." A thought suddenly struck her. "Your letter—you said you wanted to stay here for a few months. I don't understand. Surely you want a divorce as soon as possible."

"I'm afraid it's more complicated than that." Now his voice was stiff.

"I don't see how."

He took a breath. "Kim has always known that I was married."

Suzanne knew that he would have never concealed that for a moment.

"—and she doesn't want to feel that she is breaking up a home, especially when there is a child involved. So she would like for you and me at least to try, for us to give our marriage a chance, to make an effort to work out our problems. It's very fair of her."

"Yes, it is," Suzanne agreed unthinkingly. Then she

blinked. "No, no, it isn't. It's stupid. I mean, what problems are we supposed to be working at? What problems do we have, except that you love her, not me?"

Patrick looked uncomfortable, and Suzanne persisted. "Didn't you tell her? That our marriage never had a chance in the first place, that we never really intended for it to have? Didn't you tell her that?"

"I tried."

Suzanne suddenly felt angry, hostile. "Seriously, Patrick, do you have any expectation that we will be able to solve these nonexistent problems of ours?"

"No," he said, his voice tense and knotted. "I was hoping that I could just stay here for a while; after all, we have always found it very easy to live together. Just long enough to ease Kim's feelings."

"It's just a farce then? Well, I certainly don't care about her feelings. I won't do it." She wouldn't. No one in his right mind could expect it of her.

"I do wish you would reconsider." Patrick's voice was formal.

Suzanne shook her head. "Just tell her that I threw you out, that I can't forgive you for having an affair with her. Lots of wives—"

"Now wait a minute," he said firmly. "Kim's a very moral girl."

"A what?" Suzanne couldn't believe it. "She's in love with a married man—how on earth can you call her 'a very moral girl'? What does being 'very moral' mean, that she won't go to bed with you?"

Patrick would never answer a question like that; Suzanne never expected that he would. But he didn't have to.

"And I suppose," Suzanne continued, "that part of

this arrangement is that you aren't supposed to sleep with me either?''

He nodded.

Well, that certainly explained why this conversation couldn't wait until morning, why this afternoon in Concord he had pretended to be tired, why he had been so distressed when he had awakened to find himself making love to her.

"But I don't understand," Suzanne marched on determinedly, resentfully. "If we are supposed to be giving our marriage a chance, how can she expect us to be working out our problems if we are sleeping in separate rooms?"

"Kim's a virgin," he said, his voice tight, "and she finds the notion of sex between you and me very threatening."

"I should think so," Suzanne returned crisply. "But the notion that we are trying to get back together ought to be even more threatening. If she's sure that you love her, she should go ahead and sleep with you and tell me to go hang myself. That's what I would do in her situation." Suzanne knew perfectly well that she was lying; she had no idea what she would do if she loved another woman's husband.

"You have to respect her for the way she is behaving."

"The hell I do."

Suzanne never swore; she simply never did, and Patrick stared at her, amazed.

What did he expect? Coming home and telling her first that he was in love with a teenager and then that this teenager was making him live with her, pretending they were trying to reconcile—one "hell" seemed pretty mild.

"Suzanne," he spoke carefully, "I know this is a very difficult, awkward situation, and—"

"It certainly is, but it will be a whole lot less difficult and awkward if you'd just get out of my—"

But it wasn't her house. It was as much his as hers, more in fact. True, she had lived in it, decorated it, made it the center of her life and her business, and even though she now paid half the mortgage and all of the utilities, she hadn't at first and the down payment had been all his. If he hadn't been so generous, she would have had to go back to Nick. She could hardly tell Patrick he couldn't stay.

"Well," she said crisply, "just don't get in the way."

Chapter Twelve

That was impossible. Of course, Patrick got in the way, forcing Suzanne to vary the routine of her days that had always centered first around Sarah and then her work.

What made it so difficult was that he tried hard; he genuinely did not want to disrupt Suzanne's schedule or cause her extra work. So everything, each little action, had to be negotiated, agreed upon. It was a nightmare of polite stress.

She told him, for example, that as long as she was doing the huge quantities of laundry that Sarah managed to generate, she might as well do his. She would offer, even insist, and then resent having to do it. None of his business shirts were permanent press and he wore five every week, sometimes six if they went out on Saturday. She certainly wasn't going to iron them, but when she'd go to pick them up at the laundry she'd wonder why she had to pay for laundering his shirts when he was about to leave her for a nineteen-year-old, a resentment that was completely out of proportion to the money and time involved.

Of course, it was just as difficult for Patrick. He found it hard to live with Sarah. She seemed like a very alien being to him; when she cried, he didn't know what she wanted; he didn't understand her when she spoke; he didn't know how to play with her or what she should or shouldn't do. He was stiff, uncomfortable, just as Suzanne had once worried that she would be.

Additionally, Patrick was, as she predicted, startled by the extent to which the rest of the world viewed them as a couple. His friends, delighted to have him back in Boston, were eager to see him. But his old Harvard friends no longer called him except when they wanted to play sports. The rest of the time their wives would call Suzanne, and they would all get together as couples. Patrick could not be very comfortable being viewed as Suzanne's husband by the people he assumed would continue to be friends of his and Kim's.

Nor did things at work seem to be going just as he would have liked. On the surface everything seemed fine, but Suzanne sensed that he was worried.

The firm had announced that it was giving a dinner honoring the people involved in the India project. It was to be an elaborate affair, at the Parker House, with a small orchestra and dancing. Southard-Colt occasionally put on such events to assure people that their work had been appreciated. Some people needed this kind of public recognition as much as the more usual rewards of promotions and higher salaries.

Patrick was not one of them. He had gone to India with a very specific goal in mind, to get himself a vice-presidency. The project had gone beautifully, beyond anyone's expectations, but a paycheck and a promotion were all the approval Patrick needed. He had not worked so hard to sit at the head table of a dinner-dance.

In fact Patrick almost seemed to be dreading the evening. And as they got in the car that night, Suzanne finally asked, "Are you a little worried that this is being done in place of making you vice-president?"

"Of course," he answered tersely.

"But, Patrick," she cautioned, "you're thirty-one; only one other person ever made it to v.p. that young, and that was in the early seventies when the firm was growing a lot faster than it is now."

"I know that. Why do you think I have done nothing but work for the last two years?"

Suzanne fingered the pearls that gleamed at her throat and draped down the front of her pale gold dress. Clearly he had done a few other things during the last two years besides work. But of course she couldn't say that. "You may have to wait another year, you know."

"Well, it will be a damn long year."

Suzanne knew that it was not just Patrick's ambition talking. While managing the complex India project, Patrick had come into his own as a manager, developing a management style that suited him well, relying, for example, on careful review of people's work instead of the spontaneous, sporadic praise that was so difficult for him. His nominal boss, Edward Laughlin, preferred a less structured environment and Patrick's people felt a little caught between the two management styles.

It would be a long, hard year if he weren't given the chance to start developing his own business unit, and it would be a long, hard year for whatever woman he was living with.

Men were affected by what happened at work; their moods in the evening were often entirely the result of what had occurred during the day. Suzanne had learned that from Nick; so often in their first year together she had thought him angry with her when, in truth, he was on edge because his writing was going badly.

It had been easy to learn that from Nick; he was exceedingly open, always willing to talk about himself, his activities, and his feelings. Patrick was everything opposite.

Patrick Britten, Suzanne thought, would be a very difficult man to have your first serious relationship with. If he weren't made a vice-president this year, he was going to need a lot of support from his wife, although he would never admit that he needed that support, much less explain to her how to give it. She would just have to know.

For his sake, Suzanne hoped that the girl he was in love with was enough of a woman to handle it. This nineteen-year-old Kim might well find being Patrick's wife more difficult than she could possibly imagine.

And in her heart, Suzanne believed that no one could understand him as well, could help him as much, as she could.

As they crossed the richly decorated lobby of the Parker House, Suzanne couldn't help thinking of the last time she had moved across these carpets, with their intricate gold patterns against a background of deep burgundy. It had been the night Patrick had won the India contract.

What a difference between then and now. Now they were married, they shared a house, a child, insurance policies, and the memory of bewilderingly bright passion. But they had been better friends then.

It seemed terribly sad.

Stop it, she told herself. With thoughts like this, she'd end up crying before the evening was over. They were supposed to be celebrating. Oh well, once again she and Patrick were managing to be their glummest at a celebration.

That reflection did not cheer her up.

The banquet room was crowded, and Suzanne knew nearly everyone in the room, except a few of the spouses and a small delegation of what she guessed were I.B.M. people who had been in Calcutta, working on related contracts. She was immediately surrounded by people and only dimly heard someone calling Patrick.

"Patrick, dear. Patrick, over here."

She was surprised to hear anyone calling him "Patrick, dear"—even his mother didn't dare—and as she greeted people and answered questions about Sarah, she watched him as he answered the summons. A tiny, rather flighty looking woman kissed his cheek, and his hand was warmly gripped by her tall, distinguished husband.

Suzanne had no idea who they were and so as soon as she was free, she moved to his side, waiting for him to introduce her.

He didn't. This surprised her. Whatever problems he had in his intimate dealings with people, his manners were excellent. And the two others seemed just as awkward as he. The woman's eyes were focused on the floor, and the man tilted his head, looking at Suzanne almost as if he were embarrassed.

"How do you do?" she said pleasantly since it was clear no one else was going to speak. "I am Suzanne Britten."

"I'm sorry," Patrick recovered. "This is Delilah and Frederick Chaney; we were all in India together."

Suzanne smiled and started asking polite questions about how it was to be home. Mr. Chaney responded stiffly while his wife, although she had been chattering blithely when Suzanne had approached the little group, said nothing, just glancing around the room nervously. This was very strange, Suzanne thought. What was going on?

Patrick spoke to Mrs. Chaney in a low voice. "Is K—your daughter here?"

Suzanne stiffened. These were Kim's parents.

Well, you rat, she thought furiously. *You might have warned me.*

No wonder Patrick had been so jumpy about this evening. He had known that Kim was going to be there. It would be, as far as Suzanne knew, the first time he had seen her since India, and the meeting would take place not just in front of his wife but—and probably more important to Patrick—in front of both the people he worked for and the people who worked for him.

And suddenly, breaking from the crowd, was a girl, obviously Delilah Chaney's daughter.

She was as petite as her mother, with blue eyes and a mass of lively brown curls that cascaded to the shoulders of her white dress. She was exceedingly pretty, with a fresh openness about her that must have, in the strange twists of dark Calcutta, seemed as American as the flag over the embassy.

When she caught sight of Patrick, Kim's face lit with an even brighter glow, her eyes sparkled and her smile had such simple unaffected delight that, even to Suzanne, she seemed irresistible. She hurried toward them with a light, dancing step.

"Oh, Patrick," she breathed, her hand on his arm, turning her face up as if she expected him to kiss her. "Oh, Patrick, it's been so—"

He interrupted. "Kim," he said firmly, "this is my—" He faltered and started over. "This is Suzanne."

Kim gasped and turned to Suzanne with wide, wounded eyes, a disbelieving expression that reminded Suzanne of Sarah when told she couldn't have another cookie.

I do exist, Suzanne wanted to say, but "How do you do?" seemed more appropriate, and so dutifully she

recited the words, quelling the temptation to call Kim
"Miss Chaney," thereby forcing her to call Suzanne
"Mrs. Britten." It was tempting, but too cheap a shot.

Frederick Chaney didn't seem to think so. "Mrs.
Britten," he said although only a moment before he
had called her Suzanne, "Patrick has told us about your
child. I hope she is well."

As she responded politely, Suzanne realized what he
was doing, trying hard to remind his daughter, and perhaps his wife, that Patrick was married.

Why didn't you remind them of that a year ago?

In any event, the reminder wasn't working now. As
Suzanne and Frederick Chaney tortuously threaded
their way through a conversation that neither of them
cared about in the least, Kim and Patrick were speaking
to each other in low, familiar tones. Her hand was again
on his arm, and his head was bent down to hear her.

Suzanne couldn't help noticing Kim's hands. Suzanne had always been a little vain of her own hands;
they were one of her very best features, and she
pampered them. But still she had a house and a baby
to take care of. She scrubbed skillets, cleaned up
spilled juice, bathed her daughter, and put diapers to
soak. As a result, her hands simply weren't as soft and
as fresh looking as Kim's. Suzanne's were more elegantly shaped, but they had ten years more use on
them than Kim's, and there was no hiding that.

"Those are lovely pearls." Delilah Chaney finally
said something to her. "My grandmother had a string
that my sister-in-law got, but yours are better."

"Thank you," Suzanne returned politely. To say
anything more about the pearls would embarrass the
Chaneys. Boston ladies don't embarrass others; she'd
heard that from her mother countless times.

Wait a minute, she thought. *Why should I make it easy*

on these people? "These belonged to Patrick's grand-mother," she explained sweetly, quite pleased with the spunk she was picking up from her occasionally stub-born daughter. "His parents gave them to me on our wedding day."

The words sent Mrs. Chaney back into a nervous flutter, but Kim was so caught up in her conversation with Patrick that she did not hear. Suzanne thought that a great pity.

"Suzanne." Edward Laughlin, Patrick's boss, touched her arm and immediately Patrick straightened as if to hide how absorbed he had been in Kim. "People are starting to sit down."

As she took Mr. Laughlin's arm, Suzanne noticed Kim starting to move with Patrick. Her father swiftly gripped her, stopping her, and Suzanne had a quick glimpse of a very crushed expression.

Dear Lord, what had she expected? That this would be the senior prom and Patrick her date?

How easy it was at nineteen to immerse yourself in fantasies, ignoring any of reality's unpleasantness. At nineteen, Suzanne herself had managed to ignore the fact that when you borrowed money, people expected you to pay it back.

Edward Laughlin naturally led her to the long head table, finding her place card and pulling out a chair for her. She was seated next to Patrick and, she was pleased to see, her old boss, Harrison Colt.

But when she saw Mr. and Mrs. Colt moving toward the table, their smiles warm, their eyes showing how pleased they were to see her, Suzanne, for a moment, thought she was going to cry.

She knew that in many ways, Colt cared more for her than her own father had, and suddenly Suzanne longed to confide in him, to tell him her troubles, these terrible problems she was having with Patrick, to beg him to do something.

Help me, Daddy, it hurts. Make it all better again.

But, of course, she said nothing. She was twenty-nine, not nineteen.

"Now tell me, Patrick," Mr. Colt was saying, "what do you think of that baby of yours, now that you've seen her?"

"If I had had any idea how pretty she was, sir, nothing would have kept me in India for two years."

It was exactly the right thing to say, and Patrick had said it smoothly, so smoothly, in fact, that Suzanne guessed it was rehearsed, his standard answer to questions about Sarah, an answer that he did not mean one word of.

Through most of dinner, Suzanne talked to Harrison Colt just as Patrick talked to Mrs. Laughlin who was on the other side of him. Suzanne was a little surprised that their conversation was so animated. Mrs. Laughlin was in her late fifties; her life had always centered around her home, her children, and now her grandchildren. Usually Patrick was at a loss for what to say to such women, but this time he was doing fine. Curiously Suzanne listened.

They were trading baby stories.

She could not believe it. Patrick was talking about Sarah. Talking easily, enthusiastically, telling Mrs. Laughlin things about her that Suzanne had never dreamed that he had noticed.

But clearly he had. All those times when he had stood there, with his arms folded, awkward and quiet, while Suzanne and Sarah giggled and played, he had been watching his daughter, drawn to her with an interest that he was unable to reveal to anyone but this grandmotherly person he barely knew.

Suzanne could hardly breathe.

Much too soon, William Southard, the president of Southard-Colt, stood up, breaking off all conversations. Everyone turned to him expectantly, and he began to talk about the project, how successful it had been and then briefly mentioned each member of the project team, speaking some joking praise of each, concluding, of course, with Patrick.

Suzanne sensed that Patrick found this teasing tribute quite embarrassing, and in an effort to look relaxed, he rested his hand casually at the back of her chair.

"... and when we weren't sure if we should send someone so young," Mr. Southard was saying, "we asked our most competent, capable employee what she thought, only to find out that her opinion of him was even higher than ours. That clinched it. We figured that a man had to be doing a lot of things awfully right if he could persuade Suzanne Lawrence to marry him."

The hand at Suzanne's back suddenly tensed, almost clinching in a fist.

William Southard went on, now talking only about Suzanne, apparently thinking that like many reticent men, Patrick would prefer public praise of his wife than of himself. Southard talked about how lovely and competent Suzanne was, how successful her business was, joking about how high her prices were. "And, of course, we're all worried that she is going to hire Patrick away from us; it's possible that she could pay better than we do."

How awkward this all was, how miserably awkward. Patrick didn't want to be hearing about her, about how wonderful and perfect she was; he was in love with Kim.

And poor Kim. How unhappy she must be, sitting at

some back table between her parents, hearing what a lovely, successful wife Patrick had. She must be longing to be sitting where Suzanne was, to have Patrick's hand at the back of her chair, to be hearing her name spoken with such affection and respect.

And I, Suzanne thought, *would trade places with you in a minute. Sitting up here, draped in his family's pearls is nothing. Patrick loves you, and compared to that, all this is nothing.*

The dancing started and of course, Patrick stood up with Suzanne first; he had to. They said little, and after the dance, Suzanne was pleased to notice that good prep-school manners won out over inclination. He went to Mrs. Laughlin next, obviously having decided he could not seek out Kim until he had done the duty dances.

Suzanne danced with every member of the Management Committee, and of course, so many other people knew her and liked her that Harrison Colt jokingly took one of his business cards and started drawing up a dance card for her. "Then we can all sign up in advance."

"Suzanne, are you dancing with anyone?"

It was David Stern, Patrick's best friend and now one of hers. She was a little surprised at his terse request. He had heard Mr. Colt's teasing; normally he would have joined in the joking, mocking his background, going on about how they don't have dance cards on New York's Lower East Side. But instead he looked unusually serious. "Will you dance with me?" he repeated his request.

"Of course," and Suzanne put her hand in his.

But instead of putting his arm around her waist, David unspeakingly led her through the dancing couples to one of the tables in a far, dark corner.

He held out a chair for her and then, sitting down

himself, glanced around, making sure no one could hear them. "What the hell is going on?"

"I don't know what you—"

"You do too," he said impatiently. He nodded toward the dance floor and, following his gaze, Suzanne saw Patrick. His auburn head was bent over a brown one; a white dress was pressed against him.

"What's going on?" David demanded. "That's the Chaney girl. Is it what it looks like? Did he have an affair with her in Calcutta?"

"Oh, no," Suzanne replied bitterly. "She is, I am told, a 'very moral girl.'"

"Then—"

"They are in love and want to get married."

Suzanne buried her face in her hands. What a relief it was finally to tell someone.

"Go on," David ordered.

Without stopping to consider, without thinking that Patrick's closest friend might not be the best person to tell, Suzanne did. "She was out in India with nothing to do. Patrick fell in love with her, she with him, and everything is all moonlight and roses."

"Oh, Suzanne." David's voice was anguished, and when she looked up, his dark eyes were soft with sympathy.

"It's been awful," she confided miserably. "Seeing him, living with him, all the while knowing—"

"Wait a minute; that's right," he interrupted. "He's living with you. What's he doing out there if he wants to marry her? It doesn't make any sense."

"That's the fun part," Suzanne said with bitter irony. "He and I are supposed to be 'trying.' Apparently, she insisted that we give our marriage One Last Chance before filing for divorce."

"One *last* chance? I don't see that your marriage has

ever been given a first chance." He shook his head. "Are you? Trying to work things out, I mean."

"Are you kidding? Patrick doesn't want to; we are just pretending so that people don't think that little Kim is a home wrecker. She doesn't mind *being* one, just so long as she doesn't have to think of herself that way."

David's hand was warm against her back. He was on her side; he thought she had been wronged. Everyone would. She found that comforting in a bitter, biting way.

"I would have never thought it of Patrick," David said finally.

Suzanne could hear the heavy, reluctant condemnation in David's voice, and no amount of desire to have everyone on her side could justify the false impression that he had.

"No, David." She shook her head. "It's not as it seems. Patrick has not really been disloyal to me or broken any sort of commitment."

"Oh, come on, Suzanne," he said impatiently. "Don't do the proper lady number on me. You two got married; you had a child together—don't tell me there wasn't a lot of commitment in that."

"There wasn't." Suzanne looked at him steadily, knowing that she could trust his discretion absolutely. "I know what Patrick told you before we married, but Sarah wasn't planned; she was an accident, a mistake."

"A mistake? You and Patrick?" He was surprised.

"I know, it's hard to believe, isn't it?" she answered. "But when it turned out I was pregnant, getting married seemed to make sense—for health insurance as much as anything else. But we never loved each other and we really assumed that we would get divorced when he got back. I mean, we drew up premarital contracts and everything to make it all easy and clear-cut. So don't condemn Patrick for falling in love with Kim. He had every right to."

"Well, if all this is true, why are you so unhappy?"

Suzanne fidgeted with her pearls, listening to the soft clicks as the strands fell against each other. "It's just an awkward situation, that's all."

"I don't believe you," he said bluntly. "Can you look me straight in the eye and tell me that you don't love him?"

Suzanne said nothing, staring down at the white napkins carelessly cast across the table like crumpled magnolias. Dark pools of undrunk coffee cooled in the gold-rimmed cups. After a moment, David covered her hand with his.

"Well, I could have two years ago," she said, holding her eyes wide open, trying not to cry. "I didn't love him then; he didn't love me either so he's not the blackguard he may seem."

"Perhaps not, but he is a fool," David said bluntly. "Look at you. Everything Southard said about you was true. She's—My God, how old is she?"

"Nineteen." Suzanne smiled ironically.

"Nineteen!" David cursed. "What was she doing out in India? Why wasn't she in college? Or working? What does she do all day?"

Suzanne shrugged. "Believe me, I don't know."

"Look, I danced with her. She's a warm, cuddly girl, there's no doubt about that. But do you know what we talked about? AM radio stations, for heaven's sake."

Suzanne guessed that Patrick had never thought about this, about how hard it was going to be for Kim to take over Suzanne's place in his social world. Over the last two years his friends had come to think of her as a friend in her own right. They were comfortable with her because her background was the same, because she had been to the same sort of schools they had been to. They respected her for her professional success. They liked her. Kim, who was a decade younger, who hadn't roomed with the girl who had dated someone's brother, who apparently had no career aspirations whatsoever, might find it hard to earn their affection and respect.

"She's very open and friendly," David was saying, "but she's a bit on the boring side. She sure hasn't done much."

"David, it doesn't matter. Patrick loves her."

"If he does, he doesn't deserve you."

"The point is, he doesn't want me."

The music had stopped and a couple drifted back to the table, staring curiously at David and Suzanne. So they had to get up, and then someone immediately asked Suzanne to dance. The careful politeness started up again.

At long last the evening was over. Suzanne had a headache, and she suspected from the way his hand drifted to the back of his neck that Patrick did too. Well, they were certainly entitled to their headaches. It had been a dreadfully difficult evening, and riding home with him, knowing that he would rather be with Kim, was as bad as anything else.

She was silent, dull, tedious. Kim would be laughing, giggling, making him laugh, making him happy.

Suzanne paid the babysitter, and Patrick offered to drive the girl home. It seemed rude somehow to go to bed before he got back, not that there was any reason to wait up—it wasn't as if they had anything to say to each other—but nonetheless she did.

"I'm going to take some aspirin," she said when he got back. "Would you like some?"

"Is this the psychic Miss Lawrence back in action, knowing what people need and think before they do themselves?"

It sounded like he resented her.

"No," she said. "It doesn't take much sense to realize that it wasn't an easy evening."

He followed her into the kitchen, watching her as she got out the aspirin, handed him some. She filled two glasses with water and then took her share of the pills.

"I didn't realize the pearls had matching earrings," he said. He must have noticed them when she had tilted back her head to swallow the aspirin.

"They didn't. Your parents gave them to me last Christmas. They had them made up to match."

"And I see you have a gold watch now," he commented.

Why were they talking like this? Well, why not? There wasn't anything else to say.

She extended her hand so that he could look at the watch.

"It's very nice."

Suzanne remembered the first time he had looked at something around her wrist, the night he had heard about the India contract, when looking at her gold bracelet was only an excuse to hold her hand. Tonight he looked at the watch without touching her.

"Thank you," she replied politely. "Ford gave it to me the day I brought Sarah home."

"He did?" He seemed surprised.

"Yes. You know he was with me during labor."

"That's what Mother said. I wouldn't have thought you would have wanted him there."

"It surprised me too," she answered. "But I was very glad to have him. Of course I would have made it without him, but there were certainly moments when it seemed like I couldn't have."

"Your delivery was hard?"

"Very."

"And then you had the shot for the Rh antibodies?"

"The RhoGam? Yes."

Why are we talking about this? Suzanne wondered again. He had spent the evening wanting to be with his girlfriend; what had prompted this sudden interest in Sarah's birth? He had had a year and a half to ask about it. Why now?

No, it made a certain amount of sense. If nothing else, everyone's behavior this evening had labelled Suzanne as "Wife" and perhaps that made him think about things that had simply never occurred to him to wonder about before.

His next words seemed to confirm that. "It does seem like Ford has been doing a lot of things that I was supposed to be doing."

What could she say? Of course, it was true. "I don't think he minded at all."

"No, I don't imagine he did." His voice was crisp and then he turned to put the aspirin away. He continued without looking at her. "After I move out, is my brother moving in?"

"Patrick!"

He was facing her now, leaning against the counter, his eyes blank and gray. "Is that such a surprising question?"

"It certainly is." Suzanne was suddenly furious. "It's completely—I mean, how *dare* you? Not only do you have no reason whatsoever to accuse your brother of anything like that, but it certainly also seems that you have forfeited every right to question anything that I might do." She glared at him and then started to storm out of the kitchen, only to have him seize her arm, detaining her.

"Suzanne, I'm sorry. I—"

"Get your hands off me," she ordered. "And don't tell me you're sorry. You can't possibly be sorry enough. Maybe I don't care what you think of me, but how can you, how *can* you think that of one of your brothers?"

Suzanne knew that this was not why she was angry at him, this was not what she truly wanted to be saying to him, but she didn't care. This was as good as anything.

"Don't you know how they feel about you?" she demanded.

He looked at her blankly.

"I know," she went on in a rush, "you've always been so conscious of feeling left out of the family, of not being quite a part, that you've never paid much attention to the way your brothers feel about you."

"About me?" He was puzzled; clearly he had never thought about it.

"You're their big brother, Patrick, and they adore you; they always have. You are everything they always wanted to be; and you did so much for them—"

"I didn't," he interrupted.

"Yes, yes, you did. You were the one who could get kites out of trees, who showed them how to shoot baskets better; you could do all these things that they couldn't—"

"I was older." He shrugged.

"It doesn't matter why. You were the one they could go to. Don't you remember when Brian left his turtle at the playground and you rode your bike back to get it so that your parents never found out?"

"No." He seemed surprised that she should have

heard these family stories. "No, I don't remember doing that."

"Well, they remember, all three of them remember things like that. And even now that they are men... well, part of the reason that all of them, and not just Ford, have done so much for Sarah and me is that they want to be doing things for *you*, and they know that you would never let them. I mean, Andy comes down a couple times a year and cleans out the gutters and puts up the screens, things like that. He'd probably come every week during the summer to mow the lawn if I let him. Maybe neither he or Brian do quite as much as Ford has, but I think Ford has always felt a little more threatened by you; looking so much like you hasn't been easy on him. If he is eager to take on your responsibilities, it has more to do with showing you that he is an adult than any feelings he might have for me."

"Don't you think you are just being a little naive?" Patrick was nearly sneering.

"Not in the least. You don't have a sister so maybe you can't imagine how it feels to have one, but your brothers have one now, and that's why they love me. And look here, Patrick Britten, it isn't me being naive, it's you being childish."

He froze. "I beg your pardon?" His words were knife-edged ice.

It didn't stop her. "Yes, childish. All of a sudden you've started feeling guilty, and you want to feel like someone else, namely me or Ford, is in the wrong too."

"In the wrong? What are you talking about?" he demanded.

Now they were finally talking about it. "Oh, come on, Patrick, admit it. Tonight, for the first time, you finally realized that there's no getting around the fact that everyone will think you are walking out on your wife and your child for a nineteen-year-old." Her voice underlined the last words with bitter emphasis.

"What on earth does Kim's age have to do with this?" he demanded. "It's not as if you're over the hill."

"Well, she sure makes me feel like it."

"Imagine how you make her feel. You may be carrying a diaper bag these days, but you're still the estimable Miss Lawrence. It's all I've heard since I've been back—about how wonderful you are. From my family, my friends, and then tonight—"

So this was it. Suzanne's anger vanished. He *did* resent her. All the people who had been meaning to help, who wished her well, were only making everything worse.

"Patrick," she spoke softly, "do you feel like everyone is trying to ram me down your throat?"

"Yes." He spit out the word.

"They don't know about Kim. They aren't trying to—"

"I know," he said swiftly. "But it's just part of the same old thing. People want me to react, to dredge up my feelings for their pleasure. My God, at home, every time you left the room, my parents would go on and on about how they love you, how much a part of the family both you and Sarah are—'the girls' they call you—and then they would look at me with these expectant looks, wanting me to start yammering like some besotted fool. And it seems like I can't walk down the hall at work without having people ask me how wonderful it is to be home. I'd hate it even if they were asking about—" He stopped.

"About Kim," Suzanne finished for him.

"Yes." He must have noticed the blank dazed look

on her face. "Suzanne, I realize this evening must have been awkward for you. I didn't think about that; I was concerned about Kim, and you always seem like you can take care of yourself. But"—and he almost seemed to be pleading—"it's not as if you love me. I can understand if your pride is hurt, I can see that now. Everyone does think of you as my wife, and as you say, it does look like I am leaving you, but it is only pride that hurts, isn't it?"

No, she wanted to say. *Of course, my pride is hurt, but, believe me, that's the least of it.*

"I appreciate your concern," she said instead. "But I suppose it will all be over soon enough."

Now was the time to say it. *Patrick, this isn't working; I can't take it. Please leave.* Now was the perfect time. But the words just didn't come.

Chapter Thirteen

The next day was Sunday, and they had planned to go to Concord. Throughout the day, Suzanne was painfully conscious that every affectionate gesture, every word of praise that Nat and Sally had for her was likely to increase the budding resentment that Patrick was feeling for her in Kim's behalf. Didn't he realize how devastated the Brittens would be if he divorced Suzanne? Would he use their feelings as an excuse for withdrawing from them altogether, turning his family over to her as part of the divorce settlement?

Monday, even with Patrick at work, wasn't any easier a day. Suzanne was starting to feel that she was further behind in her work than she had ever been in her life. In the last year or so, her usual routine had been to spend her mornings as a housewife and mother, spending them entirely with Sarah, settling down to her own work only after the child went down for her nap. A high-school girl came in every day from three until six so Suzanne had the whole afternoon to work uninterruptedly, and then she worked again after Suzanne went to bed. The schedule had seemed nearly ideal for a working mother.

But with Patrick home, often eating dinner with her after Sarah was in bed, she got little done in the evenings, to say nothing of how the tensions and strains of their relationship ate into her concentration when she did have time to work.

To make matters worse, her babysitter's family was on vacation this week, and so she didn't even have those extra afternoon hours to look forward to.

As she tried to do her accounts during Sarah's nap, she couldn't help wondering if the tensions around her were starting to affect the child. They had had a difficult morning, with Sarah continually wanting to play with toys and games too difficult for her, which left her frustrated and sobbing. She then got furious with Suzanne for trying to help.

After her nap, Suzanne took her for a walk as Debbie, the babysitter, usually did. Sarah started out in the stroller, but very soon insisted on being taken out. So Suzanne unstrapped her. Then her dolly had to be strapped in in Sarah's place. Sarah pushed her doll and the stroller for about a half block and then wanted to get back in the stroller. So Suzanne unstrapped the doll, put Sarah in the stroller, and started pushing it herself. Then they repeated the entire process: girl out, doll in, and a block later, doll out, girl in.

When for the third time Sarah started bleating "Up, up," Suzanne thought that she might strangle her.

At home, Sarah, used to the complete attention that Debbie gave her during "arsenic hour," got angry with Suzanne for trying to start dinner instead of playing with her. When Suzanne finally abandoned dinner, all Sarah wanted to do was pull everything out of the kitchen cabinets.

When Suzanne heard Patrick's key in the lock, dinner wasn't made, Sarah was wailing, and Suzanne was nearly ready to throw her out the window.

She glared at Patrick resentfully as he walked into the

kitchen. He looked so crisp and tidy in his dark suit and white shirt, while she was sticky with the orange juice that Sarah had spilled, or rather thrown, on her.

How nice it would be, Suzanne thought with sudden longing, to go to an office all day. She could wear white blouses again and fragile gold bracelets. She could go out to lunch; no one would spit up on her. The people she worked with wouldn't plop themselves down on the floor screaming; they would be able to go to the bathroom by themselves.

"You two look like you've had a tough day," Patrick said pleasantly.

Suzanne was not in the least interested in people who still had the capacity to be polite and pleasant. "I've had it," she announced. "She's your daughter too. You take care of her."

Patrick stared at her, clearly amazed that calm, patient Suzanne was snapping waspishly, and Suzanne glared back at him and then stomped out of the room.

She meant to stay upstairs for only half an hour, truly she did. She'd just take a shower, change her clothes and sit down for a moment, before going back down to face an unmade dinner, a foul-tempered daughter, and a hungry husband, who, she thought with an unusual pang of self-pity, was in love with a nineteen-year-old who probably never had orange juice in her hair.

But somehow the idea of a hot bath was irresistible, and as the tub was filling, Suzanne picked up a book to read. Almost randomly, she chose *Pride and Prejudice*, which she hadn't reread in years, and the lovely sparkling magic of the book propelled her straight from the tub to her bed, where she spent the entire evening propped up against her pillows reading. She hadn't done that in years.

It was, she noticed with surprise, after eleven when she got Darcy and Elizabeth, the novel's hero and heroine, safely married and settled into a life where their children would have nurserymaids and governesses to throw juice on.

She stretched and, without the least reluctance or resentment, got up to check on Sarah, suddenly quite curious how the child had survived an evening of her father's care, to say nothing of how the father had survived.

Sarah was fast asleep in her crib. Her diaper was a little inexpertly draped around her, and her nightgown was on backward, but she was quite clearly fine. She had even had a bath and her hair was combed; Patrick Britten, Suzanne reminded herself, never did things by half measures.

There was a crack of light under his door. Suzanne knocked softly and went in. He was sitting up against the pillows reading *The Wall Street Journal*, having, not surprisingly, not had a chance earlier in the evening.

She sat down on the bed next to him. "I'm sorry."

He smiled and laid the paper aside. "There's no reason to be. We had a fine time."

"You did?" Suzanne was astonished. "Tell me."

"She stopped crying as soon as you went upstairs—I guess she was pretty surprised to be left with me, but she was an angel all evening."

"She probably wanted to be away from me just as much as I wanted to be away from her," Suzanne said realistically. She could say things like that now without any doubts about herself as a mother; when Sarah had first been born, every time Suzanne wanted to escape for a moment, she worried that she was turning into as indifferent a mother as her own had been. But no longer. "What did you have for dinner?"

"I had the steak that was out, and *your* daughter, madam, had peanut butter and green beans."

"Peanut but—"

"And milk," Patrick added hastily, "lots of milk."

Suzanne laughed. "How did you come up with that menu?"

"Treated her like one of those old binary computers that just makes yes-no decisions. I would point to something and she would decide yes or no. She's good at that."

"She's better at the 'no's.'"

"Why do you think we ended up with peanut butter and green beans?" he returned. "It really wasn't so hard as I thought. She seems to know her own routine and she likes to have things done the same way they were done the day before. Is that inherited?" he asked curiously. "Is she like that because you and I are such overorganized creatures of habit?"

"Maybe," Suzanne answered, secretly thrilled by his awareness that, at least in biological, genetic terms, the three of them were a definite unit. "But the baby books do say that this is a pretty repetitive age."

"Maybe I ought to take a look at those," he reflected. "By the way, why don't you use disposable diapers?"

"I did at first, but she got diaper rash from them."

Sitting on his bed like this, talking to him about their child—it felt like the loveliest, warmest conversation they had had since they had gotten married. So what if they were talking about diaper rash?

How having a child could bind a man and a woman together. But wasn't that why they had had her? Wasn't it the need for this bond that had impelled their bodies to revolt against their minds, a revolt that had resulted in Sarah?

Suzanne couldn't tell what Patrick was thinking. After a moment, he spoke. "What did you do on days like this when you were alone?"

"Well, there haven't been too many. Of course, we had some hard times with all those ear infections, but if she really doesn't feel well, I don't have any trouble being patient. These random fits of peevishness didn't start until recently. She's approaching two, I guess." Suzanne did not add that the tension from this situation with Kim was probably gnawing at her and therefore Sarah's good humor. "But basically I had no choice. There was nothing to do when a day turned terribly long but just bear it—and pray for the weekend when I could go up to Concord. Your parents," she added, "have been wonderful."

"But still it does seem like a good thing," he reflected, "having someone else around."

"Of course, it is, but live-in fathers are becoming an increasingly rare commodity."

"Yes," he reflected, picking up the front section of the *Journal* and then laying it back down. "You have to wonder how the high divorce rate is going to affect our society in the next few generations."

As good and responsible a citizen as she was, Suzanne, at the moment, didn't particularly care how the high divorce rate was going to affect American society in the next few generations; she only wanted to know how one particular divorce was going to affect her own life in the next few years.

And Patrick had spoken with a curious awkwardness, a constraint, as if he too were not concerned about the fate of society in general.

She tilted her head looking at him, knowing it was useless to ask, worse than useless; he was less likely to tell her what he was thinking if she asked. She waited.

At last he spoke. "I had lunch with David."

Oh. It would have been the first time they had seen each other since the dance Saturday night.

"He had figured out about Kim," he continued, "and he said some pretty hard things."

"Patrick," Suzanne spoke carefully, "I think you aren't being realistic if you think we can get divorced without that happening. People are going to take sides. In this situation, with the man remarrying almost immediately, most people will side with the wife, at least at first."

He shook his head, sighing. "You're probably right. I don't know why I thought this would be so easy."

She shrugged. "You were away. It must have been hard to remember exactly how things were back here."

And suddenly Suzanne wondered if that was part of why Patrick had fallen in love with Kim. Perhaps back here, where he was firmly fixed in a group of bright, ambitious friends, knowing plenty of intelligent, accomplished women, he might not have even noticed Kim as anything more than a nice, pretty teenager.

Patrick was obviously considering what she said about his life in India. "You might be right. It was different there, like a separate world. I certainly didn't think—" He cleared his throat. "Suzanne, I hope you know that what David said isn't true."

"I don't know what he said," she pointed out.

He grimaced and glanced away, apparently unable to look at her when he spoke. "He asked me if I were staying with you just until after this year's decisions on vice-presidents were made. He accused me of using you and your popularity at the firm to get an edge on—"

"Patrick," Suzanne spoke swiftly, "I never once, not for a moment, thought you were doing that."

"I don't know. It's what it is going to look like."

"I think you'd better face the fact that there is no way you can get through this without people talking about you and misinterpreting you."

"God," he cursed, "how I hate that."

"So do I," Suzanne answered calmly. "But there's not much we can do about it now. If I understand you aren't doing that, and Kim understands it, then you are probably in better shape than most men in your situation."

But how could Kim understand? How at nineteen could she possibly understand how complicated the business world was? Did she know what kind of pressure Patrick was under? Did she understand why success was so important to this man?

"What I don't like," Patrick was saying, "is how it reflects on Kim."

Suzanne stared at him.

"It makes it look like I consider her a liability," he explained, "which of course I don't."

Now that was a sentiment that did more credit to his feelings than to his sense.

"So," Patrick continued, "I was planning to come home tonight and tell you that I would leave now, that Kim would just have to understand."

Suzanne's trained ear picked up the conditional verb tenses. "You were planning to leave? Did you change your mind?"

He took a breath. "Suzanne, ever since putting Sarah to bed, I've been thinking about her. I mean, I really don't know her at all. Any one of my brothers would have known a lot more about what to do with her than I did. And, as you said, she is my daughter too."

That was the first time he had said that, absolutely the first time. Suzanne could hardly breathe.

"And this may be my one chance to get to know her.

After Kim and I are married, I'll just see her on weekends, or whatever we work out, and there's probably a good chance that if I don't know how to take care of her, I'll just let Kim do it all. I never thought I'd say this, but I would really like to get to know my child; I would like to learn how to be her parent, so if you don't mind..."

Suzanne didn't mind, not at all. She didn't even mind that he had to say "know" instead of "love." She was just so very pleased that he was interested in Sarah; she would put up with much more tension and stress, she would even listen to him talk about being married to Kim if it would bring father and daughter together.

She smiled shakily. "If you behave yourself, I'll you babysit sometimes." She had to speak lightly; otherwise she would cry.

And then surprisingly, he took her hand and lightly kissed it. "She's a wonderful little girl."

And somehow when he let go of her hand, it dropped to his chest, and Suzanne found her fingers teasing the curled hair, her palm flattening against his skin, moving across him in a slow caress.

He was warm, and so was the room, delicious and comfortable. The lamplight was soft against the blue sheets, creating a private little world, a tiny island of glowing beauty with just the two of them in it, the two of them talking about their child, the precious child their bodies had created together. Suzanne bent her head and kissed the light where it fell on his shoulder. She moved down across his chest, touching him, tasting him, her mouth open against him, as her hands felt his shoulders, his arms. She felt him sigh and lean back. "Does that feel good?" she murmured against him.

"You know it does." His head was back, his eyes half

closed, the lids not quite concealing the green glint. He swallowed.

His hands laced through her hair, holding her head gently, firmly, encouraging her as she continued. The world seemed distant, dissolved, and Suzanne was aware of only the two of them in this bed as she explored the unforgotten shape of him, his arms, his shoulders, his leg beneath the sheet. As her hand traced down the curving cord of his thigh, she could hear his breathing deepen, she could feel his hands move caressing through her hair, she could see his muscles tense. But as her hand moved upward, he gripped her shoulders firmly.

"Stop," he gasped. "You've got to stop that."

But she couldn't see why, and for all that he seemed about to push her away, the rejection never came; he didn't, he couldn't, stop her.

She leaned closer to him, as if to bury her face in his shoulder, letting her breasts brush lightly against him.

The grip on her arms tightened, almost for a moment hurting her, and then suddenly, with a movement swift and strong, he rolled over, pulling her beneath him, tossing aside the sheet that had separated them.

It had been two years since she had been with a man, two years since she had felt a man slip his hands beneath her to fit his body to hers. Suzanne had treasured her independence; she hadn't wanted a man telling her what to do; she didn't want to feel weak and dependent, but somehow, lying beneath him, his weight on her, his hands sure and purposeful, she felt wonderfully feminine, as if she had a beauty that complemented his strength. It seemed so utterly right.

Gone was all the patient, practiced, calculated skill that she had always known from him. His own needs were too urgent for restraint, and he surged into her with a dark intensity that left her shaken and gasping.

Finally as he moved to leave her, Suzanne touched him, detaining him, and he slid down, resting his head between her breasts.

"I shouldn't have done that," he said, sighing.

"I'm not sure you were given a lot of choice," she said softly.

He laughed shakily. "It sure didn't feel like I had one." As he spoke, the silky thickness of his hair brushed against her breast. Suzanne let her hands slide across his shoulders, up through his hair. How wonderful it felt to have him here, like this.

He must have felt her sigh for he suddenly rolled away from her, onto his back, staring up at the ceiling. "I swore to myself that this wouldn't happen. Suzanne, I didn't want to use you."

She loved it when he used her name; he did it so rarely. She turned to face him, propping herself up on one elbow. "You didn't. Not at all."

He shook his head. "That's not true. I was very unfair; I thought only of myself."

"Oh, Patrick, sometimes that doesn't matter. Sometimes just the closeness is enough." *Especially when you love the man.*

And suddenly Suzanne knew why she hadn't told him to leave Saturday. She was going to fight for him. She was going to try. She was supposed to be working on her marriage; well, by God, she was going to. She had Kim's permission to try to win her husband back; she was going to do her best. She loved him too much not to.

She took a breath. She was going to face this head on. "But that's not what's really bothering you, is it? You feel like you've betrayed Kim."

Patrick had made a promise to Kim, one of the oldest, most common promises a man makes to a woman. He felt bound by his word, and he had given it confidently, certain that his conscience and self-restraint were, just like those of his Puritan forebears, stronger than any physical urges.

But he had broken that promise.

He nodded unhappily. "She's just not going to understand."

"Then don't tell her," Suzanne said immediately.

"I have to."

"You don't either. Look, Patrick, I was a nineteen-year-old virgin once. It's been awhile, but I remember. When you are that inexperienced, you just don't understand the kind of mistakes people make. You don't understand how complicated life can be. Morality is just a question of whether or not you go to bed with someone. And if Kim looks at things that way, she's not going to understand. So don't tell her; you'd only hurt her."

And as much as Suzanne absolutely believed everything she was saying, she also didn't mind in the least reminding him that of the three people in this little triangle of theirs, he and she were the only grown-ups.

So maybe she was fighting a little dirty, maybe she was exploiting advantages Kim didn't have. Kim couldn't come in his room and sit on his bed, talking about his daughter, refusing to leave when he asked her to. Kim couldn't speak softly of the mistakes he had made, understanding that no one reached thirty as blameless as they had been at twenty. Kim couldn't do any of that. But so what?

"Well," Patrick said at last, "you're probably right. I just don't want to have it happen again."

Although she had absolutely no intention of putting

it on, Suzanne reached across him to get her night-gown, letting the sheet fall from her, letting him see the pale curves of her body. She looked at him over her bare shoulder and spoke, her voice low and husky. "I don't believe you."

This was fighting dirty, this wasn't the sort of thing that a Boston lady did, and Suzanne didn't care.

Patrick grimaced. "Well, of course, I *want* it to happen again; I am human. I just don't think it should happen again."

"Well, suit yourself," Suzanne said airily and nestled down next to him.

Chapter Fourteen

"Me up! Mama, me up!"

Suzanne's little human alarm clock went off with its usual regularity, and as always, Suzanne started to slide out of bed even before she was fully awake.

But this morning there was a warmth next to her, a weight at her waist. She had nothing on, and the room was different; the bed had lost its four walnut posters.

Then she remembered. She was with Patrick. This was his bed; this was his sleeping body she was curled up against, his arm holding her. As she stirred, the arm tightened, pulling her closer against him, pulling her back down into the soft warmth.

But, like every other toddler, Sarah was utterly without sympathy for her mother's desire to stay in bed, and she continued the "Me up" refrain.

Since "Me" was now at the climbing stage and might attempt a jail break if left in her crib any longer, Suzanne eased herself out of Patrick's strong, if unconscious, embrace, slipped on her nightgown, and went to her daughter.

Sarah was standing in her crib, clutching her wooly white lamb. Her nightgown was still on backward, and her red-gold curls were tousled, but her brown eyes brightened at the sight of her mother.

Suzanne lifted her out of the crib and lay her on the changing table, the two of them cooing and giggling all the while. Suzanne was threatening to chew off little pink baby toes when she noticed a shadow across the bright green carpet. She straightened a little self-consciously.

It was Patrick, standing in the doorway, his hands in the pockets of his robe. "Are you turning into a cannibal?" he asked politely.

Suzanne decided she was not going to be embarrassed, neither by the way she talked to Sarah... nor by what had happened last night.

"Can I watch?" he continued. "I want to see how this getting dressed business is done; getting her undressed was hard enough. I can't possibly imagine getting clothes *on*."

"It does take some practice." And then just as calmly and as patiently as she had once corrected his verbs, Suzanne now explained how to get clothes on a squirming, giggling baby.

It was the start of a considerable change in Patrick's life. He began to spend time with Sarah.

She astonished him. She was quite unlike anyone he had ever met. Her notion of reading a book, for example, did not include an orderly movement through the verbal narrative; she wanted to sit on his lap and randomly turn the pages looking for pictures that she recognized. And she enjoyed the strangest things. One night he took the library door off its hinges in order to plane and sand the edge that often stuck. It was just a routine chore, something that he had been putting off doing, but Sarah acted as if it were the most fascinating thing she had ever seen; she was so curious that he had trouble not tripping over her. Then when he gave her the curled wood shavings to play with, she shrieked happily and ran off to show her treasures to Suzanne.

One day after lunch, he and David stopped in a drugstore for something, and he noticed some plastic whiffle balls. "Do you think Sarah would like one of these?" he suddenly asked his friend.

"How on earth do I know?" David returned pleasantly. "But you can probably afford one even if she doesn't."

"I suppose I can." And as he bought it he realized that this ball, which cost less than a cup of restaurant coffee, would be the first thing he had ever given her.

Wasn't he supposed to be doing more? A pearl on each birthday, with the strand to be finished when she was eighteen or something like that? He didn't know.

Taking comfort in the fact that if he did give her a pearl, she would probably swallow it, Patrick took the ball home, and Sarah loved it. She couldn't have caught it if her life had depended on it, but after he showed her how, she could pick it up and with an awkward stiff-arm movement, heave it in a generally forward direction.

"That's terrific," he praised her as he tossed her into the air. "We are going to turn you into a real jock someday."

He happened to glance over at the back door and saw Suzanne standing there with a funny, tight look on her face.

"Would you look at me?" he said, a little self-conscious under her gaze. "I used to refuse to play tennis with people who couldn't give me a decent game; now I'm thrilled when this lady pitches a ball straight at her foot."

"I'm very glad you're doing that with her," she said softly, and for a moment, Patrick thought that she was going to cry.

Why? he wondered. It was't such a big deal. He was just showing Sarah how to throw a ball. Why did that bring such a gentle mistiness to Suzanne's eyes?

Well, maybe it was just that she was concerned about Sarah's physical coordination. Suzanne herself had so little athletic skill because her own father had never once taken her out in the backyard and played ball with her. She probably didn't want that happening to Sarah.

And it wouldn't, not if he had anything to do with it. He'd teach Sarah how to shoot baskets, serve a volleyball, and play tennis. It was the least he could do.

But it did seem like very little. Not just for Sarah—whom he was increasingly regarding as someone he would do nearly anything for—but for Suzanne as well.

His staying with her had made so much sense in India. He thought they could share a house in the same almost impersonal way that they had shared his Beacon Hill apartment for the two weeks before he left for India.

But that hadn't been possible, and he could now see how difficult it was for Suzanne to have him there, how mortifying it would be for her when he left. It wouldn't look as though they had grown apart, as if they were two friends who had calmly decided not to be married anymore; it would look like he was rejecting her, and people would probably wonder what she had been doing wrong that her husband fell in love with someone else.

But she hadn't done anything wrong, and it didn't seem right that people should speculate that way.

Patrick noticed himself starting to do little things for Suzanne. Xeroxing an article she'd be interested in, buying a new book she'd said she wanted to read, offering to stop on the way home and pick up dinner. Nothing on the order of perfume, chocolate, or flowers, but honesty forced him to admit that his motive was not so different from that of men who bought these more romantic things—he wanted to keep, or at least win back, his wife's good opinion.

That was all, he desperately tried to tell himself. He just didn't want her to hate him. Nothing more. He wasn't the sort of man who needed every woman around him to be in love with him. He didn't want that from Suzanne. After all, Kim loved him, and he loved her. He just wanted Suzanne to like and respect him. That was all, he was sure of it.

Of course, what had happened when she came to his room that night was a little beyond like and respect, he had to admit that, but still it didn't really mean anything. She was lovely and willing. Of course, he had found her irresistible. He did still want her; in fact turning away from her half-open door each night seemed like the hardest thing he had ever done, but surely that was natural. They were living in the same house, after all; he frequently saw her in her nightgown, he could hear her dresser drawers open as she undressed; of course, he wanted her. But surely it was just a physical thing. It had nothing to do with the way he felt about Kim. It couldn't; he wouldn't let it.

Nonetheless, he shouldn't have made love to her. Or at least not in the way that he had. For once again, they had taken no precautions. What if she got pregnant again? He couldn't possibly leave her to face a second pregnancy alone, could he? But how would he ever explain it to Kim?

Patrick cringed, utterly unable to imagine how he had managed to get himself in a situation that so dripped with sordid clichés. A man having to tell the girl he loved that his wife was pregnant—a year ago he would have said that such things never happened to people like him, but now he clearly deserved to be right in the center of such a mess.

Finally, on a Saturday morning about two weeks later, he asked Suzanne if there were any chance that she were pregnant.

"Oh, no. My period started a few days ago."

"That's good," he said in relief. He should have known, of course, she wouldn't be so foolish as to take much of a chance.

But she surprised him. "I guess it's a good thing, but I wouldn't have minded."

"*What?*"

"I like having a child," she said calmly. "I wouldn't mind having another."

He swallowed. "Suzanne, I—"

The phone rang, saving him from having to speak.

He hadn't known what to say. He could hardly agree with her, saying that he too would like another child. It was the truth, but he couldn't say that to her. His second child would have Kim for a mother. And he just couldn't bring himself to say that he hoped that she'd meet someone who'd give her another baby.

What business is it of yours what she does after you're married to Kim?

Suzanne hung up the phone and turned back to him. "Nan Montgomery is sick; they're canceling the dinner tonight."

"That's fine with me."

"Me too, but what a waste," she sighed. "I've got a Saturday night babysitter. Maybe I could ship her off to someone else and get a finder's fee."

"Or we could go out to dinner," he said suddenly.

"We? You and I?" She was clearly surprised.

Patrick was suddenly feeling awkward, as if he were

fifteen and asking a girl out for the first time. "Why not?" he said manfully. "We might have a good time."

It was just a dinner, he told himself. Surely Kim would understand that he was more or less obligated to take his wife out to dinner once in a while. There wasn't anything disloyal in that. Kim would certainly understand.

And maybe she would have, but Patrick never gave her a chance. He didn't tell her.

Suzanne was puzzled. Not by Patrick's growing love for Sarah—to her mind, anyone with half a brain would love Sarah—but by his attitude to her. For not only was he now acting like a father, but he was, at times, starting to act suspiciously like a husband.

He probably didn't realize that he was treating her differently, she told herself. His attentiveness, his occasional tenderness, must be just linked to his love for Sarah. He might be confusing the way he felt for the child with the way he felt for the mother. Just as young children ride the subway free on their parents' ticket, so she was, in terms of Patrick's affection, spare baggage riding free on Sarah's ticket.

Well, not entirely. She saw the way he looked at her. After they went out to dinner Saturday night, after he had taken the babysitter home, after they both had checked on Sarah, he had turned to her with his eyes shining with longing.

But she had only smiled and waited, doing no more to entice him. He had felt terribly guilty about the one night they had spent together, and she didn't want him to suffer more.

Of course, she could be so restrained because she knew that going to bed with her would not be enough to coax him out of loving Kim. If she thought it would, if she thought that sleeping with her would make him stop loving Kim, she would have been in his arms so fast that he wouldn't have time to figure out whether he had opened them for her or not.

So Saturday night she slept alone. Or rather she lay in her bed alone; she was thinking too much for sleep. If she could be sure that his softening toward her, his efforts to please her, meant nothing, she should probably ask him when he planned to leave. Didn't she have a right to know so that she could get started on the misery that was undoubtedly in store for her?

But if these pleasant conversations at the dinner table, if these magazines and books he brought her, if the time they spent together, indicated the least flowering of an interest in her, she didn't dare do anything, say anything, that might force him to move out.

She was still mulling over these questions Monday morning when the phone rang.

The call was from Mona Woods, secretary to the president of Southard-Colt.

"Mona," she said in surprise. "How good to hear from you. How are you?"

"I'm fine, but not as good as you and Patrick are going to be."

"What? I don't understand."

"They had the meeting over the weekend," she said, knowing perfectly well that Suzanne would know exactly which meeting she was talking about. "And Mr. Southard is going down to the fourth floor to see Patrick this afternoon."

"Oh, Mona," Suzanne gasped. "Are you sure?"

"You know I am," Mona laughed. "I filed his notes. They are only making two vice-presidents this year, but Patrick's one."

What this would mean to him! He had wanted it so; he had worked so hard for it, and it was finally, finally happening.

"Anyway," Mona's voice continued, "I thought you'd want to know so you could be sure and be home and have everything nice for him."

"Oh, yes," Suzanne breathed. "I'm so glad I know. I was planning on being out this evening."

She immediately called the friend she was going to go shopping with and canceled the entirely unimportant mission. She looked at the folders neatly stacked on her desk and told them they could all live another day without her.

She was going to do this right. There'd been times when she and Patrick should have celebrated, times when they should have been happy, like the day he had won the proposal or the day they got married, but they hadn't celebrated. They hadn't been able to; they hadn't known how to. But now Suzanne had changed, and she was pretty sure that Patrick had too. They were going to be able to enjoy this one.

Maybe they didn't have a future together, but they would have tonight. The India project had brought them together; they, together with their child, would celebrate the final result.

She and Sarah spent the morning grocery shopping, not their usual efficient supermarket trip, but instead they bought shrimp down at the harbor, bread at Patrick's favorite bakery in Cambridge, and a standing rib roast at a little butcher who listed his prices by the ounce rather than by the pound.

She polished silver and put out candles, cleaned the shrimp and baked the apple cake that Patrick liked almost as much as Sarah did.

She could hardly wait for him to come home, and her eagerness infected Sarah. The little girl was so keyed up that Suzanne thought she might explode.

As soon as Patrick's car turned into the driveway, they both rushed for the front door. Suzanne opened it and let Sarah toddle out onto the porch.

Slamming his car door, Patrick grinned and waved at his daughter. He came up the walk quickly and swung her up, tossing her in the air. "This is no ordinary Joe picking you up, young lady."

Then he looked at her, a smile lighting up his eyes. "Guess what happened?"

"You tell me."

He settled Sarah more comfortably on his hip. "Well, I was just sitting in my office, minding my own business when who should walk in but old Bill Southard. He sits down and starts talking about the India project, about how well it went—"

How unlike himself he sounded. Not crisp and terse—"I was made a vice-president today"—but rambling and exuberant, like his brothers.

"—and I kept waiting for him to say 'but,' for there to be some catch, but he kept going on and on—"

Yes, yes, this was just how Ford or Brian or Andy would tell the story. Patrick was really very happy. It was wonderful to see him this way.

"—until at last he put out his hand and said, 'The firm will have a good year next year with you as vice-president.'"

"Oh, Patrick."

Knowing in advance didn't make any difference. She was still just as thrilled, just as delighted as if she were first hearing the news. She had never seen him this happy.

But when she put her hand on his arm and stood on

her toes, just then Sarah, still keyed up and laughing, yanked at his hair. He winced and turned toward her, and Suzanne's kiss landed on his cheek unnoticed.

She tried not to be disappointed. There'd be time for kisses later. "Well, tell me. Who else made it?"

"That's the wonderful part—for me at least. Steve Shirley."

"Steve Shirley?" Suzanne blinked. "That's a surprise."

Steve Shirley was a man in his late fifties who had joined Southard-Colt just a year ago. Although he had left the federal government at the undersecretary level, the younger people at the firm would be surprised, even disgruntled, that he had been made a vice-president so quickly.

Suzanne, knowing the firm as she did, understood exactly why Patrick had called Shirley's appointment good for him. People's natural resentment at the success of others would all be deflected onto the other man. "Britten I can understand," they would say, "but why Shirley?"

This was all working out so perfectly for him.

"Did they give you stock options?"

He told her about the new compensation package as they all trooped happily into the kitchen. He deposited Sarah on the counter, and steadying her with one hand, he picked up the phone and dialed. Suzanne had no idea whom he was calling. His parents perhaps. Wouldn't it be lovely if he were this eager to tell them? If he wanted them to share in his success?

As he waited for an answer, Patrick ruffled Sarah's soft curls. "Where's your nose, princess?"

Sarah adored this game, and, giggling, she pointed to her nose, but before they could get on to ears or eyes, someone on the other end answered the phone.

"Hi, it's me," he said into the receiver. "I've been trying to get you all afternoon."

And Suzanne, going rigid with shock, had to stand there in the middle of her own kitchen, with fresh shrimp and champagne in the refrigerator, a rib roast in the oven, silver, china, and flowers waiting to be put on the table, and listen while Patrick told Kim about being made a vice-president.

"Sure, I'd love to buy you dinner," he was saying. "That sounds great. I'll be over in—no wait a second..." He looked over at Suzanne. "Was I supposed to babysit this evening?"

Silently she shook her head.

"Then it's fine," he said into the phone. "I'll see you in twenty minutes."

And then with a quick kiss for Sarah and a "Don't wait up" for Suzanne, he was gone.

She was numb. Blank, dull, and numb. Patrick had chosen to spend the evening with Kim. Despite all his plans not to see her while living with Suzanne, tonight was just too special, and he wanted to be with her. This was something he wanted to share with her, celebrate with her, not with Suzanne. It made sense. A new job, a new wife—this was the future. What difference did the past make?

Wordlessly she put Sarah in the high chair and gave her the shrimp for her dinner. Suzanne wasn't hungry anymore. There was no reason to slice the roast; she'd put it away and they'd have it cold tomorrow.

Cold roast Boston. That was the phrase used to describe old-time Bostonians. Unremittingly proper, cold roast Boston had perfect manners, unshakable morals and no warmth or sparkle. If ever a young man of his generation seemed on his way to deserving such a label, it would have been Patrick Britten two years ago.

But he wasn't like that anymore. This evening had made that so clear. What he had done tonight, coming home to Suzanne and calling Kim in front of her, had been a piece of inexcusable rudeness that he would have been incapable of two years ago. But he forgot himself this evening—he was so relaxed, so delighted, so truly and spontaneously joyous, that he just hadn't thought.

For Patrick Britten to be so caught up in joy that he wasn't thinking was a change that had to involve as profound an alteration in his character as there had been in hers.

He was now capable of happiness. What she had learned from Sarah, he had learned from Kim. And of course, he loved her for it.

Miserably Suzanne bathed Sarah, and, desperate for comfort, held and rocked the little girl until she fell asleep. Finally she had to cross the hall to her own empty room.

It was still very early, but slowly she got ready for bed.

She'd been fooling herself. It had been so easy during these last few weeks to start thinking of the three of them as if they were a family. When after dinner Patrick would share his grapes with Sarah and listen to her new words, Suzanne could imagine him someday helping their child with her calculus homework. When he had brought her that new book, she had imagined he was bringing her his heart. She had allowed herself to hope. How stupid. What an incredibly stupid mistake.

It was over. Patrick would come home tonight, she knew that, but he wouldn't stay. Within a day or two, he would move out and divorce proceedings would start.

"Marriage isn't for keeps anymore." He had said that two years ago and unhesitatingly she had agreed. But how she wished it was. That would have been one advantage of cold roast Boston. Surely some of the most proper Bostonian men were occasionally tempted by the way brown curls brushed against a pair of nineteen-year-old shoulders, but they didn't leave their wives, the proud women who ran their homes, who gave birth to their children, who stood beside them in receiving lines at charity balls, wearing black silk and their grandmothers'—

Their grandmothers' pearls.

Kim would want the pearls.

She could never, never give the pearls to Kim. They were hers; they'd been given to her. And not even by Patrick. They had been from his family. To her, from them.

She remembered that June day, how nervous she'd been, how awkward she'd felt—she didn't love their son, she wasn't really becoming a part of the family— but they had been so warm, so welcoming that none of that had mattered at all.

For the first time in her life, Suzanne felt like she was a part of a family. She had brothers and parents. To give up the pearls would be like giving up the Brittens, and she didn't know how she could stand that.

But wouldn't that be what would happen? Patrick and Kim would have Sarah on holidays and weekends. They would take her up to Concord. It would be Kim who would have those long, lovely conversations with Sally. It would be Kim whom Andy and Brian would try to teach tennis to. It would be Kim standing in front of Patrick when they all lined up on the porch for pictures.

And, really, what did pearls matter in comparison to that?

Miserably Suzanne sank down at her dressing table. Gleaming in front of her was the silver set that Patrick had given her the first Christmas he had known her. She fingered the brush, tracing the delicate vines. It was the only gift he had ever given her; he didn't know when her birthday was or remember when their anniversary was. This mirror, comb, and brush would be the only gift she would ever get from him.

Except Sarah. She was from him. "Let me give this to you," he had said during those darkly bewildering moments when they had each learned just how strong passion can be. He had given her this child that day, and Sarah knew that there could never be a gift as precious.

She picked up the silver mirror, remembering what sort of person she had been when she had first looked into it. Patrick had come to stand behind her that winter afternoon, and when she had turned to thank him, it had again been like looking in a mirror, seeing not a physical reflection this time, but a psychological one.

They had been alike in those days, too alike to love one another. But Suzanne had changed.

For a moment, she wished that none of this had ever happened; she wished that she were still Miss Lawrence, impeccable, self-reliant, detached. Miss Lawrence had never suffered like this; she was incapable of it.

But no. She didn't mean that; she didn't want to be Miss Lawrence again. For all the anguish that lay ahead of her, she would rather be as she was now, open, loving, flexible.

Who was it? Tennyson? "'Tis better to have loved and lost, than never loved at all."

She'd never really understood those lines before,

never really understood that loving will always change a person. But love had changed her, turning her into the sort of person she had always dreamed of being, into the sort of person she had always envied. Loving Patrick and Sarah had made her able to love herself.

Even if she did not have Patrick, she had his child and she had this new self. Her life was fuller and richer than she could have ever imagined it to be two years ago. True, it would be better if he loved her, better beyond all imaginings, but even so—

The front door scraped open.

Chapter Fifteen

Suzanne straightened in surprise. It was not even ten o'clock. What on earth was Patrick doing home this early? Curious, she pulled on her robe and went downstairs.

He was standing in the hall, his eyes frowning and tired. At the sound of her footsteps, he glanced up. "Has Andy called?"

Andy? "Why, no. Was he supposed to?"

"No, I just hoped he would," Patrick sighed. "I've been out looking for him. I went to his dorm and all over. I don't know where else to look."

"You've been out looking for Andy?" This made no sense. "Where's Kim?"

"Kim?" He looked a little blank. "I took her home about an hour ago."

"An hour ago?" He would have been out with her for less than two hours. Why? "Patrick, has something happened to Andy? Is he all right?"

He laughed, a short, bitter laugh. "I guess you could say something happened *to* him, although 'in front of him' would be more like it."

"What on earth are you talking about?"

"We—Kim and I—ran into him."

Mirrors and Mistakes

Suzanne's hand flew to her throat. "Oh, no."

"It was awful." Patrick ran a hand over his white, tired face. "He was across the street, and at first, he was so happy to see me, dodging cars, calling out my name...and yours too. But then he realized it wasn't you, and he just stopped dead, in the middle of all the traffic...."

Suzanne could see it. Andy's red-haired grin flashing and his bright, loud voice calling over the traffic noise, and then the color draining from his face, as he realized that his brother, his admired, adored, oldest brother, was with a woman who was not his wife.

"Everything suddenly seemed so cheap, so sordid," Patrick continued, "like I had no right to be with her. And I didn't. I'm *married.* I'm not supposed to be going out with other people."

Suzanne hardly knew what to say. "This is the only time that you've been out with her since you got back."

"A lot of difference that makes when I run into my brother.... Oh, God, if it had just been anyone but my brother."

Suzanne's heart went out to him. At long last, he was learning how much his brothers meant to him. She had realized it a long time ago; the bedrock of his quiet self-confidence was those years of being the adored oldest brother. That was why he had spent the last hour driving around Cambridge looking for Andy. Now that he thought he had lost Andy's good opinion, he understood just how much his brothers mattered.

"If you explain, perhaps he'll understand." Suzanne knew how feeble that sounded, but she persevered. "And you have to tell your family about Kim sooner or later."

His eyes shot to hers. "They aren't going to like it,"

he said slowly as if he had never thought about this before.

Well, of course, they weren't going to like it, Suzanne thought almost impatiently. They would be crushed. He should have realized that long ago. She sighed. When were Patrick and Kim going to come out of this little fantasy that the path of true love was going to be rosy and smooth? So far each person who had found out, first David Stern and now Andy, had been shocked and disapproving.

"Well, they'll have to know," she said tightly. "It's just too bad that it had to ruin your evening."

He had been so exuberant when he had first come home, and as hurt as she was, she was sorry that his pleasure in the vice-presidency had been spoiled. At least part of her was sorry. Another, less noble part thought that he deserved it.

"I don't know," he was saying, slowly shaking his head. "The evening wasn't all that—oh, well...." He broke off, shrugging.

Suzanne wanted to know what he was going to say. "It wasn't all that what?"

His words came out in a rush. "You understand, don't you? Why I wanted to be a vice-president? That it has nothing to do with having a better office or going to Southard's Christmas party. That it's the work. You understand that, don't you?"

"You know I do."

"Kim kept asking what my new office would be like."

Oh. Even before they had seen Andy, the evening had been marred because Kim hadn't understood. She hadn't understood at all.

Patrick couldn't care less about having a new office; he didn't care what the title on his business cards was. What he wanted was to be doing a vice-president's work, to have a vice-president's responsibilities. He wanted to develop his own business unit, go after contracts that interested him, hire people whose standards were as high as his own. The bigger office, the parties, the little perks of being a vice-president, none of that mattered in the least to him.

But that's all Kim understood about his job, the perks, the frills, the social trivia. It wasn't her fault. She wasn't shallow or stupid. She was just young, inexperienced; she knew nothing about the business world.

What a bitter moment it must have been for him, when he realized that Kim didn't understand what he did, when all his efforts and ambitions got translated into questions about office décor.

And in that moment, had he remembered that waiting for him at home was a wife who understood? Who knew what pressures he faced each day? Who understood the subtleties of his job well enough to realize what things like Steve Shirley's promotion would mean to him?

But Suzanne wasn't going to sympathize with him. This he certainly did deserve, as did any grown man who expected that a pretty nineteen-year-old was going to be able to understand him.

He started to speak. "Suzanne, I—"

The doorbell rang, and Patrick broke off, suddenly tense. "It's going to be Andy. What am I going to say to him?"

"Tell him the truth." And when Patrick looked unconvinced, she went on. "I'll be with you, Patrick." *And I'll be able to help. Do you think Kim would know what to do?*

A sudden warmth, gratitude perhaps, did flood into his eyes, and he turned to open the door.

It was indeed Andy. The porch light turned his red

hair into a flaming torch glowing in the dark; he looked young and upset.

"Pat, I just had to come." His voice was rushed. "It occurred to me that maybe I was wrong, that maybe it wasn't what it looked like, and if—" He caught sight of Suzanne. "Oh, Suzanne." He looked surprised as if he weren't quite expecting her to be there.

"Hello, Andy. Please come in." Andy seemed hesitant and so Suzanne took his arm, steering him into the living room. Patrick followed.

"Suzanne, do you—" Andy stopped, uncertain.

"Yes, I know he was out with Kim Chaney."

He flushed. "Then it's true? That he's cheating on you?"

Suzanne felt Patrick go rigid beside her. "Andy, I—"

Patrick's voice was tight with guilt, and Andy interrupted belligerently. "What is it, Patrick?" He was sarcastic as he whipped out Patrick's full name.

Patrick put his hand on Andy's shoulder. Andy jerked away, stepping back, his fist clenched, one arm pulling back. He was going to hit him.

Patrick moved a little, balancing his weight, his legs slightly apart, bracing himself. If Andy wanted to hit him, Patrick was going to let him.

But Andy's face crumpled and his shoulders slumped. "Oh, Pat," he pleaded. "Why are you cheating on Suzanne?"

Patrick didn't answer; he couldn't. In his own terms, he had cheated on his wife.

But Suzanne knew that Andy would think differently. He was young enough to share Kim's rather adolescent morality. Kim undoubtedly thought of herself as having done nothing wrong simply because she had never gone to bed with Patrick. She had flirted with him, teased him, fallen in love with him, but that was all right because she hadn't slept with him. She was still a virgin; that made the rest of her behavior irreproachable.

Life was more complicated than that.

But like Kim, Andy was young, and Suzanne turned to him, saying what Patrick probably considered irrelevant. "She's not his mistress, Andy. They're not having an affair."

Andy frowned. "Then I don't get it." He turned to Patrick. "Is she your girlfriend or not?"

Suzanne held her breath. Now was the time for Patrick to say the words she dreaded, the time for him to explain to his brother how much he loved Kim, how he longed to marry her, how they wanted to spend the rest of their lives together. This was it. His telling Andy would make it irrevocable; Andy would tell the rest of the family, and Patrick would have to move out, divorce proceedings would have to start.

Patrick said nothing.

And slowly, a golden, glowing bud of happiness unfolded, its leaves curling open to the sun's warmth. Suzanne knew. She knew with the kind of instinct that she was now willing to trust. Patrick was not talking about his future with Kim because he no longer believed in it.

They might not have discussed it; nothing had been settled yet, but there was simply no doubt. At last he had seen it. He and Kim were not right for each other. He was a man, and she was still a girl, not yet capable of doing a woman's work.

Suzanne felt that it wasn't right somehow to be standing here, feeling as she was, with Andy and Patrick still bewildered and unhappy.

"Why don't I go make some tea?" she said and left the room, immersed in a happy fog.

It wasn't too long before Patrick joined her in the kitchen. If he noticed that she hadn't done one thing toward fixing tea, he didn't say so.

"Andy's left."

Suzanne tried to be sympathetic to how he must still feel. "Patrick, it will be all right. It really makes a difference to him that you didn't sleep with her."

He shook his head. "There are plenty of ways to be unfaithful to your wife without going to bed with another woman."

"Of course," Suzanne answered, "but Andy doesn't know that yet."

"I hope you're right."

"I usually am," she smiled.

He laughed softly. "I used to think that about myself." He walked over to the refrigerator, opened it, but then closed it without looking in. "I really did love her."

Suzanne said nothing. He'd tell her if he wanted to.

"Part of it was... I don't know, but I just think I was ready to fall in love. I was pretty shook up by what happened between us in Washington. I didn't think I was capable of such primitive sorts of feelings, and then living with you afterward—well, this is going to make me sound like I don't know where babies come from, but here you and I had done something together, but it was only you, because you were a woman, who were tired and sick and pregnant."

"Nature doesn't treat men and women alike," Suzanne pointed out.

"I know, and while I've always believed—and always will—that women must have equality of economic opportunity, I spent a long time thinking that that meant you had to pretend that men and women are entirely alike, and I think the reason I'd never fallen in love before was that I kept expecting my relationships with my female friends—even the ones I went to bed with—to be a lot like my relationships with my male friends, and as a result, they were. But after Washington, after you got pregnant, all that changed, and I suppose I was ready to fall in love; for the first time I wanted to be deeply involved in a woman's emotional life and to have her involved in mine. If I had stayed here with you, I probably—oh, well, it doesn't matter; I didn't stay. I met Kim instead, and Calcutta was such a separate world that it didn't ever matter that she was so much younger or that I was already married."

Suzanne nodded. College too had been such a separate world that differences in backgrounds and habits hadn't seemed to matter; only when she and Nick had moved back into the mainstream did they discover that their relationship could not work.

"Actually her being so young might have been a part of it," he went on. "I think not only was I ready to be in love, but I was also ready to be a parent. I certainly wasn't aware of it, but it's possible that when we were in Washington, it was that our physical and subconscious selves took over from our rational, conscious minds to give us the child that we were both ready for, the child we both needed."

Suzanne swallowed, blinking back her tears, thinking of the little girl upstairs, their unspeakably precious child.

Patrick smiled at her gently. "You had Sarah; I didn't, and I think my relationship with Kim was very paternal; I was always doing things for her, the sort of things I'll probably do for Sarah someday. Frederick Chaney has always traveled a lot; he's never had much time for Delilah or Kim. Kim wanted a father figure; I wanted to be taking care of someone, and we disguised it as a romance. That was the mistake.''

Suzanne thought of her own mistakes. Her debts had made her practical and realistic. Nick, the way she had allowed him to be dependent on her, would keep her from ever encouraging such overdependence again, even in Sarah. And, of course, Sarah herself, a mistake, an accident, the best thing that had ever happened to Suzanne.

Kim too would benefit from her mistake. Now that she couldn't spend her nineteenth year planning her wedding, she'd have to find something else to do, college, a job, something. She would not go directly from being a child to being a wife. She'd have to learn how to be a woman first.

But Suzanne didn't want to talk about Kim anymore. She wanted Patrick to talk about himself and her. What had he been about to say before he broke off, saying it didn't matter? Had he been about to say that if he had stayed in Boston, he would have loved her?

But, not surprisingly, he said nothing, just turning back to the refrigerator, opening it almost idly.

''Do you want something to eat?'' she asked. ''There's—''

He interrupted, his voice stiff. ''What's all this?''

Confused, Suzanne peered around him. On the top shelf next to the milk carton and the juice were two green bottles of champagne. She had forgotten. It seemed like so long ago.

Patrick lifted the corner of the aluminum foil that covered the unsliced roast; then he glanced on the top of the refrigerator where the apple cake lay covered with Saran Wrap.

''Oh, God,'' he groaned. ''You knew, didn't you?

You knew that I had been made a vice-president and this was all for a celebration."

"I knew before you did."

"And I called Kim right in front of you." He turned and faced her; his eyes were gray, exhausted. "I'm a real bastard."

"I thought so for a while," Suzanne admitted. "But you did what you wanted to."

Patrick didn't even try to apologize. It was as if he were certain that she could not possibly forgive him. "I don't know why I called her. It was automatic, I guess; in India, she talked a lot about what we'd do when this happened, how we'd celebrate. She's so festive; that's what I first liked about her. But even before we saw—no, I shouldn't say that."

"Go ahead."

"A couple of times during the evening, even before we saw Andy, I would"—he took a breath—"I'd catch myself thinking, 'Why aren't I with Suzanne?' and the whole time you'd been planning..." He stopped. He lifted his hand as if he were about to take hers, but then he let it drop without touching her. "Suzanne, there's just nothing I can ever say or do to make up for the pain I've caused you, and I'm not just talking about tonight."

"I'll be all right."

He didn't seem to have heard. "You know, I always have thought of myself as someone who didn't make mistakes, but I look back over the last two years and I've made one mistake after another. I should never have gone to India; this vice-presidency just isn't worth what I missed with Sarah. And when I came back, I should have—I would give anything if I'd been sincere about why I was here, if we really had been working on our problems."

"But, Patrick—" She sank down into a chair.

"And the irony of it is"—his voice was suddenly bitter—"that the one problem you said we had has managed to get solved now that it's too late."

"Solved? What are you talking about?"

"Don't you remember what you said that first night—you were sitting right where you are now—you said our only problem was that I loved Kim, not you. Well, that's been taken care of, but"—he shrugged—"I'm sure you don't want to hear this." He started to leave the room.

"Wait a minute." Suzanne suspected that she did want to hear this, very much indeed. "Are you saying—"

"That I love you? Yes, as a matter of fact, I am. When that doorbell rang tonight, and you said you'd be with me, suddenly I knew that I wanted you with me always. It's such a miserable, stupid cliché, isn't it? A man decides he's in love with some pretty, young thing; he uses his wife, takes advantage of her time, her patience, her body, gives her every reason to hate him, and then finally wakes up and realizes that she... that you..." He faltered. But in a moment, he cleared his throat. "Well, you don't have to worry. At least I've got the sense to know that you aren't going to welcome me back with open arms."

"I'm not?"

He stared at her, frowning, confused.

"Well, there's no doubt at all," she said lightly, happiness flooding through her, "that you do deserve to be banished to a third-rate furnished efficiency for a few months before I forgive you."

Her teasing tone stunned him. "Suzanne—"

She stood up and went to him. "Oh, Patrick, of course I love you. How could you not know that? Do you think I would have put up with all this if I didn't?''

He stared at her, but in a moment, his arms started to close around her.

As his head bent to her, she put her fingers on his lips, stopping him. "But wait." She was more serious now. "Are you sure that you aren't confusing your feelings for me with what you feel for Sarah?''

He drew back, surprised. "Oh, no, Kim's the one who should say that. I don't feel the least paternal toward you." His arms tightened again. "You're my partner, my friend, my wife, and I..." His voice grew hesitant.

She knew how hard this was for him. "No, Patrick, you don't have to say anything. Not to me. Remember? I'm Miss Lawrence, the one who always knows what you're thinking.''

"No, you aren't. You aren't like her at all. And, Mrs. Britten, I'm not going to be one of those men who never tells his wife that he loves her. Boston has too many men like that already. I love you, and I hope that you will always know that without having to read my mind.''

Suzanne sighed and leaned against him. What lovely words. In all her reading, in all the plays and novels and poems, she had never heard such lovely words.

"We belong together, you and I," he said. "Not like we belonged together two years ago, not because we are so alike, but because we love each other and because we can make each other happy, genuinely and honestly happy. I really believe that.''

"Oh, Patrick, so do I," Suzanne breathed. "So do I.''

He took her face between his hands. "Then shall we really try this time to work on our problems?''

"What problems?" she asked softly.

He looked at her blankly.

"Patrick, my love, you tell me what problems we have and I will work harder at solving them than I have ever worked at anything. But you'll have to tell me what they are because I don't know."

He stared at her, and then suddenly relaxed, pulling her into his arms again. "I'm not sure that I know either." He bent his head and kissed her, but just as passion mingled with the tenderness, he broke off. "No, I do know of a problem."

"What's that?"

"Now just how is this family—you, me, and Sarah—going to adapt to having someone around who is not a mistake? What will we do with a child that has been planned?"

Suzanne laughed, so happy that she was almost giddy. "I don't know. We probably won't know what to say to it."

"What are we going to do?" Patrick sighed with a despair that would have been a little more convincing if his fingers hadn't already started to tug at the sash of Suzanne's robe.

"No, wait," she cried eagerly, pushing his hand away. "Do you remember those two bottles of champagne? If we sit down and drink our way through both of those, then I'm sure we can, in all honesty, say that we simply did not know what we were doing. And then we can call that baby a mistake too."

"My God, Suzanne," Patrick marveled. "You are the cleverest woman I know." He let go of her and snared one of the bottles out of the refrigerator and began untwisting the wires that held the cork. "Why are you standing there? Go get some glasses."

"What's wrong with you?" she demanded. "Your leg's not broken anymore." But she hurried out to the dining room, returning just in time to thrust a crystal glass under the neck of the dark green bottle and catch the dancing gush of champagne, the golden liquid as high-spirited and sparkling as—

As they were. These two people, these two proper Bostonians, who had once been tea at four, perfectly brewed tea, elegantly served in fine china cups, they were now champagne at midnight. They were, at last, celebrating.

Patrick raised his glass. "Here's to mistakes. May we make many more of them."

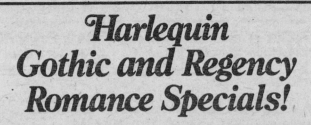